The

Rises

at

Sunset

Also by Susan Hubert

FICTION

Sabi Star

Sunrising – Book 1 of the Sunrising Series

The Sun is Bright – Book 2 of the Sunrising Series

The Full Moon

Rises

at

Sunset

A novel

SUSAN HUBERT

Cover design – Duncan Watson

Front Cover photo – Frankie Kay

Photo of the dog on back cover – Jeremy Hubert

This book is dedicated to my parents
Christopher and Moira Carver

Lineage of the Craig and Brooke families

The Craigs

Isabella Braithewaite b1877 d 1960 married Anthony Craig b 1873 d 1905
Their children:

- William b 1904 d 1904
- Oliver   b 1905 first married Emily d 1943, then married Lily
    Their children:
        - Amanda b 1940 widowed 1978
            Her children - Karen and Louise
        - Dominic b 1955

The Brookes

Celia Braithewaite b 1874 d 1956 married James Brooke b 1862 d 1947
Their children:

- Tim b1907 d 1947 married Serena b1914
    Their children:
        - Martin b1935 married Kate
            Their children   - Brian and Harry
        - Valerie b 1936 married, moved to England 1970
            Her children   - Cassia and Leo
        - John b 1939 married Molly
            Their children   - Will and Tom
        - Beatrice b 1940 married Ron Pierce
            Their children   - Sarah, Jane and Richard
- Patricia b 1909 married, moved to Australia in the 1960s
            Her granddaughter - Samantha
- Graham b1917 married his widowed sister-in-law Serena 1950
            No children

Other characters

Siphas Ngwenya	the owner of a neighbouring farm
Prince Zulu	Oliver's major-domo
Farai Ncube	the Craigs' gardener
Frank Dube	the Pierces' gardener
Gladys Khumalo	the Pierces' maid
Dumisani Lunga	Amanda's gardener
Agnes Phiri	Amanda's maid
Zachariah Mpofu	the Brookes' cook
Petros Nkala	a security guard
Philemon Nyoni	a security guard
Abednico Sibanda	the headmaster of Freedom High School
Edna Mpala	a teacher at Freedom High
Beryl	Cassia's friend and a teacher at Freedom High
Gladmore Moyo	Beryl's boyfriend and a teacher at Freedom High
Ma Moyo	Gladmore's mother
Innocent Moyo	Gladmore's brother
Precious Moyo	Gladmore's sister
Pete & Moira Fletcher	Dominic's friends
Davo &Sandy Davidson	Dominic's friends
Andre Van Staaden	owner of the Binga Resort
Darvie Peters	a rancher
Bert Goosen	a rancher
The Chesters	farmers
Ted Squires	the deputy headmaster of St. Benedict's School

CHAPTER 1

Matabeleland in the mid-1980s

THE VISCOUNT began its descent into Bulawayo airport as it was flying over the Matobo Hills. Cassia put her book down to peer out of the aeroplane window and found, even from this height, the huge granite *dwala*s were distinguishable from the grassy *vleis*. She craned her neck to get a better view of the great patchwork below her; the glowing domes of the gigantic rocks, the deep shadows they cast, the textured grasslands in between. She noticed a dirt road snaking through a *vlei*, the only hint of human habitation in an otherwise unpopulated landscape.

Her heart leapt.

She was home.

Minutes later, further signs of development appeared on the scene. A tarred road, a dam, a building, fenced fields, more roads, clusters of houses, a railway line, tall buildings. As the plane flew over the city centre, Cassia pressed her face to the window, looking for landmarks she could recognize. The cooling towers, the railway station, the racecourse, residential suburbs fanning out from the city centre.

The Viscount lurched as it prepared to land and a short while later they were braking along the runway, the engine roaring, the propellers slowing.

Cassia gathered her possessions and joined the queue of fellow passengers edging up the aisle towards the exit. Once through the door, she paused at the top of the steps, relishing the sun on her face and a gust of wind blowing through her long, blond hair. She glanced at the airport building, and could see people waving on the balcony. As she strolled across the tarmac, she felt like Lauren Bacall in "Casablanca", wondering who awaited her on the balcony. She considered looking up and waving back, but chose not to.

A tractor with a trailer load of suitcases chugged nearby and disappeared around the side of the building while Cassia walked into the arrivals hall situated under the balcony. The airport terminal had barely changed in the years she'd been away, except for the customs and immigration officials, who were now all black people, as opposed to the last time she'd passed through this building, when they'd all been white. Although they scrutinised her work visa with care, the officers greeted her warmly, but she hated that she could not call herself a "returning resident", in this, the country of her birth.

Two men offloaded the suitcases from the trailer, while a third dragged them along a rack to spread them out. Cassia found hers, loaded them onto a trolley, which she discovered had stubborn steering, but she manoeuvred it through the wooden door into the foyer, her heart thumping with excitement.

She stopped for a moment to look for her relatives, but recognised no one at first. Then she spotted her Aunt Bea's rounded figure and animated face, deep in conversation with another woman. Cassia glanced around for her cousins, but none of them were there.

She guided the tricky trolley towards her aunt, who was still chatting to her friend. Bea hesitated when she looked up and noticed Cassia, and then a warm smile spread across her face, deepening the creases surrounding her shining eyes. She rushed towards Cassia with her arms outstretched and pulled her into a tight embrace.

*

'I'm so thrilled to be home,' Cassia said as they exited the airport parking lot. 'I've missed you, the rest of the family, and this country more than words can express. I can't wait to see everyone and everything.'

'Yes. I'm sorry Sarah and Jane weren't able to meet you too. Neither of them could get away from their work, but you'll see them later,' Aunt Bea said.

After a brief pause, Cassia said, 'That's great. We'll have plenty of time to catch up.'

'Exactly. What a lovely young lady you've grown up to be. My girls will be so envious when they see your beautiful, natural hair. Their hair styles take far too much blow drying and curling.'

Cassia laughed. 'I'm just too lazy to bother.'

'You understand you're going to find many changes here, don't you? With all of us, and especially the country, now that it's Zimbabwe and no longer Rhodesia.'

'Of course, but it's still home. The geography and weather haven't changed, and my family is still made up of the same people. That's good enough for me.'

Bea's lips twitched, and she gave Cassia's arm a brief pat.

Cassia stared out of the car window, enthralled by the scenery; the long strands of yellowing grass swaying either side of the tar road, the cloudless blue sky meeting the wide, open landscape everywhere she looked, the glimpses of the city each time they crested a rise. She sighed. 'This is what I've missed so much. This space.' She waved her hands in front of her as she breathed it all in. After another kilometre of silence, she spoke again. 'Oh look. I can see some high-rise buildings. I can't remember them before we left.'

'There's been plenty of development in the years you've been gone.'

'Amazing, when you think there's been a war, and sanctions, and all that.'

'Yes. We've been through difficult times, but hopefully we're over the worst now.'

'I hope so too,' Cassia said.

'You'll notice lots of street names have changed,' Beatrice warned when they were driving through the town.

'That doesn't surprise me. They were colonial names. I'm sure I'll learn the new names soon.'

*

Only her young cousin Richard came home for lunch and then disappeared as soon as he'd finished eating, saying he had plans to meet his friends. This disappointed Cassia, but she pretended not to mind. She said she was jet lagged, dirty and tired, after her long journey and needed time for herself. After taking a shower, she closed her bedroom curtains, lay down on the single bed and fell asleep at once. When she woke and looked at her watch, she saw she had only slept for an hour. She listened for noises in the house, but all she could hear was the twitter of birds and the hum of a gardener outside.

Now that she was over her initial excitement, she felt down-hearted and unwelcome, perhaps because she'd been looking forward to returning for so long. She told herself she must not rush to judge anyone. She and her cousins, Sarah and Jane, had been such good friends when they were little, she had expected them to have come home at lunchtime to say hello. But why should they? Bea told her they had opened a small clothes shop in the middle of town, called "Sarah Janes' ", where they employed several seamstresses to make clothes they had designed. Their initiative impressed her, and she understood it must keep them busy, so she mustn't read anything into their not coming to meet her. All her cousins were bound to be different now.

She threw off the light blanket and swung her legs over the side of the bed, then opened the curtains and gazed out of the window at the lush green garden and sparkling pool visible behind a flowerbed. She left the bedroom and walked through to the living rooms, noticing the green wall-to-wall carpeting throughout the sitting room and dining room, and the chintz lounge suite and oak dining room suite had not changed. There was no one in either of these rooms, so she strolled into the hall and across the polished parquet floor to the kitchen, where she saw the maid ironing in the laundry. Her white apron and coloured uniform shimmered in the sunlight shining through the window next to her.

'Would you like tea, Madam?' the maid asked as soon as she saw Cassia.

'Oh no, thank you. But please don't call me "Madam". My name is Cassia. I'm the Pierces' relative from England, although I was born here in Zimbabwe. My mother is Mrs Pierce's sister.'

The maid said nothing.

'And what is your name?'

'Gladys, Madam.'

'I don't think you worked here when I used to visit back in the 1960s, did you?'

'No, Madam. I only started working here in 1981.'

'Well, nice to meet you Gladys, and please try not to call me madam.'

Daddy would roll his eyes if he heard all this "madam" business, Cassia thought as she walked through the French door from the sitting room onto the veranda and sat down in one of the metal chairs. One reason they'd moved to England was that her parents disapproved of the vast gulf between "us and them", as her father

5

used to refer to the racial divide. He predicted it would cause a great deal of trouble in the future, and she acknowledged he was right, as there had been a bitter bush war for independence. At least that was over now and all races were theoretically on the same level, yet it was clear Gladys had difficulty calling her anything but "madam". Odd that, Cassia thought.

A voice from the garden made her jump, breaking her train of thought.

'Can I put a cushion on your chair, Madam?' She whirled around to find the gardener walking up the steps onto the veranda, carrying a pile of cushions. He looked at her and then his chocolate brown face crumpled into a multitude of wrinkles. 'Missus… Missus Cassia,' he stuttered. 'Missus Cassia, how are you?' He plonked the cushions on the metal table and wrung his hands together in delight.

Cassia's mind raced as she tried to remember his name. 'Frank?' she asked.

His smile widened further. 'Yes Madam. It's Frank… Frank Dube.'

'Wow. I'm amazed you are still working for Mr and Mrs Pierce. If I remember, you'd been here for many years even before we left.'

'Since 1961, when the madam and the boss first married.'

'That is a long time.'

'I have lived in the *khaya* out the back ever since then.'

'And your family?'

'They live at my rural home in Lupane, Madam… And how is your family? Madam Val, and the boss? And how's the other *picannini*, Boss Leo?

'Everyone is well, thank you, although Leo is now grown up like me. My family is still in England.'

His forehead furrowed. 'We need them to come back here to Zimbabwe like you.'

'They won't do that, although Leo may visit me here one day.'

'That will be good, Madam.'

He put a cushion on each of the chairs, after which he shuffled down the steps and across the immaculate lawn to move a hosepipe from one flowerbed to another.

*

Cassia met the rest of the Pierce family that evening. Uncle Ron, with his hair so heavily oiled she noticed the tooth marks from his comb, and Sarah and Jane, both smartly dressed in the outfits they'd worn to work; big shoulder pads and nipped-in waists, designed by them and sewn by their seamstresses (they told her when she asked.) Cassia thought they appeared much trendier than she in her bright floral trousers and pink cotton blouse.

'So what school will you be teaching at?' Ron asked her at dinner.

'It's called Freedom High.'

'Never heard of it.'

'I believe it's a new school, built after Independence,' Cassia said. 'It's in a suburb called Luveve.'

'Luveve? Good God. How strange.'

Cassia noticed Sarah and Jane sharing an amused look. 'My friend Beryl has been teaching there,' she went on, 'for more than a year. She and I were at Uni in Bristol and she suggested I join her at Freedom. She says it's very rewarding teaching there.'

'Mm,' Ron said, cutting another slice of his steak.

Knives banged and forks scratched on the crockery as they continued eating their dinner.

'And your parents? How's everything going for them in Bristol?' Ron asked when he'd swallowed his next mouthful.

'They're in excellent form, thank you.' Cassia's mother had told her that their decision to move to England, because they disapproved of the white dominated politics, had not gone down well with the rest of her family. She hoped Ron would not mention this now.

Bea may have had the same thought because she butted in with a big sigh. 'I miss my big sister Val so much. It's always sad when family members live far apart. Maybe now you're here, we can talk them into coming back for a visit.'

'That would be nice.'

'At least I have my mother and stepfather, and both my brothers nearby, so I can't complain too much,' Bea said.

Sarah yawned. 'So what will you do until the school term starts?'

'I hope to spend as much time as possible on the farm.'

Bea rested her knife and fork on her plate and wiped her mouth with her table napkin. 'Granny is so looking forward to having you. She phoned earlier to say she and Graham are coming into town tomorrow to welcome you back. They'll stay the night with us, like they usually do.'

'That's great, Aunt Bea. I can't wait to see them.'

'Granny wanted to take you back to the farm the next day, but I asked her if you can stay here for a few more days, as I could do with your help. I'm arranging a Garden Club meeting this weekend, you see, and I'd like you to help me with this.'

'Of course. I'd be happy to help.'

'I'm having it at the farm, in Lily Craig's garden, so you can come out with me then, and stay on with Granny afterwards.'

'Mum is the chairlady of the Garden Club this year, so she's pulling out all the stops,' Jane said.

'And that's why I've chosen Lily's garden as the venue,' Bea said. 'She has the most glorious garden. I've invited an expert pruner from Harare, and this woman will show us how we should prune our roses and other shrubs. With spring just round the corner, we'll need to prune everything soon. I've told everyone to bring their secateurs and gloves, and Lily has said we can use her rose bushes to practise on. Her rose garden is magnificent.'

'Sounds like it'll be fun,' Cassia said, smiling at Sarah and Jane, who were pulling faces at their mother. 'But you have an impressive garden here, Aunt Bea, and I see you still have the same gardener. Frank.'

'Oh yes. Good old Frank. But my garden is nothing compared to Lily's.'

'Plus, Frank does all our pruning,' Sarah laughed. 'In fact, I'd say this will be the first time most of the members of your Garden Club will ever have pruned anything, Mum.'

Bea screwed up her face, but couldn't help giggling. 'You may be right, Sarah.'

Bea continued telling them what she wanted to do at her Garden Club meeting. She was determined to make it a function they would all remember, little knowing, as she discussed it now, that she would never forget this particular gathering of the Garden Club, but not for the reasons she was hoping.

CHAPTER 2

THE SOUND of gunfire rattled and echoed through Oliver and Lily's bedroom window, waking them up. Their eyes shot open and Oliver's dog, Jimbo, who slept in his basket next to the bed, leapt out of it, barking. Their son Dominic's dog, Luna, was staying with them, and he joined in with the barking.

'What the hell?' Oliver said, lifting himself onto his elbow and cocking his head. 'Shut up, Jimbo. Luna, be quiet.'

The shooting continued. Popping and banging, followed by rapid gunfire. Then it stopped and they could hear nothing but their own breathing. Lily put a hand to her chest as if to control her pounding heart.

The dogs growled.

'Shush,' Oliver said. He eased himself off the bed and stumbled to the window.

'Careful, Oliver... don't open the curtain. Maybe, maybe there are people in the garden,' Lily stammered.

His hand froze on the curtain and he stood for a moment, unsure. Then the gunfire began again, and he ducked down. A rally of shots went on for what seemed like an eternity, followed by silence once more.

'Bloody hell. It sounds like World War Two all over again,' Oliver said. 'I'm trying to work out where it's coming from. It sounds far away.'

'Yes, thank goodness. Could it be from Sunlands?' Lily's face was ashen and her hand trembled as she pushed a strand of hair from her face.

'No, I think it's coming from the compound. I'd better dress and go down there to find out what's happening.' He hobbled through to their dressing room, trailed by both dogs, and pulled a pair of trousers from the cupboard.

Lily followed too. 'Oliver, please, you can't go rushing off to see what's going on. Let's phone Sunlands, rather. They may know more than us.'

'At my age, I don't rush anywhere,' Oliver said, 'but remember, Serena and Graham spent last night in town. To meet what's-her-name from England.' He fumbled as he did up his shirt buttons.

'Cassia.'

'Yes, and, with John and family still fishing on the Zambezi, and Martin et al. in South Africa, we're the only ones here on the farm at the moment to sort things out. I can't just ignore this gunfire.' By now, he was fully clothed. Lily pulled on her dressing gown and followed him as he tentatively opened their bedroom door onto a wide veranda stretching along the length of the house. For the first time ever, Lily wished the design of their house was different and the bedrooms did not lead onto this open veranda. She couldn't remember feeling this scared, ever, during the Independence War.

The gunshots started again, individual bursts this time. They both jumped, and the dogs barked.

'Shut up,' Oliver told them. 'I'll leave you boys in here, rather.' He closed the bedroom door on the dogs and stood outside while he listened. 'Yup, it's coming from the compound. Let's go to my study, and I'll phone the police.'

'I wish Dominic was here,' Lily whispered as they shuffled down the veranda.

'Yes, me too.'

They never locked any of the doors opening onto the veranda. This'll have to change, Oliver thought as he opened his office door and walked in. He picked up the telephone, and then almost dropped it again when a figure appeared at the door. 'Good God, Prince, you gave me a fright.'

'Sorry, sorry.'

'What's going on?'

'Ah...*Varume*, Sir. They are in the compound.'

'*Varume*? What do you mean, *Varume*? Not THE *Varume*, I hope?'

'It is, Sir, with their red...' Prince pointed to his head. His hand was shaking. Fear dripped from him. 'The police are with them,' he finished.

Oliver's eyes widened. The *Varume* were a special brigade of the army, deployed in Matabeleland to "keep the peace", but many worrying rumours were circulating about the methods they employed. 'Oh God, not them! With the police, you say? I was about to phone them. What on earth is going on?'

'I don't know, but you need to come now. They have shot Zachariah and they say you have to take him to the hospital.'

'Zachariah? Do you mean Martin's cook?'

'Yes Sir.'

'Where is he?'

'At his homestead.'

'But that isn't in the compound.'

'No. The *Varume* left him there and went to the compound.'

'The *Varume* shot him?'

Prince said nothing.

'Is he badly injured?'

'I have been told he is.'

Oliver looked at Lily. 'What are we going to do? I can't leave you here alone with all this going on.'

'The shooting appears to have stopped now.'

'That makes it even more ominous.'

'Yes. I'll put on a dress and come with you. While I'm changing, ask Prince to fetch some blankets in case we need them for Zachariah. I'll meet you at the car.'

Ten minutes later, they were hurtling down the road in Oliver's Peugeot 404 station wagon towards Zachariah's homestead, Prince on the back seat and the dogs behind a grille in the rear. Their house was several kilometres from Zachariah's and they saw no one as they drove.

'Strange,' Oliver muttered. 'Everyone should be on their way to work now.'

'The *Varume* are not allowing anyone to go to work. They have ordered everyone to stay in the compound,' Prince said.

Oliver raised an eyebrow at this.

They stopped next to the rough mopane pole fence surrounding Zachariah's huts. As they glanced in the direction of the huts they observed a figure lying on the path; blood-stained clothes, bare feet, and arms splayed in surrender.

'Good Lord!' Oliver said. 'Who is it, Prince?'

'Hardwork, if I am not mistaken.'

'You didn't say anyone else was injured.'

'I wasn't here. They did not tell me.'

'You stay here, Lily, in case we need to make a quick getaway. Prince, come with me and let's see what's happening.'

Oliver crouched next to Hardwork, searching for a pulse in his outstretched arm. There was none. He moved his fingers over Hardwork's wrist, feeling for a throbbing vein, but his arm was limp and the veins were still. Oliver let out a small moan. He turned Hardwork over and sucked in his cheeks when he saw his face; wide open eyes, blood smeared across his cheek, a deep gash on his forehead exposing his skull. Oliver closed Hardwork's eyes with a trembling hand.

'Go back to the car and fetch the blankets, Prince.'

Once they had covered the body with a blanket, they searched for anyone else in the vicinity. The hut doors were all shut, and there was no sign of life except for the chickens in their elevated coop, which was also built from mopane poles.

'Anyone here?' Oliver called. 'It's Mr Craig.' He paused, waiting for a response, but there was none. 'Where is Zachariah?' he tried again. 'I am here to take him to the hospital.'

The door of one hut opened a crack. Noticing this, Prince shouted: '*Vula. Sijahile.*' He pushed the door. '*Ungaphi uZachariah?*'

The young boy standing at the door stepped aside to reveal another body lying on the floor at the back of the hut under a thin blanket, curled in the foetal position, his arms over his head. Oliver's heart missed a beat. Was he dead too?

They stepped into the smoke-smelling dark hut, and a woman sitting on the floor let out a quivering wail. To Oliver's relief, the person lying on the floor moved. It was Zachariah.

'Ah, old man, I'm... I'm so sorry,' Oliver said. 'Where are you wounded?' The woman pulled back the blanket covering him to reveal a pool of blood underneath his torso. Blood covered his shirt, too, and a blood-soaked piece of rag was tied around his shoulder.

'Right, I see. Your shoulder... Anywhere else?'

'*Hayi.*' Zachariah whispered.

14

'We need to stem the bleeding, and then I'll take you to Mpilo Hospital.' Oliver beckoned Prince to come and help turn Zachariah over, with the woman and young boy supporting him. Oliver unbuttoned Zachariah's shirt and pulled it off his shoulder. He winced as Oliver removed the rag. Blood dripped from the wound.

'We can't have this. We need something else to push into the wound to stop this bleeding as best we can. Ask these people for an old towel, Prince.'

Fear flashed across the young boy's face when Prince told him to fetch a towel. He glanced at the open door.

'It's okay,' Prince said. *'Akula muntu phandle ngaphandle komfazi wakhe.'*

The boy returned soon with a threadbare towel. Oliver folded it lengthwise and pushed it hard against each side of the wound, Zachariah shuddering and crying out as he did this.

'Sorry Zac, but it has to be done,' Oliver said. He pulled off his belt and wrapped this around the towel to secure it in position. 'Now, can you walk? We need to get you to the car.'

'*Yebo*,' Zachariah murmured.

They stumbled towards the car and Lily clambered from the front passenger seat, where she'd been sitting, to open the back door. Zachariah eased himself into the back seat. His wife was about to push in beside him when Lily led her around to the door on the other side of the car and directed her to climb in there.

'What's your name?' Oliver asked the young boy.

'Tobias. I am the son of Zachariah, and she is my mother,' he said.

'I think you should stay here, Tobias. Is there anyone else in any of the huts?'

Tobias shook his head.

'Take him, in case the *Varume* come here again,' Prince said. 'I will stay.'

Oliver didn't like the idea of this. Prince had been with him since the 1940s when he was a young man. Prince's father, Gonda, worked for his mother from the turn of the century until he died in the 1950s. He hated the idea of abandoning Prince, but, as if he could read his thoughts, Prince said: 'Don't worry, I will hide if the *Varume* return.'

*

They arrived at the casualty department of Mpilo Hospital and Lily rushed in to tell the attending staff they had someone in the car with a gunshot wound. To her relief, the nurses reacted immediately and pushed a trolley towards the car. Oliver opened the back door to reveal Zachariah slumped against his wife. After a moment's discussion, one nurse hurried back into casualty to find help, while the second nurse leant into the car to see how best to remove Zachariah from the back seat. With more nurses soon at the car, it took little time to place Zachariah on the stretcher and wheel him into the outpatients. Zachariah's wife and son slipped from the car and followed, while Oliver asked Lily to park the car in the shade and wait there. He expected they'd be at the hospital for a long time, so was relieved when he walked inside to see Zachariah already in one of the cubicles, surrounded by nurses, a drip in his arm and his wound being attended to. With all of this under control, he went to check on Lily in the car park. On his way, he noticed Zachariah's wife and son sitting on a wooden bench near the reception, glancing up and down the passage, their faces blank, their clothes full of blood. Appreciating how lost they must be, he hesitated, thinking how best to deal with everything that needed to be done. He told them to stay where they were while he went to check on his wife.

He found her in the car park under a shady tree.

'I think the best thing is for me to take you and the dogs to Amanda's house and leave you there,' he said on reaching her. 'I'll come back here to sort out the admin, and then return to the farm with Zac's wife and son. I need to see what's happening there.'

Lily's face hardened. 'For goodness' sake. You're far too old to be dealing with things like this.'

'I know, but I can't just run away and wait for everything to return to normal. When we get to Amanda's, phone Graham and tell him to meet me back at our house. Don't forget, the police and *Varume* are there. Hopefully, they'll have things under control.'

'From the way Prince was talking, it sounds like they're the cause of all this.' Lily paused. 'I didn't want to say anything in front of the Zachariahs, but do you think they are looking for dissidents?'

'I don't know what it's about,' Oliver said. 'I guess that could be a possibility. There have been so many dissident-related incidents since Independence, we've been lucky not to have had any trouble before now.'

'Yes, I've sometimes wondered how we've got away with it for so long.'

'Well, that's changed, and I'm afraid I need to get back there as soon as possible to find out what's going on.'

Oliver dropped Lily at Amanda's gate and drove straight back to the hospital. There, the nurse at the casualty reception told him they had taken Zachariah to surgery, and he found Zachariah's wife and son still sitting on the bench. He asked them if they wanted to go back to the farm with him and they both immediately shook their heads. Tobias said they would stay with a relative who lived in the neighbouring suburb of Mzilikazi. Oliver felt in the top pocket of his shirt for the small notebook he kept there, and for some money. He tore a piece of paper from the notebook and wrote Amanda's telephone number on it. Handing money and the piece of paper to them, he said they must phone when they needed help again, then he headed back to the farm, dreading what he might find when he got there.

He saw no-one as he drove down the dusty farm roads. On reaching his home he stopped his car beside the turning circle behind the house and switched off the engine, listening for activity. There was none. It was eerily quiet, despite being a normal working day. He climbed out of his car and was on his way to his study to ring Bea and find out if Graham was on his way back to the farm, when Prince made another sudden appearance.

'What the heck, Prince. Thank God you're safe, but please, stop sneaking up on me like this, will you?'

'Sorry Sir, but you need to come quickly.'

'Again? Now what?'

'The *Varume* have forced everyone to the school. This is a big problem.'

'What? The school? Why?'

'For questioning… but it is not good.' Prince averted his eyes, avoiding further discussion. All he said was: 'Bring the lorry for transport.'

'The lorry? You mean the cattle lorry? Transport for whom?'

'Hurry, Sir.'

'And you? Are you coming with me?'

Prince was silent.

'Right. You stay here then, and hide again, if necessary. Mr Graham Brooke may arrive soon, and you can tell him where I've gone.'

When Oliver reached the school fifteen minutes later, he parked the lorry on the dirt road outside and walked through the gate. Seeing no one about, he went around the side of the admin block to the playground, which was surrounded on three sides by classrooms. He knew the school layout because his family had built it over many years, adding new buildings as the number of children increased.

Staring at the playground, he discovered why Prince was so afraid.

Grown men were lying shirtless on their stomachs in the dirt, a carpet of brown flesh, and the *Varume* were walking on their backs. Despite his shock, Oliver noticed how young the *Varume* appeared, only teenagers, as far as he could tell. They were grinding their heels into the men's backs and poking them with their rifles. Some men were crying in pain. Taking stock of this, Oliver glanced around and observed two groups of people huddled either side of the playground. Children made up one group, women the other. He stared in bewilderment at their terrified faces and the smirking *Varume* herding them as if they were animals. Intermittent sobs cut through the banter and shouts from the *Varume*. As he watched, one of the older girls was dragged from the group of children. A man pushed the bayonet attached to his rifle into her back and must've told her to run, because she took off at high speed to the group of women. Other *Varume* jeered and laughed as she did this. That's when Oliver noticed the policemen standing in the background, watching what was going on, doing nothing.

Without thinking of the consequences, he stormed across to an older looking man, standing with the policemen, assuming he must be in authority.

'What the fuck is going on here?' Oliver burst out. 'These people live and work on my farm and you have no right to treat them in this manner.'

A look of surprise flashed across the man's face, quickly turning to contempt. His eyes narrowed.

'We are conducting our business. It has nothing to do with you. Leave us.'

'I... I will not leave,' Oliver stuttered. 'I have a responsibility to these people,' he waved his hand towards them, 'and... and I will stay until you have finished your business.'

The man licked his lips, then took a cloth from his pocket and wiped his face. His eyes moved in the direction of the other *Varume*, who had stopped what they were doing and were staring at him, confused.

'Leave us,' he spat at Oliver. 'I do not want to see you here again while we are making our enquiries.'

Oliver steeled himself to walk away. He knew it was futile to continuing to argue.

'Thank you. I will wait for them on the road outside.' He turned and strode back around the admin block to where the lorry was parked, his hands shaking, his heart racing. On reaching it, he clambered up the steps into the cab and reversed through the gate so he could turn the lorry to face the way he'd come. He then drove a short distance along the road. He parked in the shade of a large, leafy combretum and switched off the engine, forcing himself not to panic.

He heard nothing from inside the school grounds for what seemed a long time until suddenly people began pouring out of the gate, civilian people, he noticed with relief. He recognized many of them. When they saw the lorry, they surged at it and, without hesitation, began clambering onto it, pushing and shoving as spaces quickly filled. The back of the lorry was soon packed to capacity, but this did not stop more people from climbing on. They scaled the metal poles that made up the sides, finding places to shove their feet, clinging to whatever they could. Oliver dared not leave the cab. Some people scrambled in through the passenger door. He lost count of how many. They squashed themselves on the bench behind the front seats and three people managed to fit in the passenger seat next to him. A young man shoved a baby through the window. It was bundled into the back seat, screaming and kicking. The air became heavy with the smell of sweat and fear. At last, when Oliver could see no one left on the road, he started the engine and drove slowly down the dust road, keeping the engine revs low, fearing any sign of panic may cause a foolhardy reaction from the *Varume*. He headed to his house a few kilometres away, his head spinning with what he had seen and the predicament they were now in. He had no idea what was going to happen, but he knew he could not leave these people at the school with those *Varume* and policemen there.

Graham rushed out of the house to meet Oliver as he pulled up next to the garage, with Prince just behind him. 'What the fuck...?' he said, staring at all the people in the lorry. Oliver opened the cab door and fumbled to find the ladder with his foot so he could climb down, but his leg was shaking so much he kept missing it.

'Here, let me help you,' Graham said, guiding Oliver's foot onto the top rung. He helped Oliver lower himself down the ladder, but even when Oliver was on the ground, he looked shaken. He held onto the lorry door to steady himself, his face drained of colour.

'Prince has been filling me in on what's been happening,' Graham said, 'but I wasn't expecting this.' He pointed at all the people on the lorry.

No one said a word, but, as if some comment was needed, the vehicle gave a sudden groan from the weight of its load.

'Neither was I, I can assure you,' Oliver said, feeling his composure beginning to return. 'I'll tell you what happened at the school a little later, but suffice to say, I couldn't leave them there.'

'Please Sir, we all need to stay here,' Prince said, pointing to the area behind the garage, within their security fence.

'Ah,' Oliver said, staring at the hundred plus men, women, and children. 'Um...' He looked at Graham.

'Why can't they go back to their own homes?' Graham asked Prince.

'*Hayi*, Sir... the *Varume*... *Hayi*.'

'What?'

'No Sir.'

'He's right,' Oliver said. 'From what I saw at the school, we need to stick together until this threat is over. I suppose we can make…um… make space in the barn and the…' He glanced at the clear blue sky. 'At least the weather is warm.'

'We never had to deal with anything like this during the war,' Graham said.

'I know.'

They stared at everyone in the lorry again.

'We'll have to say yes then, and hope things return to normal pretty damned quick,' Graham said to Prince.

'Thank you, Sir.' Prince said, and with this, the multitude began climbing off the lorry, dropping onto the ground, picking themselves up, helping others.

'What about Hardwork?' Oliver asked Prince once the commotion had died down. 'We will need to bury him.'

'Yes Sir, I will take some men now to do so. And then we will return here where we are safe.'

Oliver was not so sure, but he said nothing. His mind was reeling, wondering how they would support so many people and for how long.

CHAPTER 3

THE TELEPHONE in the Pierces' hallway rang, and Richard ran to answer it, hoping one of his friends was confirming their plan to meet later at the Holiday Inn Nightclub.

'Oh hello Granny, how are you?' He made little effort to hide his disappointment. 'I'll call Mum for you.' He yelled for his mother and left the receiver on the table before returning to the veranda. Amanda's daughter, Louise, had dropped in earlier that day to welcome Cassia back to Zimbabwe. Like Richard, she was in her final year at school. It was the school holidays at the moment and while she was using them to prepare for her A level exams in November, she was always looking for excuses to get away from her books.

Bea strode into the hall from the kitchen. After picking up the phone and greeting her mother in her usual cheerful manner, she fell silent.

'Oh Mummy. This sounds terrible,' she eventually said.

There was silence again while she listened to Serena.

'You say over one hundred people... Goodness gracious... All within the security fence. Where on earth are they all going to the toilet?'

Cassia, who had been half listening to her aunt's conversation, wondered what her grandmother was telling Aunt Bea. 'They're having an odd-sounding conversation,' she said to Louise and Richard.

They halted their own conversation to listen.

'Yes, I understand Mummy. Of course, we can't hold the Garden Club meeting in Lily's garden anymore. Don't worry. I'll come up with another plan.'

She ended the call and walked through to the veranda, a warm glow spreading across her cheeks. She sank into one of the chairs.

'What was that about, Mum?' Richard asked.

'There's been trouble on the farm. *Varume* have turned up and have been intimidating the workers. Running around with rifles, shooting at them.'

'God, them! Have they killed anyone?'

'One person we know of.'

'Oh no.'

'Who?' Louise asked. She travelled out to the farm often with her mother and knew many of the workers there.

'Granny didn't say. But Oliver had to rush another person who had been shot to Mpilo. Lily came into town with Oliver and is now at your house, Louise.'

'Oh wow, this must've happened soon after I left. Is the other man okay?'

'Apparently, yes, although he'll be in hospital for a while. Lily tried phoning us to tell Granny to stay here, but the phone was constantly engaged,' Bea said.

'That will be because of you, Richard, always on the phone,' Louise said.

'Exactly.' Bea gave Richard a long stare and then continued. 'So when Lily couldn't get through to us, she phoned Sunlands and discovered that Granny and Graham had just arrived back there.'

'Gees. That's scary,' Richard said. 'Are they okay?'

'They say they are, although they will stay with Oliver at his house for the time being. Lily will remain in town with you and your mother, Louise, although she'll no doubt want to get back to the farm as soon as possible. All the workers are too petrified to return to their own homes in the farm compound and are now camping in the barns behind Oliver's house. There are over a hundred people there.'

'Wow, that's awful,' Cassia said.

'Yes. Granny says they were all forced to go to the school this morning. Apparently, the situation turned out to be pretty nasty. She says it was by the grace of God that Oliver went there in the cattle truck. Heaven only knows what could have happened to them if he hadn't. He said the *Varume* were treating the people appallingly. Poor Oliver, he was shaking like a leaf when he got back to the house with all of those people.'

'He brought them all back to his house in the cattle truck?' Richard said.

'Apparently.'

'Wow. So what were the *Varume* doing?'

'Granny didn't say. I'm sure we'll hear the details soon.'

Cassia had been listening wide-eyed to all this. 'I still don't understand. Who are these *Varume* and why were they treating the farm workers so badly?'

'I guess you don't know what's been happening here since Independence, do you?' Louise said.

'I know some of it. I know there have been some incidents where people have been hurt and some even killed. I know about those poor tourists who were abducted on the road to the Victoria Falls, for instance.'

'It's more than some incidents,' Bea said. 'Since Independence, more people have been killed in Matabeleland and Midlands Province than during the war. It's way worse for farmers and their workers now than it ever was then. The worst part is no one knows what's really going on, and also, they don't have the support and back-up they had during the war. Before Independence, farmers could get onto their agric-alert radios and ask for help if anything threatening occurred. This no longer exists. Now there is this special brigade that we call the *Varume*, supposedly sorting things out, but we hear more bad things than good about them. Today being a case in point.'

'But Granny, Graham and Oliver are safe, aren't they?' Cassia said.

'Granny says they are. But she pointed out something else.' Bea inhaled. 'I can't hold my Garden Club meeting in Lily's garden anymore.'

'Wow. That's true,' Cassia said. 'What are you going to do?'

Bea pursed her lips and sighed. 'I'm not sure. It's such a shame. I was so looking forward to hosting it there. It would have been such a treat for the members of the Garden Club to look around Lily's beautiful garden.'

'You must admit, Aunt Bea,' Cassia said, 'how absurd it is that you can't have your Garden Club meeting at your chosen venue because hundreds of people are now using it as a refuge from danger.'

Bea stared at Cassia, as she thought this over. 'Oh deary me, yes. It is a most bizarre situation, isn't it? No one knows how long these poor people will need to stay there, or if trouble could flare up again. At least some of the neighbours are bringing them food.'

'Bet you're wishing you hadn't come back to this country after all, hey?' Richard said to Cassia.

'No, no, of course not. I'm surprised, that's all, because we weren't aware of any of this in the UK. I thought your lives returned to normal when the war ended and the Africans got what they wanted; i.e. their independence.'

'Well, that's the irony. Our lives are more normal than they were during the war,' Bea said. 'For instance, during the war, all young white boys were called up for compulsory national service as soon as they left school. This was always a terrible worry for everyone, especially as the war escalated and many died. I lived in dread for when Richard would be called up, but thank goodness he was still too young when the war ended. Older men had to do their bit, too, and many were killed.'

'Like my poor dad,' Louise said.

'Oh yes, dear Louise. We do all miss him so.' Bea leant forward and patted Louise's knee. 'On the whole, though, it was a great relief when the war ended and we thought everyone could put down their weapons. The end of the war also allowed us to drive around the country freely. You see, in the late 1970s, when the war was at its height, we always had to drive in convoys whenever we travelled from one town to another, as protection from ambushes on the open roads. Those convoys ceased after Independence. So I'd say Independence brought both good and bad, although the current problems only effect people in rural Matabeleland and Midlands Provinces. Not in the towns, or elsewhere in the country.'

'Well, I'm sorry it's happening anywhere.'

'Us too. There's nothing we can do about it, except get on with our lives as best we can. And, on that note, now that we've put you in the picture, I need to decide what to do about my Garden Club meeting. Should I cancel or change the venue, to here, for instance?'

'Cancel,' Richard said.

Louise flung Richard a dirty look. 'Of course you need to have it, Bea. You're the Chairlady. You've been looking forward to holding this meeting all year. Your garden is perfectly suitable, especially with all your poppies and larkspur in full bloom.'

'Then you need to make sure Frank prunes nothing until afterwards, so you can still have your pruning pro teach the members how to prune their shrubs,' Richard joked.

Bea ignored him. 'Right then. I'll inform everyone that the venue has changed to here. At least this will make it much easier to organise.'

Louise glanced at her watch. 'I guess I'd better go home and see how poor Lily is. She'll be pretty shaken after what has happened.'

'She's not the only one,' Cassia said as she saw Louise out.

*

That afternoon Cassia's friend, Beryl, also came round to the Pierces' to welcome Cassia back. She'd telephoned the previous day to make arrangements, and when Cassia found out about the problems on the farm, she'd tried to cancel but failed to get through to Beryl on the school telephone.

'Things are tense here,' she warned Beryl after greeting her when she arrived. They were standing in the Pierces' paved parking area, between the house and the gate, next to a bank of yesterday, today and tomorrow shrubs in full bloom. The sweet scent from these flowers wafted about them.

Beryl glanced at the house and garden, taking in her lovely surroundings. 'Oh? Why?'

Cassia explained what was happening on the farm and Beryl looked more and more surprised as the story progressed.

'I wish I could understand what it's all about,' Cassia concluded. The contrast between their present setting and what she was describing was not lost on her.

Beryl ran a hand through her thick red hair. 'It does seem strange. Why would your farm workers be afraid of their own race? A special brigade of soldiers, you say?'

'Yes. I don't know why, but apparently they are.'

'I find this hard to believe. I mean, the black people in this country are now free from suppression, and yet you say they are being treated badly by these soldiers.'

'That's how it appears.' Cassia sighed. 'My family seems to think their workers are safe for now, staying in their security fence. Some of the other farmers in the district are helping by dropping off food for all the people there.'

Beryl's lips tightened. 'White farmers?'

'I didn't ask.'

'Mm.'

Cassia wondered what Beryl was implying. She didn't want to delve further, so instead she said: 'Do you want to come in and meet my aunt?'

Beryl glanced at the house. 'No. Now is not a good time. Why don't I return tomorrow, rather, and I'll take you back to Freedom so you can see what it's like there?' She hesitated. 'But, be warned. It is very different from here.'

'I'm sure I won't mind. I look forward to seeing it tomorrow.'

When Beryl arrived back at the Pierces' the next morning, Cassia again invited her in to meet her aunt, and again she declined.

'They won't bite, you know,' Cassia said.

'I know. But, seeing this house and how they live, I doubt we'll have anything in common.' Cassia was quiet while she mulled this over. Maybe she was right, but the Beryl she knew in England would have been more tolerant and open minded.

Cassia walked back into the house to pick up her bag and say goodbye, then she and Beryl were soon on their way, travelling in Beryl's blue Datsun 120Y down the Hillside Road towards town.

'Ah, I love this view,' Cassia said as they crested the top of an elevated part of the tarred road, giving them a view of the town centre in the distance. They stopped at a traffic light and Cassia pointed to an old-fashioned looking house with a derelict cart in the garden, next to the intersection of two main roads. 'You're not going to believe it, but that's where my relatives lived when they first came to this country around 1900. That old cart may have been theirs, although I can't say for sure.'

Beryl glanced at the property. 'Really?'

'Well, they lived on the plot, but in a small house made of corrugated iron. It was knocked down shortly after they sold it, and this house was built in its place.'

'It must've been pretty impressive in its day,' Beryl said, 'although it is rather run down now. Hopefully it'll be torn down too. Black people don't want to be reminded of their colonial past, and who can blame them?'

Cassia pursed her lips. What was up with Beryl, she wondered. Where had this radical attitude come from? She hadn't been like this when they were students together in Bristol.

They drove into town and turned west down Eleventh Avenue towards what Cassia remembered in the old days they called "the locations", and which Beryl now referred to as the "high-density suburbs". This was the part of town where the black population lived before Independence, as opposed to the "low-density suburbs" where the white population lived.

'The segregation was very real,' Beryl said, as if Cassia didn't know already. 'The Indians lived in another part of town and the mixed-race people had their own areas. The problem with Rhodesia was that this segregation was forced. Thank God it's all changed now.'

'So, have any white people moved to the high-density suburbs since Independence?'

'I've only seen a few expats like myself, although lots of blacks have moved to the low-density areas. Of course, most black families still live in the high-density suburbs, but many send their children to schools in the low-density areas, if they can. They think the schools there are better.'

Cassia found her head reeling at all this talk of "high-density" and "low-density".

They turned into the Luveve Road and, a few kilometres later, down a narrow tarred street, separating two rows of squat bungalows. Each house was in a small yard, but none of them had gardens with flowers and lawns, like the Pierces' garden.

Cassia pointed this out and Beryl's face tightened.

'That's because the people who live here choose food security over frivolity,' she said. They continued along the street for a few more blocks. 'That green plant you see in all the yards, which looks a bit like overgrown spinach, is a vegetable called chomolia. Everyone grows it because they can pick off a few fresh leaves for one meal and leave the rest of the plant intact for other meals.'

'Have you tasted it? What's it like?'

'Delicious.'

'I see banana and mango trees growing in lots of yards too.'

'Yes, and mulberry trees. They grow easily here.'

'I rather like this part of town. The houses may be small, but the area is tidy.'

Beryl smirked. 'You reckon, when you compare it to your aunt's house?'

Cassia stared out of the window. She was finding Beryl tedious. 'Some people live in big houses, others in small, Beryl. It's like that all over the world. It's life.'

A young boy ran across the street in front of them at that moment. He was chasing a homemade ball made from a stuffed plastic bag tied with a piece of rubber, and Beryl had to brake and swerve to avoid hitting him.

'Bloody hell,' she shouted. 'I could have run him over.'

Cassia smiled at the youngster and lifted a tentative hand in a wave. The young boy's face lit up and his friends laughed.

'*Khiwa, khiwa,*' they cried, giggling and dancing around.

'That means "hello white people",' Beryl said, waving at them and driving slowly forward.

'If I remember, it doesn't mean that, exactly,' Cassia laughed.

'Mm, well, something similar.'

Beryl turned into the school gate and brought her Datsun to a halt, giving Cassia a chance to take in the scene before them; an open, dirt parking area with the school buildings behind. These buildings were extensive one story blocks, made from bricks with asbestos roofs. The classroom doors opened onto verandas stretching along the front of each building. They looked as if they'd been whitewashed at some stage but, judging from their grimy state, they hadn't been redone for some years.

Beryl edged her Datsun around a small traffic circle in front of the school. It was covered in browning grass and surrounded by rocks, also whitewashed, with the Zimbabwean flag flying on a flag post in the middle.

'I'll take you to where I live,' Beryl said, 'and afterwards I'll introduce you to the headmaster, Mr Abednico Sibanda.'

'So do you live alone right now?' Cassia asked.

'Sort of, although my boyfriend stays with me often. On the quiet, of course, because we don't want the school children to know about us. He lives with his mother and siblings in a suburb called Makokoba, otherwise.'

'I didn't know you had a boyfriend. What's his name?'

'Gladmore Moyo. You'll love him. He's so interesting,' Beryl said.

CHAPTER 4

EARLY DAWN, and Dominic Craig lay on his bunk listening to the water lapping against the side of his boat. He always slept in the cockpit on his boat cruises. He had had the yacht built when he returned from England in 1980. It was a seven-metre cabin cruiser, based on a Matilda. Before the construction started, he sat down with Bulawayo boat maker, Chris Carver, and together they changed the design to enlarge the cockpit. This allowed him to convert the seats into bunks, providing him with four berths – two in the fore-cabin and two in the cockpit. He liked to sleep in the cockpit, under the stars.

Today was the last day of their cruise and, as always, Dominic was sad it was ending. He enjoyed sailing his yacht on Kariba; a vast expanse of freshwater covering a total distance of two hundred and eighty kilometres from one end to the other. It took him five days sailing up the lake against the prevailing wind and three back, sailing by day and mooring up at night, and always depending on the winds. The area is sparsely populated but teeming with big game visible from the water. This was the third time he had done the trip since Independence and it had been as enjoyable as ever. During the final years of the war, before Independence, he would never have dreamed of doing anything like this. There would have been the danger of meeting terrorists crossing the lake from Zambia, the country on the northern shores. But all this had ended with Independence, with the "terrorists" now known as "freedom-fighters". They had won freedom for the majority, and everyone could get on with living their lives the way they wanted, and Dominic counted himself fortunate that he knew what he wanted.

He had travelled enough after school and compulsory army call-up to know that Africa was where he belonged. There was much about Africa he found frustrating, but also much that he loved, and the wildlife was at the top of his list. He could not imagine living in a country where he could not interact with African animals. He found their presence so enriching. This sailing trip, for instance, would have been much less interesting if it hadn't been for the wildlife they'd seen along the way. The animals they viewed on the shoreline – herds of buffalo, elephant, zebra, impala and warthog. The animals they saw in the water – mainly crocodiles and hippos in the bays they moored in every night. And the bird life everywhere – fish eagles soaring above them, calling their eerie cry, whistling ducks flying low across the water, Egyptian geese strutting along the water's edge, cormorants roosting in the dead trees off the shoreline. Encountering all this meant a great deal to him, and he never wanted to live without it. This had triggered in him a positive attitude towards his country, while many of his countrymen saw only doom and gloom. He was thankful he did not regard his life in Zimbabwe this way. Instead, he looked forward to his future, taking over his elderly father's management responsibilities on the family farm. There were two other managers on the farm, besides his father, and Dominic would be the first in the next generation to assume a management position. He hoped others in his extended family would follow suit.

Reaching his decision to forge ahead in Zimbabwe had not been easy when so many people he knew were leaving the country after becoming disillusioned by the outcome of the war. He found this unsettling; firstly, because it meant the community he had been brought up in was disintegrating, and secondly, because he knew the exodus of skills would take generations to replace.

His soul searching had reached a climax when he fell in love with an American girl who came to stay on the family farm a few years ago. Initially, she appeared to enjoy being on the farm as much as he did and involved herself in many projects but, after a few months, her attitude changed. She regarded the farm as too isolated, the projects boring, the people frustrating. "Khaki fever" has worn off, she used to joke with him. She talked him into returning to the States with her and for a year he worked as a farm labourer in her native state of Colorado. Although he found himself again in the great outdoors, with a fair amount of its own wildlife (but tame by his standards), his life there did not excite him the way Africa did, and they finally agreed to part ways.

The odd thing about what was going on in Zimbabwe right now was that while many people (mainly locals) were leaving, many others (mainly foreigners) were applying for jobs and moving to the country. From 1965 to 1980, the international community imposed severe sanctions on the country, but after Independence, they lifted these sanctions, and the country opened up again. This had produced many changes in their lives, and the most notable, on a personal level, was the steady stream of relatives, friends, and friends of friends who now came to stay with them on the farm. Before Independence they had hardly ever had foreign visitors, but now, it was almost as if they had issued an open invitation to anyone who wanted a gap year, or an "African Experience", or just a change of scenery. Right now, his second cousin from Australia, Samantha

Gardner, had come to the farm for a visit, and Dominic had invited her to join them on their sailing trip.

Dominic's old school friend Pete Fletcher, and Pete's wife, Moira, had also joined them. Pete was an experienced sailor and had a Fireball, but this was only good for racing and couldn't make a long cruise like this, so he had jumped at the invitation when Dominic asked him. Pete and Moira slept on the two bunks in the fore-cabin, and Samantha had been sleeping in the cockpit with him.

He stopped his morning musings and glanced across the cockpit at her. Dew had made everything damp, and he could see that she had tucked her head inside her sleeping bag to keep herself dry. He often did this, too, in the early hours of the morning, when the dew was at its heaviest, but, before this, he loved the feel of the cool night air on his face and listening to the night-time noises. The plop of fish jumping, the gentle tap of the mainstay against the mast, water lapping against the boat's sides, the grunt of the hippos, the roar of lions far away.

Although it was August, the first month of spring, the cockpit was hot for most of the day, with only a small square of shade cast by the sails. The girls found this daytime heat uncomfortable, so they spent most of their time lying on the front bunks inside the cabin with the front hatch open. This allowed a cool breeze to blow through the hull, even reaching Dominic and Pete in the cockpit, where Dominic helmed the boat and Pete trimmed the sails according to the wind direction.

When arranging these sailing expeditions on Lake Kariba, Dominic always invited another boat to join him. He preferred having more than one boat, in case anything went wrong, because the only other vessels they ever saw on the lake were kapenta fishing rigs and a ferry. The kapenta rigs operated in the waters near the towns of Kariba, on the north-eastern shores of the lake, and Binga, on the south-western shores, with the ferry travelling between these towns. Otherwise, the lake was empty of other vessels.

This time Dominic had asked Davo and Sandy Davidson to join them in their yacht, a smaller, two-berth cabin cruiser called a C Sharp. Every night, they tethered their boats together and tied up to one of the thousands of dead trees along the lake's shoreline.

Dominic had discovered, on his first sailing trip on Kariba, that if he moored the boats on the shoreline every bug, beetle and flying insect in the vicinity flew into their lights after dark, but if he tied to a tree fifty metres off the shoreline, they had none. Of course, they always had to check first that there weren't any hippo nearby, although most hippo moved off if the boats came too close. But crocodiles were a different story, and most nights, someone would shine a torch across the water to pick up their red eyes. They would always see at least one, so no one dared dip a finger or a toe into the water. Last night, however, Davo drank more brandy and coke than he should have and threatened to dive into the water "just for the hell of it", much to the consternation of Sandy and the other girls.

They'd all had too much to drink, probably because it was the final night of their trip, and Davo said it would be a waste of energy carrying any of the hooch they still had off the boat. Stupid bugger, Dominic thought. It's no wonder everyone was still asleep. Most nights, they'd exhibited relatively controlled behaviour, with everyone climbing into Dominic's bigger cockpit for dinner and then playing cards. These games became ever more competitive as the cruise progressed, with Moira, who was the overall winner, keeping running totals of their nightly scores.

Dominic looked at Sam again, still sleeping with her head inside the sleeping bag. Thank God things had not ended the way they were heading, he thought to himself now. She had sat next to him while they played cards, her leg constantly rubbing up against his, touching his arm, giggling at his every move. For one moment, he thought a starlit romp could have been a fun way to end the trip, but then he considered who she was, and he changed his mind. Samantha was the granddaughter of his father's cousin, Patricia, so they were distant cousins, but Patricia was a domineering busy body and it was best to keep her at a distance. The Gardners had left Rhodesia back in the sixties, but Dominic still remembered this about her. So, no, he didn't want to get entangled with her granddaughter, Samantha, however brief, in case it got back to her. When the evening wrapped up and the girls clambered onto the Davidsons' boat to clean their teeth and pee discretely off the back, as they did every evening, Dominic climbed onto the roof of his cabin and sat there, with his back against the mast, staring at the shine of the moon on the water, waiting for everyone to go to bed. He knew he might cramp Pete and Moira's space a little, but at least Samantha wouldn't flirt with him up there. That was the only problem with these boat trips. It was difficult to get away if you needed to. At least it was pleasant watching the ripples on the water, and the night became even more agreeable when the dark hulk of a bull elephant came down to the water to drink. Dominic sat watching him, marvelling at how such an enormous animal could be so quiet. When he finished drinking, he wandered up the bank again, and Dominic saw this as his cue to retire too. Checking there was no further movement on the boat, he slid off the roof and into his sleeping bag in the cockpit.

As if Samantha had been following the replay of last night's events in his head, she emerged from her sleeping bag and gave him a bright smile. 'Morning.' She pushed her fingers through her tousled hair, then stretched and writhed about like a cat. 'Shit, I'm feeling rough this morning. And you?'

'Not too bad.'

'You're probably better off than me, sitting up on the roof for a while and sobering up before going to bed.'

'Yeah.' His eyes flashed over her face, and he wondered if she knew he'd done this to avoid her. Maybe. He sensed some tension behind her smile.

He felt in the cubbyhole next to his bunk for his t-shirt. Finding it, he flicked it over his head and shoved his arms into the sleeves. 'Now you're awake, I'll put the kettle on for tea.' He swung himself onto the seat dividing the cockpit from the cabin. A small galley with a two-plate gas stove was situated just inside. 'Coming in,' he warned Pete and Moira, in the fore-cabin. 'Hope you're decent.' Ignoring the rustle of sleeping bags, he scooped up water from the lake to fill the kettle and then lit the gas stove.

'Morning,' Pete said. 'What's the weather like? I can't hear much wind.'

'No. It's still pretty calm, but we're in no hurry to get to Binga, so we can wait for the wind to pick up.'

'Speak for yourself,' Sam said as she pulled herself onto her elbow to peer at the calm lake. 'I can't wait to loll in the hot springs at the Binga Resort. The thought of this has kept me going these last ten days.' She laughed at her joke.

'Howzit guys,' Davo piped from where he stood on the deck of his boat, wearing nothing but a pair of black boxer shorts. He rubbed his bronzed chest. 'Have you *okes* got hot water? Our gas seems to have run out and I need a cup of coffee right now.'

Dominic said: 'Hot water coming up shortly, pass your mugs over.'

Davo stepped from his boat onto theirs, pushing Dominic's sleeping bag to the bottom of the bunk and sitting down. He smiled at Sam, who was still in her sleeping bag, leaning on her elbow. 'Morning Beautiful.'

'Hardly,' Sam muttered, 'but hopefully a good deal better than you look. You sure burned the candle at both ends last night.'

Davo's hairy face twisted into a crooked smile. 'Speak for yourself, Madam. But hey man, we had a *lekker jawl*. Nothing that a strong coffee won't sort out.'

Dominic arranged the mugs in a row on the seat next to him, asking for tea and coffee orders. Once everyone had yelled their preferences, he spooned instant coffee into some mugs and put tea bags into others, before pouring in the boiling water. He then opened the icebox next to the seat he was sitting on and searched for a bottle of milk. They had replenished their ice stocks in Kariba town, but that was four days ago and most of it had now melted. Probably a good thing their trip was ending, he thought.

'So what's the story?' Davo asked, slurping his coffee.

Dominic glanced at the calm, golden-coloured water surrounding them. 'We've still got some bacon and eggs left over, so let's have a final fry up while we wait for the wind. Hopefully, after this we can have a good run into Binga. We might even fly our spinnakers. It should only take a couple of hours. When we arrive, the girls can walk up to the resort and spend the afternoon in the hot springs, while we take the boats out of the water and sort everything out.'

'I'll join the girls in the hot springs,' Pete called from the front bunk.

'No, you won't,' Dominic said, rummaging around in the tiny cupboard below the galley, looking for the frying pan.

*

As they approached the Binga harbour a few hours later, they could see someone standing on the jetty looking out towards them. Sailing closer, Dominic recognized Andre Van Staaden from the Binga Resort.

'Useful having him there to catch us when we come in,' he shouted to Pete, who was sitting on the front deck with Moira. He released the jib, which started flapping in the wind, the jib sheet flicking from one side of the deck to the other. Sam was sitting on the roof of the cabin, her back against the mast. 'I'll turn into the wind as we approach the jetty and you can throw him the painter, hey Pete.'

'Okey, dokey.' Pete called back. Most of the times they'd come into shore, he'd had to leap off the boat and control it, preventing it from ramming too hard into the jetty or the beach. Andre was an experienced boatman, and he readied himself to catch the painter even before Pete said anything to him. Pete threw it, then leapt onto the jetty after it to help Andre steady the boat. Dominic tossed the stern painter to Pete, who pulled the stern in and tied it to the jetty while Andre secured the bow.

'Thanks man,' Dominic said. 'I'll fetch my vehicle so we can offload our kit into it before we take the boat out of the water.'

He felt on the shelf above the galley for the keys of his Land Cruiser and stepped off the boat, taking a moment to steady himself after being on water for so many days.

Andre put out his hand to shake Dominic's. 'You have a pleasant trip?'

'The best. The winds were great, the weather perfect. Company questionable... but that's life. You can't have everything, can you?' Dominic raised an eyebrow at Pete.

Andre straightened his glasses. 'Well, you're all looking healthy enough. As brown as berries, that's for sure.'

'Yes, we've been wearing nothing but our cossies and boxers for the last two weeks. But hey, here come's Davo's boat. We'd better help him in. Throw me your painter, Sandy,' he yelled.

Davo steered his C Sharp to the other side of the jetty. Andre caught the painter and pulled the bows in while Dominic grabbed the stern to pull it against the tyres hanging down the sides of the jetty.

'Thanks, *okes*, bloody brilliant,' Davo said. He tossed a few things from his cockpit onto the jetty.

Andre joined Dominic as he went to collect his vehicle while Pete and Davo let down the jibs. Both main sails were flapping loudly but they wouldn't let these down until they'd removed everything that needed taking out of the boats, otherwise they'd get in the way.

'I'm afraid my main reason for coming here wasn't to help you in,' Andre said. 'I had a call from your father.'

Dominic stopped walking. 'Is he okay?'

'He is, but there's been an incident on your farm.'

'Oh God, what? Dissidents?'

'No, *Varume*, apparently. They've been terrorising your labour, who are now all staying inside the security fence around your homestead.'

'What? Since when?'

'He says they've been there for two days.'

'Fuck.' Dominic stared out at the calm-looking expanse of blue water, spreading all the way to the horizon in the east and west, and across to Zambia in the north. 'And here I've been chilling on the lake, having a great time, while my poor old man's been dealing with this.' Dominic looked at his watch. 'I've still got a lot to do sorting out my boat. It's not as if I can rush back there this minute. Do you know if my dad's cousins are on the farm? And my mother?'

'Your father told me to tell you that your mother was there, and he mentioned, umm, was it Graham and Serena, if I remember rightly?'

'Yes. They're the cousins. But they're all old and shouldn't be dealing with shit like this.'

'Can I tell the others what's happened while you drive your vehicle to the jetty?' Andre asked.

'Yes please,' Dominic said. 'Maybe we can get things done quickly enough for me to set off this afternoon.'

42

By the time he'd driven his Land Cruiser to the jetty, Pete had taken over.

'Andre has told us what's happened and we've made a plan. You're going to drive back to Bulawayo in my car as soon as you're ready, and the rest of us will stay here and sort out the boats, after which we'll go up to the resort, where we'll stay the night, and then head back tomorrow.'

Andre nodded his head. 'Come back with me now to the hotel, Dominic, and I can give you a few cokes and some sandwiches for your journey.'

Dominic looked at everyone. 'Thanks. I really appreciate this.'

Sam grabbed Dominic's arm. 'Do you want me to come back with you, as we're talking about my relatives too?'

Dominic narrowed his eyes for a moment. 'No, don't worry. You stay here and enjoy the hot springs. Hopefully, things on the farm won't be as bad as they sound, but it'll be easier if I get back there on my own.

CHAPTER 5

WOOD SMOKE filled the air as Dominic drove down the dirt road towards his parent's house, the acrid smell wafting through the open windows of Tom's Peugeot 505 sedan. This car was new and nippy, especially when driving up the steep hills out of the Zambezi escarpment, and Dominic got back to the farm in a little over four hours, an all-time record for him. He would phone the Binga Resort later, as soon as he had assessed the situation, to let the others know whether they could bring his boat back to the farm and swap cars, or whether they should carry on into town in his Land Cruiser.

Dominic's heart sank when he drove up to the gate of his parent's security fence and found it shut tight and padlocked with a thick chain. They'd always kept the gate locked during the war, but hadn't felt the need to do this once the war was over. But here they were again, locking it. Damn, he thought. Petros, one of their security guards, came running from behind the garage and Dominic's heart sank further when he saw he was carrying a gun, something else they thought they could do away with after the war.

'*Yebo*, Petros, *litshonenjani*,' he said, driving through the gate. Petros locked it behind him and came to the garage where Dominic was parking the Peugeot. 'So what's going on?'

'Everyone is scared, so they are staying inside the security fence.'

'Scared of what?'

'They have heard rumours of people being killed for harbouring dissidents. The *Varume* came and were interrogating people, and shot Hardwork and Zachariah. Hardwork was killed, and now they are scared there will be more killings. They have heard terrible stories.'

'Hardwork. Oh, no!'

'*Yebo*.'

'And Zac?'

'He is still at Mpilo. Your father took him there.'

'That's awful, Petros.'

'*Yebo*.'

'So tell me, are there dissidents here?' He wondered if Petros would tell him, even if there were. He felt for Petros, and anyone else in his position, because this situation caught them between the proverbial rock and a hard place. If there were dissidents in their compound, and he informed on them, they or their comrades could kill him, yet if he didn't inform on them, the *Varume* would come for him. They'd shown what they were capable of by killing Hardwork. Poor bugger. Had he been harbouring dissidents? He'd worked for them as a cattle handler since he was a young adult. Surely he hadn't been involved in anything untoward?

Petros's reply was adamant: 'There have never been dissidents here.'

'I hope you're right. If there were, they would be after us *makhiwas* you know? Surely no one wants trouble like this?'

'Not us *madalas,* but we can't tell with youths. They talk, it can sway their minds.'

'If you hear of anyone, you'll let me know, won't you?'

'*Yebo,*' Petros replied.

Dominic picked up the small satchel he'd brought back with him and made for the house. While walking across the back lawn, he glanced over at where everyone was camping, between the sheds and the security fence. Lots of small fires had been lit, on which women were cooking their evening meals. The faces of those close to the fires shone deep orange in the firelight. He recognised many of them, but he didn't want to talk to anyone else now. It had been a long day. He dropped his bag in the hall, wondering where his parents were, as he walked into the kitchen to get a beer from the fridge. He grabbed the beer and went back through the hallway and out onto the veranda where he found them, sitting in their usual chairs, having their evening drinks, his mother's favourite Roger Whittaker LP playing on the stereo inside the sitting room; behaving as if nothing stressful was happening, as if their back garden was not full of their workers taking refuge.

Dominic kissed his mother's cheek and flung himself into the chair next to his father. 'Howzit?' he said.

'As you see us,' Oliver replied. 'A bit of a mess, if we're honest.'

'But you're okay?'

'We're holding up, but glad you're back, dear boy.'

Dominic smiled weakly. 'Me too. Have there been any more incidents since…. was it yesterday?'

Oliver said: 'No, the day before. Your mother stayed in town the night after the incident but insisted on returning yesterday. The Greaves were passing on their way to Nyamandhlovu and she got a lift with them.'

Dominic said: 'I'm sorry I was out of comms for so long.'

'None of us were to know something like this would happen when you left.'

'How was your trip?' Lily asked. 'Did you have a good time? Did Sam enjoy herself?'

'I'm not sure it was quite up Sam's street, but for me, it was as enjoyable as ever. I left Sam at the Binga Resort, thought it better not to bring her back in case things were a bit hairy here. Besides, she was desperate to spend time in those hot springs.'

Lily said: 'Yes, Patricia would not like her grandchild being anywhere near danger. She'll have her on the next plane back to Australia as soon as she hears what's been happening here. Nevertheless, I'm pleased you enjoyed your trip.'

'Where are Graham and Serena?'

'They've been staying here since this happened. They're bathing right now, but you'll see them at dinner.'

Dominic took a swig of his beer. 'Petros gave me the lowdown. He told me about Hardwork and Zac, and said people were being interrogated about harbouring dissidents in our compound. Do you think they are?'

Oliver leant back in his chair and joined the tips of his fingers. 'It is impossible to tell. I hope not.'

Dominic said: 'Yup, it's hard to understand why all this is happening, isn't it? The war is over. Everyone should be happy.'

Oliver said: 'The racism before Independence has turned into tribalism now.'

'Hard for us to fathom.'

Oliver grimaced. 'Yes, it's not good... what's been happening... on any level. It was worrying seeing the heavy-handed way the *Varume* were treating our labour during their so called "interrogation".' He described what had happened at the school.

While he was talking Lily left them to go and check on the dinner, unnoticed by both men.

'Fuck Dad, you shouldn't have done that,' Dominic said when Oliver finished telling him about his behaviour at the school. 'They could have shot you.'

'I know, I know. I was acting on auto-drive and it was only when I got back to the house that I realised how rash I'd been.'

'Was Mum with you?'

'God no. She was in town with Amanda. As I said before, she only returned yesterday.'

'Bloody hell Dad. You all need to be more careful.'

Oliver licked his lips, looking abashed for a moment. 'Yes, dear boy, you have every right to give us a bollocking, but we have learnt our lesson now.'

'You reckon? Mum shouldn't have come scurrying back here straight away.' He clapped his father on his back.

'I know, but she insisted.'

'So, tell me, have we got our entire labour force and their families here?'

'No, yesterday we divided them up and shovelled half of them across to Martin's place while the other half remained here. It was getting congested having them all here, and it doesn't make much difference whether they're staying inside our security fence or Martin's. Martin and Kate are still in South Africa, but we've got armed guards at all the homesteads now.'

'Well, that's good. Are all the labour staying inside the security fences all the time, or are they going out to work during the day?'

'They were at work today.'

'I guess that's a step in the right direction. We can't carry on like this for very long. They have to go back to their homes at some stage.'

'I thought you should go to the police tomorrow and talk to the member-in-charge. You have a good way with most people, especially as you are fluent in Ndebele. Try to get some sense out of him. Check if their lives are in danger.'

'Okay, I'll do that.'

*

The member-in-charge of the local police station did little to reassure Dominic that everything would return to normal. In fact, he considered everything normal as it was and saw no issue with *Varume* forcing the local population to go to the school and be treated like animals. When Dominic mentioned the men being made to strip off their shirts and lie on the ground while the *Varume* walked on their backs, the policeman categorically denied anything like this had happened. He called Oliver's version of events "an exaggeration", waving his hand at Dominic and telling him his father had misunderstood what was happening. Dominic was reluctant to get into an argument with a police official so he did not contradict him, despite feeling uncomfortable, knowing this man was fobbing his father off. His discomfort grew when he asked the member-in-charge if it would be safe for their labour to return to their homes and was told that they must, they had nothing to fear, but they must attend *pfungwis* each weekend as they needed to be "re-educated."

They held the first of these *pfungwis* that Saturday, the same day as Beatrice's Garden Club meeting in town. While Bea was adding the finishing touches to what she hoped would still be an enjoyable gathering of gardening enthusiasts, despite the last minute change in venue, the young children living on the farm and surrounding areas were being forced to gather at the school, on a day they would never normally go there. After the incident earlier that week, none of their parents dared challenge the command issued by the police that they must attend.

Later that afternoon, Prince related to Dominic in Ndebele what had happened, and Dominic relayed this to his parents. According to Prince, when the children arrived at the school, the teachers ordered them to assemble in the playground and sit on the dusty ground, where they remained all morning, listening to lectures about the evils of colonialism. They were told about the sacrifices the freedom fighters had made and the hardships they had endured so that everyone could now be free. The teachers delivered these lectures, and they did not let up till noon, at which time they gave each child *sadza* for lunch. The children ate this with their hands out of large iron pots.

'The *sadza* they ordered us to donate, I've no doubt,' Oliver muttered, but said no more when he saw Lily scowling at him.

Dominic continued relating what Prince had told him. After eating, the children had to gather again in the playground and this time the teachers taught them liberation war songs. Someone beat a drum, and the teachers encouraged them to dance while they all sang. They dismissed the children at four o'clock.

'Well, well,' Oliver said. 'What a very long day for small children. Did they enjoy themselves?'

Prince's head did not move. Only his eyes slid toward Oliver. 'Yes, Sir.'

'Mm. You reckon? Well, at least it's now over. They've listened to the lectures and they've learnt the songs. They have been re-educated.'

'No, Sir, we have been told we need to attend *pfungwis* every Saturday.'

Lily shook her head. 'Surely not. All of you?'

'Yes.'

'But why the small children? Saturdays are the time they need for themselves.'

'The police gave instructions to the parents,' Prince said. 'Sunday will be their day for playing.'

There was silence. They all felt uncomfortable about this latest development. They had heard stories about workers on other farms being subjected to *pfungwis*, but this was the first time they had experienced it here.

Oliver said: 'Oh well, I suppose you need to ready yourself for your session, eh, Prince?'

Prince stared at his feet. 'Yes, Sir.'

'Maybe you should stop calling me sir,' Oliver said. 'Mr Craig is fine with me.'

Prince's eyes flashed again in Oliver's direction. 'No, Sir.'

Oliver's heart went out to him. They had known each other for so long, and no one had ever messed him around like this. 'Well, you go off now, good man. I hope everything will be fine.'

Prince licked his lips. 'Thank you, Sir.'

There was an uncomfortable silence while they waited for him to go.

Lily was the first to speak. 'It's indoctrination, pure and simple. Surely they don't need this?'

Dominic patted his mother's arm. 'You'd think not, but hey, we don't know what goes on behind the scenes. Maybe they do need to be re-educated.' Trying to make light of it, he said: 'They need to learn not to call you two sir and madam, for starters, although I can't see that happening in a hurry.'

The sound of a vehicle coming up their drive interrupted him. They weren't expecting anyone, and they glanced at each other.

'I'll see who it is,' Dominic said, rising from his chair.

He returned with John and his two sons, much to everyone's relief. They had returned from their fishing trip earlier that day.

'Thank goodness it's only you,' Lily said.

'Yes, what are you doing here?' Oliver asked.

'We decided you guys could do with our support,' Will said.

Lily said: 'But what about Beatrice's Garden Club? I thought you'd all be heading straight into town so Molly could attend.'

'I suggested she go with Mum and Graham,' John said. 'They need a break after all the tension out here this week. Molly will stay with her folks tonight, and Mum and Graham will stay with Bea. They'll all return tomorrow. I would have tried to talk you lot into going, too, but I know you wouldn't have gone.'

'No,' Lily said, 'even though I know it will be an enjoyable event.'

'Of course it will,' John agreed. 'If there's one thing my sister is good at, it's entertaining.'

'Oh yes,' Lily said.

'But, as for you guys, it's not much fun out here right now, so once we'd finished unpacking the car, we thought we'd come over.'

'Kind of you, John,' Oliver said.

Lily leapt up and gave John a hug. 'Absolutely. You've always had a good heart, despite being such a naughty little boy in the classroom when I taught you all those years ago.'

'Someone had to be,' John laughed.

'You'll stay for supper, won't you? We're having spaghetti bolognaise, and there's plenty. In fact, why not stay the night? Safety in numbers, and all that, eh?'

'Right, that sounds like a good plan. Thanks. But hey, what's been happening today? Is that drumming I hear in the distance? Has the *pfungwi* started?'

'What do you mean, it's been going on all day,' Oliver said. 'First the poor children. Now it's the adult's turn. They'll be at it all night, I've no doubt.'

There was silence while everyone listened. The rhythmic sound of faraway drumbeat was obscured by the chirping of crickets in the garden and a flock of babblers causing a riot as they flew into a tree. The rattle of a beetle nearby followed this and then a francolin screeched in the bush beyond the security fence.

'Normal evening sounds. Pity about the drumming in the background,' Lily said. 'We often hear drumming from the compound and we usually enjoy the sound, but somehow it seems sinister this evening, doesn't it?'

The drumming stopped and someone started yelling at the top of his voice.

John said: 'Bloody hell, now that does sounds sinister. They're getting a right ear-bashing, aren't they?' He took a slug of the beer he'd brought with him.

Oliver said: 'They are indeed. I don't think we need to listen to it. Dominic, please put your mother's favourite Herb Alpert LP on the stereo. His trumpet drowns out most extraneous noises, doesn't it Lily, my love?' He smiled at her.

'I'll help you, Dom,' Will said, 'and while we're there, who wants another drink? We mustn't forget that Saturday night is party night, eh?'

*

For weeks, the Craigs and Brookes endured the incessant chanting, singing, and drumming that emanated from the *pfungwis* held at the school. This noise, although from afar, annoyed them, as they assumed most attendees didn't want to be there. Talk about being brainwashed, Dominic thought. Is this what their so-called freedom means?

He decided he would see their neighbour and friend, Siphas Ngwenya, about these *pfungwis*. Siphas had bought the farm next door from their long-term neighbours, the Beamishes, when they sold it and moved to England in 1980. The Ngwenyas were strangers in the area when they bought the farm, but the Craigs developed a friendship with Siphas and his wife after Lily and Oliver went round to meet them when they first arrived, taking a cockerel and a hen as a welcoming gift.

'This will surprise them,' Oliver had said, 'but we need to embrace the new Zimbabwe if we intend living here, and being friendly with our neighbours is the first step.'

Some family members had disagreed.

'Martin thinks you shouldn't have done that,' Martin's wife, Kate, said to Lily when she found out about their visit to the Ngwenyas'. Her maid, Flora, had told her. 'Martin says we should stick to our own kind and not fraternise with the locals. It surprised Flora as well.'

'I've no doubt,' Lily responded. 'Her only experience of white people is working for them.'

'There's nothing wrong with that. I treat her very well,' Kate said. 'She often confides in me, telling me about her family and children, and I'm always giving her my old clothes and other things. But I'm certainly not going to sit down and have cups of tea with her, like you did with the Ngwenyas.'

'I know you're fond of Flora,' Lily said, 'and I'm sure she appreciates everything you do for her. Of course you can't change the mistress/maid relationship you have with her; you'd both be uncomfortable if you did, but the Ngwenyas are different. They aren't domestic helpers. They are our neighbours and social equals.'

Kate snorted. 'Honestly Lily, excuse me for being so frank, but you can be so naïve. Don't you know he was a *gook* during the war? Our security forces would have captured or shot him, and now you're taking him and his wife a pair of chickens and pretending they're on an equal social footing to us.'

Lily blanched, but refused to back down. 'The war is over, and we must stop looking back, or call him a "*gook*" or a "terrorist". Now we refer to him as a freedom fighter. We all need to move on, Kate. Imagine the progress this country could achieve if we overcame our racial prejudices and united.'

This conversation had taken place years ago, shortly after Independence. Mrs Ngwenya had died since then, and the Brookes still had no contact with Mr Ngwenya, while the Craigs saw him from time to time when he paid them a visit. They mostly met about farming matters, and a respectful civility had developed between them. It was exactly because of his wartime credentials that Dominic went to see Siphas Ngwenya now about the *pfungwis*.

He pulled into his yard and switched off the engine of his Land Rover, hoping Siphas would have heard him arrive. Luna sat in the passenger seat of the vehicle, growling at the Ngwenya dogs as they sniffed the wheels. Dominic had removed the doors from the cab, to enable him to hop in and out easily when he was driving around the farm, and he had taught Luna to stay inside unless he was told he could jump out. Despite this, he continued to bristle and growl at the Ngwenya dogs.

'Shush,' Dominic said to him, also remaining seated in the cab, staring at what had once been Mrs Beamish's impeccable garden, remembering when it had been as lovely as his mother's. Like his mother, Mrs Beamish had taken great pride in her garden, as had her mother-in-law before her, and between them, they'd also overseen the creation of a small piece of paradise. The Beamish ladies had spent years learning about the best plants to grow in these semi-arid conditions. They had arranged the sinking of wells and trained one gardener after another to plant, water, prune, weed, and mow, transforming the dry bush into lush green lawns, thriving indigenous trees, and flourishing flower beds. With sadness, Dominic observed that all of this had disappeared. It seemed that Siphas had no interest in gardening except to grow food. Could you blame him, living here alone, Dominic wondered? He stared at the miserable chomolia plants growing on ridges outside the veranda and the scruffy yard filled with dry, dead mealie stalks, which were lying on the bare ground where the luscious lawns had once grown. The

Beamishes had enjoyed a stunning view from their home, but this was now blocked by a washing line, filled with washing, either pegged or hitched to the barbed wire drooping between two cock-eyed and rusty poles. Mrs Beamish's greenhouse, the place where she'd propagated a vast assortment of plants, was now a chicken coop. From where he was sitting, Dominic could see that the shelves where she'd kept her seedling trays were half eaten by white ants, and the door was hanging crooked by one hinge. The chickens were milling around the garden, scratching the bare ground.

Another scrawny dog appeared at the glass door leading onto the veranda. On seeing Dominic's Land Rover, it hopped through a broken pane of glass and ran up to the vehicle, barking. This encouraged the other dogs to bark again, and Luna gave another low growl as they ran around the vehicle, yapping, their skinny tails bristling above their thin bodies.

'No, boy,' Dominic said. 'You stay where you are and behave yourself.'

Luna glanced at him and gave a quick wag of his tail before turning his attention back to the dogs outside.

The commotion must've motivated Mr Ngwenya to check what was going on, because he soon appeared at the glass door. Dominic heard the high-pitched rasping of the metal frame scraping the concrete floor as he pushed the door open. It, too, was hanging by one hinge only, causing it to droop forward when Siphas let go of the handle.

'Shut up!' he yelled at his dogs. They stopped barking and crawled under an overgrown bougainvillea bush next to the driveway from where they could watch the proceedings.

Dominic told Luna to stay where he was, and he slid out of the cab.

Mr Ngwenya gave him a welcoming smile. 'Hello Dominic, how are you?'

'Well, thank you, and you?' Dominic said.

'Still struggling. Our borehole pump has packed in, so we now have to draw water from the well with buckets.' As if on cue, a woman walked past them at that moment with a bucket on her head. She gave a small curtsey, before continuing to the house. 'My house girl,' Siphas explained.

'Have you pulled the pump up to check what's wrong?'

'No. We don't have the equipment to pull up borehole pumps.'

'Ah. Would you like me to send my guys here tomorrow morning with our tripod? They'll get it up in no time, and Kenneth, our mechanic, may detect the problem straight away. He's pretty good.' As Dominic said this, he wished his parents had given the Ngwenyas' a tripod as a welcoming present when they'd first moved in, instead of the chickens they'd brought them, much to the ridicule of the Brookes.

'Thank you, I would appreciate that very much,' Mr Ngwenya said.

Dominic paused for a moment. 'There's something you might help me with; that's why I've come to see you.' Siphas looked at Dominic, waiting to hear what this was. 'You know about the trouble we had on our farm. The incident at the school?'

'Of course. Some of my labour were forced to go there too. They told me afterwards that if your father had not arrived when he did, more people may have been killed.'

'I hope not,' Dominic said.

'Your father is a brave man, but he needs to be careful. There are evil people around. Your father was lucky this time. The *Varume* were so surprised when he arrived and started shouting at them, they didn't know how to handle him, so they let him and the others go.'

'You reckon?'

'Yes. Terrible things are happening these days. We hear worrying reports about these *Varume,* although we are not sure how true they are. They cover much up.'

'But why? The country is independent now. Everyone should be happy.'

'We are from different tribes. Tribalism has replaced racism.'

'Is that so?'

'This is happening.'

Dominic traced his foot in the dirt, trying to make sense of what he was hearing. 'I wanted to ask you about these *pfungwis.* They take place at our school every weekend. Are people being forced to attend because of tribalism?'

'Partly.'

'Must they endure what sounds like brainwashing?'

'They are simple people.'

'But shouldn't adults be allowed to choose?' Siphas said nothing, so Dominic continued. 'Is there any way to stop these *pfungwis?* I have known many of the people my whole life who are being forced to attend, and they don't deserve to be treated this way.'

Siphas puckered his lips. 'I steer clear of politics. It is a dirty game at the moment. However, my brother is involved in politics. I will ask him if there is anyone he can talk to.'

'Thank you. I will send Kenneth and some guys from the workshop here tomorrow to look at your borehole pump.'

*

The *pfungwis* at the school stopped after this. Dominic told no one about his conversation with Siphas Ngwenya. He didn't know what Siphas meant when he mentioned "bad things happening", but he sensed it was best not to talk about it to anyone else for fear of bringing whatever this was closer to home.

CHAPTER 6

WHEN CASSSIA first made plans to return to Zimbabwe, she thought she'd spend the weeks before school started staying with her grandmother on the farm. She and Serena had always been close, and she'd always loved spending time at the farm.

Visiting the chapel was at the top of her list of things she wanted to do when she got there. Isabella Craig had had this chapel built near the school in the 1920s; the school where the recent dreadful incident had occurred and where the *pfungwis* were now being held every weekend. In the late 1940s, Isabella, a prolific artist, encouraged school children to paint murals on the chapel walls, transforming a plain building into something special. As a child, Cassia remembered being riveted by these murals. They depicted the school children's own interpretations of bible stories, so all the people in the murals were black, all the structures were mud huts, and the backgrounds contained rocky *kopjes* and African animals and trees. The children filled every interior wall of the chapel with these murals, from the roof to the floor, and they painted them in flat tones, but using vibrant colours. This, together with their size, made them very striking. Cassia longed to see them again with adult eyes and feared for their safety amidst the unpleasant incidents occurring near there now.

Of course, her plans to spend time on the farm had to be shelved. Even Amanda, who visited the farm often, was told to stay in town, and Sam did not go back there after returning from Binga. Instead, the Brookes brought her possessions into town, and she flew back to the safety of Australia, within the week. Only those who lived on the farm stayed there, and they encouraged everyone else to keep away until things settled down again.

This was disappointing for Cassia. Not that she disliked being in Bulawayo with Aunt Bea, but she still found her cousins, Sarah and Jane, difficult. She had hoped their joint effort in helping Bea arrange her Garden Club meeting (which was a great success, despite the last minute change of venue) would bring them closer, but this had not happened. Then, sharing their interest in fashion and design, and again hoping to reignite their friendship, she offered to help in their shop as a sales assistant, for no wage, in the weeks she would be around. But they turned her offer down and remained indifferent towards her attempts at friendship.

She wondered if Aunt Bea noticed this coolness. Bea said nothing, but Cassia could see she was attempting to include her in her own activities, probably because Sarah and Jane were not. So Bea invited her to attend her monthly book club at a friend's house, asked her to fill in with tennis on the Pierces' tennis court when one of their usual four could not make the weekly session, and found herself included in a "girl's lunch" at the Peking Restaurant, where the average age of the "girls" was forty. She appreciated Bea's efforts to include her in all these activities, but she felt bad she had to do this for her. However, when Amanda's daughter, Louise, invited her to join her gang at The Granada Restaurant and Nightclub, where they spent an enjoyable evening dancing and listening to the local band, Special FX, she found herself the oldie of the group, as Louise and her friends were still at school, albeit it in their last year.

She got away from the Pierces' house, whenever possible, by borrowing Aunt Bea's Renault 8 and visiting Amanda and Louise at their home, where she felt more welcome and relaxed. She wished she'd gone straight there when she first arrived in Zimbabwe, instead of to the Pierces' home, but Amanda was a more distant relative than Aunt Bea, and when she was making her plans, it never occurred to her that Sarah and Jane wouldn't want her around.

*

Finally, the time came for Cassia to move to the cottage at Freedom High School, but again, things did not go as she had envisaged or wanted. Freedom was completely different from what she was accustomed to, which would have been fine with Beryl's support. However, upon arrival, she quickly realised Beryl would not provide this.

Aunt Bea drove Cassia to Freedom with her eyes darting from right to left. She told Cassia she'd never been to this part of town before and because it was unfamiliar territory for her, she insisted on bringing Frank with them, "in case we need backup". He sat on the backseat of her Renault 8 with Cassia in the front passenger seat next to her aunt. Cassia hoped he was enjoying a change from his gardening.

'These townships really aren't that bad,' Aunt Bea said several times.

'They're called "high-density suburbs" now Aunt Bea.'

'Huh. They'll always be townships to most of us, won't they, Frank?'

'Yes, Madam.'

'You see.'

They arrived at Freedom High, and Cassia directed her to the cottage. She parked the car outside but left the engine running.

'Would you like to come in and look around?' Cassia asked.

'You know what, maybe next time. I've got a lot to do today, so we'll need to get back ASAP. Frank can help you with your belongings while I stay here.'

Cassia had two large suitcases, which Frank carried into the cottage, while she carried a variety of small bags and a hat. Beryl was standing in the sitting room as they entered, her jaw locked, her arms crossed against her chest.

'Hi Beryl. Um…. Are you okay? Is something wrong?'

'Can't you carry your own stuff?'

Cassia glanced at Frank. 'He's happy to help. You okay there, Frank?'

'*Yebo.*'

'Right, well, bring them this way.' She ignored Beryl and walked the few steps to her bedroom, but stopped dead in the doorway. There was no furniture in the room, and when she turned to ask Beryl why not, she found she'd disappeared. 'Well… I suppose you can leave the suitcases in the corner over there. Thanks Frank,' she said to him. She strode back to the car to fetch the last remaining bag and say goodbye to her aunt, again followed by Frank, who slid onto the back seat, without question, and closed the door.

'Call if you need anything,' Bea said as she reversed her Renault away from the cottage, before changing into first gear and heading for the front gates of the school. Cassia decided she looked like a chauffeur, with Frank sitting in the back, waving to her as they glided around the school roundabout. She smiled to herself at the thought of buying her aunt a chauffeur's cap as a joke, but her smile faded when she re-entered the cottage and found Beryl hovering in the passage next to Cassia's bedroom door.

'Ah, there you are, Beryl. Why is there no furniture in my room? I thought you said you'd arrange with Mr Sibanda to have a bed and a wardrobe put in before I arrived.'

'I decided it wasn't necessary.'

'Sorry?'

'Most of the staff who teach at the school don't have beds or wardrobes. There is no reason why you should be different. You can sleep on that sleeping mat,' she pointed at the grass mat in the middle of the floor, 'like the rest of us do. It'll be good for you.'

Cassia walked into the small room and plonked the bag she was still carrying on the mat. She glanced at her suitcases and other bags in the corner. 'So tell me, Beryl, why will it be good for me to sleep on a mat on the floor?'

Beryl pushed a strand of her long, matted hair from her face. 'It will allow you to empathise with your fellow teachers and pupils.'

'Empathise?'

'Yes. The first time Gladmore slept in a bed was when he was twenty-one years old. Can you imagine what it must've been like to have never had a comfortable place to sleep his entire childhood?'

'Of course I can't imagine it, except... it must've been pretty uncomfortable. But at least he wouldn't have known anything else.' Beryl opened her mouth to say something, but Cassia continued. 'As for me, Beryl, you know very well that I've never in my life slept on the floor, so I won't be able to sleep properly. I'll get a sore back... and... and sore hips. In fact... sore everything.'

Beryl wasn't interested. 'Try it for a few days. You'll soon get used to it. Did you bring blankets like I told you to?'

'Yes, I did. I also brought sheets, pillows and pillowcases.'

'So you'll be a lot more comfortable than anyone else here.'

'You think so? I can't see the need for sheets if I'm on a grass mat on the floor.' As she said this, she resolved to ask Aunt Bea to buy her a bed and something to store her clothes in, and bring them here, even if Beryl didn't approve. After making this decision, and not wanting to fall out with Beryl on their first day as roommates, she changed the subject. 'Is Gladmore going to come to the cottage soon?'

'He will stay here some weekends when the headmaster and pupils aren't about.'

'Where did you tell me he lived, again?'

'With his family in a small house in a suburb called Makokoba. I'll take you to see it. It might help you climb off your pedestal.'

Here we go again, Cassia thought. 'Honestly, Beryl! I'm not on a pedestal. There's nothing wrong with wanting to sleep in a bed. I've always slept in a bed. But yes, I'm interested to see what it's like where he lives in Makokoba, and to meet his family.'

'I'll ask him if we can go this weekend then.'

'Great.'

No sooner had they put this spat behind them another difficulty became apparent; the ablutions. These were a separate structure from the cottage and comprised a communal long drop toilet, known as a Blair latrine, and a concrete shower cubicle. Black algae grew in the corners of the shower cubicle and it only had a cold water tap. She knew these basic facilities were not of Beryl's making, so resolved to say nothing, but Beryl noticed the fine crease develop between her eyes and she became defensive.

'Are you going to complain about this now?'

'No, but I am going to struggle with it,' Cassia muttered. 'Sorry, but that long drop... smells.'

'Throw ash from the fire down it if you can't take the whiff of human excrement. You know what, Cassia, you really are showing your privileged colonial upbringing, aren't you? Gladmore and his family have used long drops their whole lives.'

'It's not because of my "colonial upbringing" that I don't like using long drops. It's because the modern world has moved on from them, and my family brought me up in the modern world, as did yours. I can't think of anyone in the UK who would use a Blair latrine in this day and age. Bet you never used one before you came here? The only time I have, is when I went on a road trip with my family to the US and we camped in the Bureau of Land Management areas. I didn't much like them then either... and there's nothing wrong with admitting this. My actual point, though, is that I wasn't expecting ablutions like this... but I'll get over it, so take that scowl off your face. I guess I should have checked them out when I came here before and then I wouldn't be so shocked.'

'And as for forcing that poor old man to carry your suitcases.'

'Frank? I didn't force him.'

Beryl snorted. 'Huh. You reckon?'

'For goodness' sake, Beryl. Stop it, before we come to blows. He's worked for my aunt for years and she is very fair with the people she employs in her house and garden. They probably wouldn't have jobs if it wasn't for her.'

Beryl stomped off, and Cassia retreated to her bedroom, but discovered there was nothing to do in there. With no furniture, she couldn't unpack her suitcases, and with no bed, she couldn't make herself comfortable. So she went back through to the sitting room where Beryl was sitting on the floor, her back against the wall, her legs drawn up to her body, her long java print skirt pulled over her knees. Cassia felt a wave of sympathy towards her. Why was she so angry? Was it because she had become more aware of Cassia's "colonial background"? This had never been an issue before, but it seemed, after a year of living in Zimbabwe, it now was.

'I'm sorry, Beryl. I don't mean to sound like a princess. It's just that I was in comms with Steve and Dave from uni, who have also come to Zim as expat teachers, and from what I can make out, they have comfortable housing at the schools they're teaching at, with beds, hot and cold running water and flush loos.'

'Steve, Dave… do I know them?'

'I don't think so. I only got to know them after you'd left.'

'Well, they're probably teaching at what were formerly whites-only schools. The government built those schools with all the mod cons.'

'Dave told me he's at a former whites-only school, Milton High. But Steve is teaching at a school somewhere near here, I believe, in the "high-density suburbs", as you call this side of town.'

'So, if Steve is at a school near here, and they have running water and flush loos, the government probably built it during the colonial era. The Zimbabwe government built Freedom High after Independence.'

Cassia's eyes narrowed at this contradiction, but she forced herself to stay silent. Beryl needed to lighten up and stop being so sensitive about "the evils of colonialism", but she knew she couldn't convince her of this by arguing with her.

*

Cassia soon got to know Gladmore well, both in the staffroom and when he came round to their cottage, and she was relieved to discover that he was a lot less radical than Beryl. At first, she had wondered if Beryl's extreme opinions were due to him, but it did not appear to be so. He never lectured her, or told her what she should or should not be doing, and thankfully, Beryl followed his example. On one of his visits to the cottage, Beryl mentioned that Cassia was interested in seeing where he lived. He thought about this for a moment, then suggested they pay him a visit the following Sunday, as he was playing soccer at Barbourfields Stadium this coming weekend.

*

Gladmore was waiting on the road outside his house when Beryl and Cassia drew up to his gate on the prescribed day. After parking her car on the side of the road, Beryl walked around it to double-check that she had locked all the doors, including the boot.

'Welcome to "the ghetto", aka Makokoba township,' Gladmore smiled at Cassia. 'It is one of the oldest high-density suburbs in Bulawayo.'

'Really?' Cassia glanced up and down the neat-looking street with small bungalows on either side of it. 'I wouldn't call it a "ghetto", though.' She had found the drive from Freedom High to Makokoba intriguing. Most of the houses they passed were small and needed a lick of paint, but from what she could make out, the suburbs were clean and well maintained. No shabby shacks, erected haphazardly, as she would have expected in low income, high-density housing areas in Africa. The suburbs reflected careful planning. The houses were semi-detached or detached, and they all appeared to have their own small yard with fruit trees and vegetable gardens, and she recognised the ever popular chomolia plants. On their drive to Gladmore's house, they passed an athletic stadium, two-story apartment buildings, an open-air street market, a Catholic church, and a large beer hall.

As they walked through the wire gate into Gladmore's yard, he explained he lived here with his mother, brother, and one of his sisters. Cassia could see that the house was too small for so many people, hence the reason for "high-density," she decided. There was also an outhouse, separate from the main bungalow, with galvanised water pipes and a breather pipe. This must be the bathroom, or kitchen, or both, she thought, and she smiled to herself as she recalled Beryl's lecture about Gladmore not having ever had running water or a flush loo. She kept these observations to herself, though, as she followed him through the front door into a small, dark room. The curtains and windows were closed, so it took a few moments for her eyes to adjust to the darkness, and then she noticed two people sitting on a sofa in the room. Gladmore introduced them as his mother, Ma Moyo, and his younger brother, Innocent. Both Cassia and Beryl bent to shake their hands awkwardly as neither of them rose to greet their guests. Beryl had told Cassia she'd met Gladmore's family several times, so it surprised Cassia how cool their greeting was. Maybe the Moyos didn't approve of her relationship with Gladmore? Whatever, Ma Moyo invited them to sit down, pointing to a narrow wooden bench along one wall, while Gladmore drew up a wooden stool and sat near his brother. No one said a word for what seemed like a long time, and Cassia felt uncomfortable with the tense atmosphere pervading the room. Everyone was behaving so formally, no one appeared relaxed.

'Cassia is Beryl's friend from England,' Gladmore eventually said, 'although she was born here. She and her family left for the UK in 1970.'

'Oh.'

Another long silence followed this.

The conversation continued in this stilted manner for a few minutes until Ma Moyo heaved herself from the sofa and shuffled to the door, saying she would bring the tea.

'Can I help you, Ma Moyo?' Beryl asked.

'No, thank you.' She closed the door behind her.

The atmosphere improved with Ma Moyo out of the room, yet they were still awkward in each other's company. So different from when Gladmore visited them in their cottage, where he was always easy-going and relaxed.

Beryl smiled weakly at Gladmore, and Cassia glanced about the room, at the sunken sofa where Innocent sat, Gladmore perching on his homemade stool, a small table in the corner, and the homemade bench she and Beryl were sitting on. There was a single light bulb hanging from a beam holding up the asbestos roof. She noticed the curtains were pieces of material nailed to the walls, and there was a calendar from the previous year on the wall behind the sofa. A print of Jesus Christ, his arms wide open, his halo encircling his head, his heart drawn on the left side of his chest, hung above the door Ma Moyo had disappeared through.

'So I'm guessing you're Roman Catholics?' Cassia said, breaking the silence.

'Yes,' Gladmore and Innocent said together.

'Gladmore was lucky to go to Makokoba Mission School, which we passed driving here, where he received a good Catholic education,' Beryl said. 'You went there, too, didn't you, Innocent?'

'Yes,' Innocent said.

The door opened and Ma Moyo re-entered, carrying a tray of enamel mugs and a brown teapot. A young girl holding a large red plastic bowl and a tin jug followed her. This girl came up to Cassia and knelt on the floor next to her. A twitch played across her mouth, but she said nothing and did not make eye contact.

Beryl noticed Cassia looking around, confused. 'This is Ma Moyo's daughter, Precious,' she said. 'She has water in the jug for you to wash your hands.'

'Oh wow,' Cassia said, glancing at her hands.

'It's the African custom to wash your hands before eating or drinking. Put your hands above the bowl so Precious can pour water over them,' Beryl said.

Cassia did this, rubbing her hands together while Precious poured a trickle of water. 'Thank you,' she murmured as she took the small cloth Precious gave her to dry her hands. It would have helped if Precious had looked at her, but she did not, nor at anyone else as she made her way around the room, kneeling in front of each person and pouring water over their hands. No one said anything while this ritual took place. When Precious finished, she took the jug and bowl out of the room but soon returned with a tin plate with biscuits arranged on it. Lemon creams, Cassia noticed. Beryl rifled in her handbag and produced another packet of lemon creams, giggling as she showed them to Ma Moyo.

'I bought these for you. I know they are your favourite.'

'Thank you, my dear. You are very kind. Put them on the table, Precious.'

'Would you like me to pour the tea?' Beryl asked.

'Don't worry, Precious can do it.'

Which she did, asking no one how they liked it, so they were all given mugs of sweet, milky tea. Cassia always drank hers black, with no sugar, so she had to force each mouthful down. Precious slipped from the room once she had served the tea and biscuits without having said a word to anyone. Cassia would have thought she was mute if she hadn't heard a sudden stream of loud talking coming from behind the door. She wondered who Precious was talking to.

Meanwhile, their conversation remained stilted as they kept to the only subject they had in common: Freedom High School. But even then, the discussion remained superficial.

*

The children at Freedom High were a delight to teach. There was never any back-chatting, or muttering snide remarks, or giggling amongst themselves. It appeared they were desperate to learn, but Cassia soon found there was one lesson few people at Freedom had learnt. Time keeping.

Despite the scheduled start time of seven-thirty and finish time of one o'clock every weekday morning, staff and pupils drifted in and out of the school gates at all times of the day. They arrived late, they left early, they all did their own thing. It started from the very first day of term, and, to give Mr Abednico Sibanda his due, he lectured the pupils about it at assembly, and the staff later at the staff meeting, but everyone ignored him and continued to do what they pleased. Unfortunately, Mr Sibanda did little to prevent this. He would stand at the school gate for a few hours in the mornings, but when teachers arrived late, he would laugh and tease them, and make obsequious jokes about their excuses. Anyone would have thought he was standing there to welcome them, not to instil discipline. The school gate was near Cassia's classroom and she watched these goings-on every morning with growing frustration. He was less tolerant with the children, but this did not worry them. They avoided him by either waiting further down the road until he'd gone back to his office, or otherwise by climbing over the wall behind the school to get in.

Cassia would have been less annoyed if it hadn't been for Edna Mpala, who taught in the classroom next door. She never arrived at the school before the third period, and her pupils ran riot every morning until she got there. The headmaster, standing at the gate nearby as he always did, would hear them, yet he did nothing to stop the problem, and always had a long, friendly chat with Edna when she arrived late. After weeks of trying to teach above the commotion from next door, Cassia eventually started going to Edna's classroom and giving her students work to get on with until she arrived. She told Edna she was doing this, and how awkward it was for her, and Edna responded with a charming smile and a promise to be there on time the next day. This was yet to happen and, worse still, she never appeared in the least embarrassed by her continued tardiness.

CHAPTER 7

A FEW WEEKS after the *pfungwis* ceased, Cassia's wish came true. Her family said it was safe enough for her to visit the farm.

Bea arrived at Freedom after school on the Friday, minus Frank this time, to fetch Cassia and take her back to her house. Serena and Graham were there, having spent the previous night in town, and they drove back to Sunlands with her after lunch.

She sat in the back seat of their Mercedes 190D, remembering the landmarks they passed on the way, and recalling her family's history. Her grandmother was first married to Grandpa Tim, and they'd lived in the main house on the Brooke's section of the farm, Sunlands House. They'd had four children; Uncle Martin, who was the oldest, then her mother, then Uncle John, and finally Aunt Bea. Grandpa Tim died in a drowning accident in 1947, when his children were still young. Polio had left him crippled, and a nurse was his primary carer. On the day he died, he'd asked his nurse to drive him into town from the farm after a heavy rainstorm, and the swollen river washed their car off a low-level bridge. Every time the Brookes and Craigs went to town and back, they passed this place. In the 1960s, a new high-level bridge had been built next to the low-level bridge, but the original one remained and served as a reminder of poor old Grandpa Tim. Cassia wondered what her grandmother thought every time she passed this bridge. She would love to ask her, but of course she couldn't, not with Graham driving the car right beside her. When they passed it now, she glanced at Serena, but she was facing the front and showed no visible reaction to the significance of the spot. Cassia decided it would have been different if her mother was with them. Her mother claimed that the circumstances of her father's death haunted her, and this became worse when Serena married Graham, Grandpa Tim's younger brother in 1950. Cassia's mother hated Graham. As Cassia sat in the back seat of their Mercedes now, thinking about this and staring at Serena and Graham's heads, she wondered why her mother disliked him so much. She and her cousins called him Gramps, at Serena's insistence, and as far as Cassia was concerned, he seemed nice enough. Bea got along with him, just like she did with most people, unlike her mother.

When Graham and Serena married, Graham moved out of his little cottage on the farm and into Sunlands House, where he, Serena, and Serena's four children had lived until Martin and Kate married in 1960. After this, they moved into Graham's old cottage, where they were heading now.

John and Molly had married as teenagers a few years earlier than Kate and Martin. Serena allocated them the house on Sunlands where Graham's mother, Celia, had lived until her death in the 1950s. Sunlands House was always earmarked for Martin, as the eldest son, but Celia's house was big enough for John and Molly, even with Molly already expecting their first baby.

There was so much interesting, intertwined family history, Cassia thought, a history she'd hated leaving behind when they emigrated to England. Her mother often said there were two main reasons they'd left the country; one, because she disliked her stepfather so much, and two, because she and Cassia's father disapproved of the government trying to hang onto power by declaring Independence from Britain in 1965. Cassia had never thought either of these reasons warranted the upheaval and isolation from the rest of their family this move to England had caused.

They turned off the main tar road now and onto the dirt road to the farm. As they did this, Cassia twisted in her seat to read the large sign post on the corner. It listed all the farms this road headed to, and who owned them. Growing up in Rhodesia, she had always found these minor details intriguing. There were thousands of these signs, scattered on hundreds of intersections of farm roads, listing the farms and the owners. It must've been a tremendous job, done decades ago, updated every time a farm changed ownership. For her, these signs listed magical places, with their names conjuring up fascinating images. She read the list now:

BRIGHTSIDE – O A Craig – 4km

SUNLANDS – T P Brooke – 7km (She wondered why no one had ever changed it)

WHISPERING PLAINS – R M Beamish – 15km

SPRING GRANGE – E E Rushmore – 22 km

MANDALAY – M N Little – 35km

Serena turned in her seat and noticed Cassia craning her neck to read the sign. 'Are you trying to recall all the people who lived around here?' she asked.

'I don't remember anyone other than us and the Craigs,' Cassia said. 'I never went further along this road than Sunlands, although I always wanted to.'

'You don't remember the Beamishes?'

'No.'

'They sold their farm as soon as Independence was declared.'

'When the British stabbed us in the back,' Graham muttered.

'Let's not get onto that topic,' Serena said. She smiled at Cassia. 'Going back to the Beamishs' farm, they sold it to a Mr Ngwenya and emigrated to England. I haven't ever met Mr Ngwenya, but Graham says he's only running a few cattle on his farm, and leasing out the rest. And the Littles sold their farm to the Tates. You must remember them?'

Cassia thought for a moment. 'I remember that coloured man, Mr Tate, who lived at the school.'

'Yes, he was the headmaster until he retired. It was his son who bought the Little's farm in the late 1970s when coloured people could buy places other than in areas designated for them.'

'Wasn't Mr Tate very friendly with Oliver's mother?'

'Oh yes, for many decades. Unfortunately, the friendship has not continued with his son. I'm afraid he dislikes us.'

'But why?'

'He doesn't like white people per se. A slap in the face after everything Isabella did for his family. But the son expected her to have done more. He doesn't understand that the society she lived in hampered her.'

They drove over a grid and through the gate onto their farm, then continued along the dirt road, passing the track heading to Oliver's and Lily's house. 'Dominic lives in the cottage next door to them,' Serena said. 'Do you remember it? Oliver built it by combining two rondavels, for the governesses who taught here for many years. The last governess to work here was Lily. After her, we sent our children to boarding school.'

'I have a vague memory of the cottage. What's Oliver and Lily's story again?'

A half smile flittered across Serena's still beautiful face. 'Their story is like the book, "Jane Eyre", except, unlike Mr Rochester, Oliver did not have a mad wife locked away in an attic.' She laughed at the thought. 'His first wife died years before Lily arrived here…. and he didn't even have an attic.' She laughed at her joke. 'No, but seriously, his first wife died during the war. It was a terrible tragedy because she was only twenty seven and Oliver was hiding in Italy. He'd escaped from his war prison and was being hidden by the Italian Resistance, so he didn't know she had died for quite some time. After the war, he and Amanda hated living together, as they had been complete strangers. He hired Lily to teach her and provide company, along with Bea and John, giving her time to bond with her father without going away to school. It was a good move. They are now very fond of each other, and he and Lily have had a very happy marriage.'

They reached Sunlands Cottage and Cassia's attention turned to her surroundings. How she had always loved her grandmother's home. A gorgeous thatched cottage set in a lush tropical garden.

Cassia opened the back door and climbed out, pushing away the two excited Labradors who had bounded down the steps to greet them.

'Down Rudy, behave yourself Buster,' Graham shouted.

'It is so wonderful to be here again,' Cassia said, bending down to pat the dogs' heads. 'I just wish it was for longer and I didn't have to go back to town on Monday.'

'Me too, darling.' Serena said. 'But there will be plenty of other times you can come out. I've made plans for you to see as much of the farm as possible during your visit.'

*

Serena's first plan for Cassia, made with Lily, was met with resistance at Brightside when it was disclosed the following morning.

Dominic was sitting on the veranda of his cottage, drinking an early morning cup of tea, Luna lying in a sunny spot next to him, his pet duiker, Grey, nibbling a bush nearby. Lily opened the garden gate and Luna changed from sleeping to running in a split second, as he rushed across the lawn to greet her. Grey disappeared over the fence.

'Down. Down, boy,' Lily said as she walked towards the cottage, pushing him away from her.

'He's just happy to see you, Mum.'

'You reckon. I call it badly disciplined.' She patted his head as she slipped into one of the metal chairs on Dominic's veranda. It felt cold after the cool night. Luna put his head on her knee and she stroked it as she inhaled the fresh morning air. 'Serena's granddaughter, Cassia, came out to the farm yesterday. She's staying the weekend with Serena and Graham.'

'Dad told me.' Dominic sipped his tea.

'When Serena discovered you were off to the other side of the farm this morning to check on your cattle, she thought it would be a grand idea if you took Cassia with you.'

'I can't. I've got too much to do.'

'Oh dear. Serena phoned yesterday evening to ask if this would be okay. I came here to ask you, but you weren't around, and I noticed you didn't come back until late.'

'I was out at the Basin Paddock, heaving a stupid cow out of the gully it had fallen in to.'

'Oh dear, and did you manage?'

'Eventually.'

'Thank goodness.' She paused, waiting for Dominic to say something else, but he did not. 'Well, anyway, Serena phoned me back later to check if you had agreed and when I told her I hadn't spoken to you, she said she was sure you wouldn't mind and she'd have Cassia ready by six-thirty this morning.'

Dominic glanced at his wrist watch. It was six-fifteen, and he intended leaving in the next five minutes. They were spraying the cattle in the Galletas Paddock, at the top of the farm, and it would take at least half an hour to get there on the rough farm roads.

'Well I can't. Sorry for that, but I've told the guys I'll get there by seven. I'll be late if I have to swing past Sunlands to pick her up.'

Lily stared at a lizard sunning itself on the step. 'You asked if I could come with you. You said you needed to check the cattle numbers, and you asked me if I could help you. Did you find someone else?'

'No.'

'Can you get her to do it, then? I'm sure the cattle guys won't notice if you're a few minutes late.'

Dominic said nothing as he pushed his feet into the soft leather of his well-worn *veldskoens*.

Lily continued. 'She's ready and waiting and Serena has arranged all the food and drink she'll need for the day, with lots for you, too, no doubt.'

Dominic shook his head. 'You and Serena are the worst, Mum. You really know how to get your own way, don't you?'

'Absolutely not. But thank you darling.'

*

What the fuck, Dominic thought when he first saw Cassia, standing on her grandmother's front step, waiting for him. Where does she think she's going? Cassia would have been mortified if she knew his thoughts. She was wearing a pair of khaki shorts, with a bright white t-shirt tucked into the shorts, and a leather belt around her waist. Over this, because it was still chilly in the early morning, she wore a brand new Barbour jacket. On her feet she had a pair of sparkling white socks under a pair of brand new *veldskoens*. She had bought them at the Bata Shoe Shop in Bulawayo the week before, especially for her trip to the farm. She finished off her outfit with a large-brimmed straw hat, which she had also bought the week before, at the Jarios Jiri Craft Shop in Bulawayo.

She bounced down the steps and rushed up to Dominic as he was sliding out of his door-less Land Rover and thrust her hand towards him in a greeting. He took it, a half smile playing across his lips as he considered what she would look like at the end of a dusty day with his cattle. She mistook this for a friendly gesture and she shook his hand warmly.

'Thank you so much for agreeing to take me with you around the farm today,' she said.

'Well, yes. I hope you will not be bored. We're going to be spraying cattle.'

She eyed the two men standing in the open back of the Land Rover, both wearing green uniforms and each with a rifle slung over their shoulders. Beside them, his paws on the side, his tail wagging, his mouth stretched in a wide smile, was a dog.

'This is Petros and Philemon. They come with me when I go to more isolated places on the farm, like where we're going today.'

Cassia attempted to sound casual as she said: 'Ah, hello, nice to meet you.' She patted the dog in the hopes it would prevent him from leaping off the back of the vehicle.

'And his name is Luna. He also comes with me everywhere on the farm.'

'Hello Luna,' she said, still patting him. 'Um, let me collect the picnic basket Granny had her cook prepare. I'll just be a moment.' She ran up the steps and grabbed the basket.

'I'll put that in the back. Everything will melt if we leave it in the front.' Dominic took the basket from her as she was about to place it on the floor of the cab and wedged it behind the spare wheel. 'I don't know if you've ever been in a Land Rover before, but the cab floor gets boiling hot from the engine.'

'Oh yes, I'd forgotten that. I remember now from when we used to visit the farm when I was little.'

Cassia climbed into the passenger seat and noticed the doors were missing. Dominic explained he took the doors off for a cooler cab on the farm.

'And there's no chance of us falling out?'

Dominic laughed. 'Not unless you lean out too far.'

Cassia wasn't sure. She grabbed the small handle on the dashboard and clutched it with both hands. Once they were on their way and she relaxed, she removed one of her hands from the handle and felt in her Barbour pocket for her large sunglasses. The sky was clear blue, and she found the light was too bright and glaring for her eyes. She also removed her hat and held it in her lap because gusts of wind kept billowing through the open cab, flipping up the wide brim. The last thing she wanted was for it to blow off and Dominic having to stop to retrieve it. Dominic watched all these goings-on out of the corner of his eye, but he didn't say a word. The engine was noisy as he revved along the dusty, sometimes very sandy road.

After a long period without talking, Cassia said: 'We're heading in a northerly direction, aren't we?'

'Yes, up to the top end of the farm where we keep one of our beef herds. There isn't much there besides the cattle fences, one borehole we sunk a few years ago, and, of course, the cattle handling facilities.' Cassia did not know what "cattle handling facilities" were, but she didn't want to ask. She'd find out soon enough once they got there, but Dominic explained anyway. 'You know, a race and all that.'

'Ah ha,' she said, although she didn't know what he was talking about.

'We haven't even built a plunge dip there, like we have elsewhere on the farm,' Dominic continued. 'We're thinking it may be more efficient to spray the cattle instead of making them leap into a trough.'

'Ah ha.' Cassia recalled watching cattle being dipped when she visited the farm as a child. She remembered being enthralled, as they leapt into murky brown water, smelling strongly of chemicals, then swimming the three or so metres to the other end, where they would clamber out and walk up a small cement slope while the water drained off them and back into the trough. She remembered she'd become distressed when the smaller animals struggled to climb out, and the larger ones would catch up with them and scramble over them. On consideration, she couldn't remember any of them ever coming to harm.

'So you enjoy cattle ranching?' she asked.

'I enjoy lots of things about it, but, to be honest, I'm helping my dad out at the moment. He's too old to spend long days in the scorching sun, like we'll be doing today.'

'I can imagine.'

'On this farm, Martin is in charge of the dairy and the dairy herd, John is in charge of the crops and irrigation, and I check on the beef herds. Way back when, my dad did everything after his cousin, your grandfather Tim, died back in the forties, until Martin and John started getting involved in the dairy and the cropping.'

'Right. And what does Graham do?'

'Still flies his plane a bit. Not like he used to when he ran his air charter company. He used to fly people all over the countryside then. Now, he just flies when he feels like it.'

They continued their journey in silence while Dominic concentrated on the road. It had deteriorated as the area became more remote. Cassia was relieved they were no longer conversing. She had struggled to hear what he was saying above the roar of the engine, made worse because Dominic spoke in a low voice. She refrained from requesting him to speak louder, thinking they were not acquainted well enough.

A while later, they crested a hill and Cassia gasped. On the road, a short distance in front of them, were three antelope. Dominic took his foot off the accelerator, and the revving stopped.

'What are they?' Cassia whispered,

'Eland' Dominic whispered back. 'All bulls.'

'Of course, I always loved eland. Just shows how long it's been since I was last in the bush that I didn't recognize them. Eland and kudu were always my favourite.'

'I'm surprised we haven't seen any kudu yet. I usually see lots, but in small groups. Eland move in big herds on this section of the farm, unlike kudu. This area also has a lot of sable.'

'Ah, sable. Another of my favourite antelope.' She exhaled. 'In fact, I love all wildlife. I so miss the bush and the wildlife when I'm in England.'

At that moment, a family of warthog ran across the road in front of them; Mum, Dad and four babies, their tails straight up in the air like periscopes.

'Just look at them,' Cassia said. 'They're so cute.'

Dominic glanced in his rear-view mirror, then leant out of the cab and growled at Luna, who had his front feet on the side of the vehicle, preparing to leap out and chase the warthog. He licked his lips and wagged his tail as he glanced at Dominic. His plan thwarted.

'We'd better get moving,' Dominic said. He pressed his foot on the accelerator again and the vehicle bumped forward with a clatter. The eland disappeared into the bush. 'No worries. I'm sure we'll see more,' he said, although the noise of the engine was again making it difficult for her to hear what he was saying.

They spotted some kudu around the next corner but Dominic didn't stop, as he needed to get to the cattle. When they arrived, he parked the Land Rover under a tree near what he told Cassia was the "race". He told her he was parking there so she could sit in the vehicle and record the information he needed, as he called it out.

'I suggest you sit in the back, so you can see and hear better,' he said, rummaging behind the seat and bringing out a dusty old bag full of writing books. As he tossed the bag into the back of the Land Rover, his shirt lifted and Cassia noticed he was wearing a holster with a pistol in it. This shocked her. In the meantime, the two guards jumped off the back of the Land Rover and headed into the thick bush surrounding the "cattle handling facilities". She saw now that this comprised the race, which was a straight passage made of gum poles, about ten metres long and eighty centimetres wide, with a large metal clamp at the end leading into small enclosures partitioned off by wire fences. These fences were held in place by straight wooden posts cut from trees and bushes. Cattle stood in the enclosure behind the race with men milling around them. Dominic walked over to talk to them, while Cassia climbed out of the cab and walked to the back of the Land Rover, where she slid her bum onto the tailgate. Dominic returned to the vehicle, searched the bag, and took out a book and pen. He turned to a page with a long list of numbers.

'Each cow has a number,' he explained, 'and when it comes through the race, this number will be called out. You need to find their number and tick off that they're present and correct. Okay?'

'Yup, I think I can do that.' Cassia noticed this had been done many times before, the last time being the previous month, judging from the date written at the top of the last column. She wrote today's date at the top of the next empty column. Meanwhile, the men started whistling and shouting, encouraging some cows to walk into the race. At first they were reluctant, but once one trotted in, others followed, dust billowing, some bellowing. One man ran to the clamp and, as the first cow was about to move through it, he slammed it closed so that she was caught in the clamp by her neck. After the initial shock she settled down, making Cassia realize they must be used to this sort of thing, although the other cows standing behind her still pushed and shoved while someone thrust a gum pole behind the last cow in the race, squashing them tightly together.

One man sprayed all the cattle as he walked down the race with a spray pack on his back. Dominic walked with him, lifting their tails so he could spray underneath them. A third man walked with them, reading their tattoos and calling out their numbers.

'Se-ven-ty eight, f-or-ty three.'

'Did you get that?' Dominic shouted.

'Yes,' Cassia said.

'You've ticked it off?'

'I'm just looking for the number. Umm…' Her eyes darted up and down the list, and she breathed a sigh of relief when she found it. 'Okay,' she yelled as she ticked it off.

'Se-ven-te two, sex-ex-ty sex.' The man called out the number of the next cow.

'Get that?' Dominic shouted.

'Ah, no,' Cassia said. She couldn't make out the pronunciation.

'Seventy-two, sixty-six,' Dominic said.

Cassia's eyes scanned up and down the list of numbers again, wishing they were in numerical order.

'Got it?'

'Um… okay, yes.'

When all the numbers were called out and checked off by Cassia, the cows were released from the clamp. Dust wafted everywhere and Cassia glanced at her t-shirt, which was fast changing from white to light brown. She brushed some of the dust off it with her hand, but this only made it worse, leaving a large brown smear across her shoulder.

Once the cows left the race, the men began whistling and shouting again. The next batch entered the race and the entire process was repeated. The morning proceeded in this way until all one hundred and forty-five cows were sprayed and had had their numbers ticked off. Dominic also treated wounds and other problems whenever he found them on any of the cows. He made Cassia record everything he was doing.

By the fiftieth cow, she was feeling dusty and parched, but she dared not tell anyone. From what she could make out, hers was the easiest job, sitting in the shade in the back of the Land Rover, ticking off numbers and writing the odd note. Her only difficulty was finding the numbers, which she did always manage to do eventually, although she had to delay proceedings from time to time when she was looking for them.

She noticed that after about one hundred cows, one guard appeared from the thick bush and spent some time making a small fire, on which he put a tin can of water. He added salt to the boiling water and then stirred in mealie meal from a packet, thickening it.

The workers milled about and chatted to each other after they released the last animal, while one man joined Dominic at the Land Rover.

'This is the foreman, Kefi,' Dominic introduced him to Cassia.

'Hi Kefi.'

'*Yebo* Madam.'

'Kefi is going to give you the list of cows that have had calves since I was last here. You'll need to record which cows they are and what the calf's number is. You'll find a list at the back of the book. Each number will start with this year, as it's the year they're born, and then you'll write the number Kefi gives you after this. What number are we at now, Kefi?'

Kefi consulted the book he had in his hand. 'Thrity-five, Sir.'

'Right. So you'll carry on from thirty-six, Cassia. You've found the list?' Cassia nodded as she scanned yet another long list of numbers. 'Good. So who's the mother, Kefi?'

'Seventy-nine, one hundred and five.'

'Write that down, Cassia, followed by thirty-six, and then you'll write whether it's a bull or a heifer by writing a B or H after its number. What is it Kefi?'

'Bull, Sir.'

'You got that Cassia?'

'Um…. Can you just give me the mother's number again please, Kefi?'

While Kefi and Cassia proceeded with this task, Dominic removed the now filthy glove he had pushed onto his hand at the beginning of the proceedings. He flicked the glove around a few times to remove the cow dung on it, then turned it inside out and threw it into the back of the Land Rover. It landed next to Cassia and a splodge of cow dung splattered onto her shorts and t-shirt. Despite thinking this was unnecessary, she said nothing.

'Oops, sorry,' Dominic said. 'I thought I'd got it all off.'

It didn't take long for Kefi to give Cassia the cow and calf information, after which he went to join his mates, who were still strolling amongst the cows.

'Why don't we have some of whatever you brought in your picnic basket?' Dominic suggested.

Cassia slid off the tail gate, stretched her stiff limbs and yanked the basket from behind the spare wheel. It was filled with plastic containers and a flask. As she opened them, revealing egg sandwiches in one, ham sandwiches in the other and crunchies in the third, Dominic sauntered off again to chat to the workers, followed by Luna, who had been sleeping underneath the Land Rover for most of the morning. Cassia saw a small round trough in the enclosure where the cows were, and the men were washing their hands in it. Luna ran to this and leapt in, splashing all of them.

'Out boy,' Dominic yelled. Luna jumped out and shook himself, this time spraying everyone near him, but he quickly escaped from the enclosure when a cow charged at him, with another one in pursuit. Cassia glanced at her own hands, which were so dusty her life lines showed up as brown cracks but, after seeing the cows chasing Luna, she was reluctant to walk through them to wash her hands in the trough. However, her problem was soon resolved because, after more chit-chat between Dominic and the men, one of them walked to a collapsible wire gate and opened it. With this, the cattle ran in a stampede out of the enclosure in a haze of dust. It amazed Cassia how quickly one hundred and forty-five cows could disappear into the thick African bush. The men wandered off to their fire and their pot of *sadza* while Cassia walked to the trough to wash her hands. Luna saw her and ran over to join her, leaping into the water again, splashing her this time. She looked at what had been her white t-shirt, deciding she'd have to throw it away when she took it off. She could only laugh at how naïve she was to have worn white. After giving her hands another wash, savouring the cool water, and deciding to enjoy Luna's splashes, she strolled back to the Land Rover where she found Dominic munching on the sandwiches. He tossed a crust to the now muddy Luna and poured two cups of hot tea from the flask.

'Oh, I don't know if I want tea in this hot weather,' Cassia said.

Dominic peered into the basket again. 'I see nothing else in here to drink, and I've drunk all the water I brought in my water bottle.'

'Oh.'

'You can always drink the borehole water running into the trough. It'll be fine.'

Cassia hesitated, but she needed a drink. She made a mental note that the next time she travelled anywhere on the farm she would bring her own bottle of water, but in the meantime she'd prefer to drink tea than risk the water being pumped into the trough. The tea was surprisingly refreshing and went down well with the sandwiches, but, still feeling dehydrated, she threw caution to the wind and took her mug to the trough where she gulped down two mugs full of the water. It was warm and limy tasting, but it quenched her thirst.

'So how did you find all of that?' Dominic asked. 'I hope you weren't too bored.'

'No, it was fascinating, and you kept me too busy to be bored.'

'Well, thank you for helping. It's something that needs to be done often, so I appreciate your effort.'

Cassia glanced at him, wondering if he was taking the micky out of her, but no, he looked serious. 'Not at all,' she said. 'It was a good excuse to spend time in the bush, which I love. You're welcome to call on me anytime you need help, whenever I'm on the farm, that is.'

Dominic eyed her over his mug of tea. 'Great.' He took a final swig, then tossed the dregs out and put the mug back in the basket. 'When the men have finished eating their *sadza,* I have to drive them back to their houses. We can go home via the dam afterwards, if you like. Do you remember it?'

Cassia's eyes widened. 'Oh yes, we used to have such fun there when we were little. Sailing Optimists and what-not. If I remember, you had another type of yacht, as you were too old to sail an Oppy.'

'I had a Laser.'

'Bea told me you're still a keen sailor?'

'Yes. I sail a Fireball here, and sometimes my dad's GP as well, and I have a cabin cruiser called a Matilda, which I sail up and down Kariba when I get the time.'

'I was told you did this recently.'

'Yes.' He glanced at his watch. 'If we make it to the dam on time and there's still a good wind, I'll give you a short sail before taking you back to Serena's.'

CHAPTER 8

CASSIA RETURNED to the farm the following weekend, this time for Oliver's family birthday party. It was still a few weeks until his actual birthday, but the South African Universities were on their ten-day vacs at the end of September, and Martin's sons, Brian and Harry, and Amanda's elder daughter, Karen, were home. Lily thought it would be more fun to have them at the party too. Not that Oliver was close to Brian or Harry, but he was very fond of his eldest granddaughter, Karen. Lily didn't ask Oliver if he wanted a party. She knew he would say no, as he had done every other time she'd asked him in the many years they'd been married, but he always enjoyed the parties she arranged for him, so she resolved to just get on and do it. It would make a pleasant change after the dreadful time they'd had.

The story of how he'd been born prematurely on their farm in 1905, when his mother came out for his father's funeral, was family folklore. Back then, the farm was a very different place from what it was now. When they'd bought it from the BSAC in 1905 there were no fences, no roads, no houses, no dams, no dip tanks, no barns, no fields, no school, no chapel, no compound. The only sign of any human habitation in the area then had been a couple of mud huts in which a white man was living with a black woman and their children. So, by being born on the farm when they first bought it, Oliver was the personification of their history here. But, furthermore, he had become the key figure in the farm's development, with his greatest achievement being the construction of the dam in 1947/48. This dam had transformed the area from a dry, dusty, arid, barely productive stretch of Matabeleland bush into the highly intensive, incredibly productive farm it now was. The old saying, "water is life", could not be more true when describing how this dam had transformed their lives. Water is needed to farm successfully in Matabeleland and Oliver was one of the first farmers to recognize this and do something about it.

The dam had initially been built to irrigate crops, but when it became apparent, there were no hippos or crocodiles living in it, (unlike many other dams in the country) it became a place for recreation too – for picnicking, swimming, sailing, water skiing, and fishing. In the 1960s they'd built a campsite there, a place where they could leave their boats and camp the night if they wanted. When the war intensified in the 1970s they ceased staying overnight, although they did still use it sometimes during the day. Now, in the 1980s, they had been putting the campsite to full use again, until the recent problems had occurred.

Lily hoped these problems were now behind them and made plans to have the party at the dam, even though it made the task more difficult; lugging the food and drinks there, arranging guards to patrol the vicinity, sending staff down earlier to clean the place and lay the fires. However, she decided all this would be worth it. The area behind the campsite was elevated and had views in both easterly and westerly directions and, with the moon full this weekend, they would be able to watch it rising while the sun was setting. She and

Oliver had celebrated this dance of nature many times, and she knew it would make his party more special if he could watch it again there.

The whole family would be at the farm for the weekend. All five Pierces were to stay with Serena and Graham, plus a friend of Richard's, so Serena asked Lily if Cassia could stay at Brightside with them. Martin and Kate's house was full, too, as both their sons had brought girlfriends home, and John and Molly didn't have any extra space either. They had Molly's parents staying from town, as well as Will and Tom, and Tom's girlfriend. Lily was delighted to have Cassia, as they only had Amanda and her daughters with them.

They arrived the Friday afternoon before the party and, after leaving their bags in their respective bedrooms, they gathered on the veranda for tea and birthday cake. Any misgivings Oliver might have had about the party dissipated when he saw the look of joy on Lily's face as she dished out slices of chocolate cake to her guests. They sat in the armchairs on the veranda, the tea and cake set on the table in the middle.

'Here, let me pour the tea,' Amanda said, pushing back her chair so she could reach the big enamel teapot more easily. 'So where's my brother?' she asked as she poured and handed out the mugs.

'He's down at the dam making sure everything is in order for the party tomorrow,' Oliver said.

'I hope he is also checking on the boats because I plan on having a sail with him.'

'Of course, he wouldn't dare not take you out,' Oliver said with a chuckle. It was a never-ending source of satisfaction to him that, despite the fifteen-year gap in their ages, his two children got along so well. Elegant Amanda, bush-happy Dominic, yet they had many common interests. Of course she had lived on the farm until she married and had loved her upbringing there. As an affirmation of this, she came out often to stay. This was the first time she'd been back since the problems, making it even more special having her now.

'So how is the teaching going, Cassia?' Karen, Amanda's eldest, asked. She was studying to be a teacher at the University of Cape Town.

Cassia hesitated. She was still processing how she felt about her position at Freedom High. 'I love the children,' she said. 'They are desperate to learn, and so well behaved. The only fault I have with them is they are frequently late for class. However, I have found that when I threaten to punish them, they attempt to arrive on time. They really try to do what they are told, unlike many of the students I taught in the UK.'

'You taught at a comprehensive school, right?' Karen said. 'Maybe the children would have been more responsive to you if you'd been at a grammar school.'

Cassia hesitated. 'Yes, well…'

Sensing she didn't want to talk about her job, Oliver drained his tea and stood up. 'Who wants to come with me to check on my cattle? I need to look at a cow that's been poorly. We've given it tetracycline these last few days and I want to see how she's doing.'

'Is it far away?' Cassia asked, thinking about the trek she'd been on the previous weekend.

'No, it's in the Bowl Paddock. But I intend driving the long way back, around the fields. Who's coming with me?'

'Yes please Granddad,' Louise said. 'We love going around the farm with you.'

'Do you need me to stay and help with dinner, or preparations for tomorrow?' Amanda asked Lily.

'No, the kitchen staff and I have everything covered. However, there are some last-minute things I need to do, so you go, and I'll see you later.'

By now the dogs were leaping around, knowing an activity was imminent. 'Thank God Dominic isn't here with his hound,' Oliver said. 'Then there would be real scrum.' It was more chaotic when Amanda and the girls came because they always brought their dog, Kevin. He and Jimbo now sprinted to the end of the veranda where they stopped and waited for everyone to follow, then they darted to the garage and leapt into the back of the open Land Rover, barking and snapping at each other.

'Shut up and behave,' Oliver shouted as he climbed into the driver's seat.

*

The following day, Lily sat back in her canvas deck chair, relaxing for the first time that day. The lunch was over, the dirty plates removed and taken back to the house in the old mule cart by Farai, and the flasks of tea and tins of cakes and biscuits set out on the picnic table for everyone to help themselves during the afternoon. Later Farai would return, again in the mule cart, with replenished cooler boxes of beer, wine, gin and tonics, and platters of snacks, for everyone to enjoy while they watched the sun go down and the moon rise.

Lily placed a finger on her mug to feel the temperature of her tea. It was always difficult drinking hot tea out of a tin mug, and she blew over it to cool it off as she glanced out at the dam. Her view of the dam was broken by several trees and shrubs, but she could still see yachts moving across the water. There was enough wind today to make sailing fun. She recalled the many times they had come down to the dam for a sail and the wind had dropped, leaving them stranded in the middle of the water, or in various bays. She used to enjoy sailing a Laser when she was younger, and on one occasion, when her boat would not move for lack of wind, she'd jumped out and swum to the shore, towing it with its painter, and then walked in the shallow waters along the shoreline, pulling it behind her, as she trudged in and out of all the bays until she eventually got back to the place where they kept their boats below the camp.

Today no one would have problems returning to the jetty below the campsite. She could see Dominic beating across the main bay in his Fireball with Jane crewing for him, out on the trapeze, her legs straight, arms clutching the jib sheet, doing her best to prevent the boat from tilting too much. She knew Dominic loved the boat tipping until it was on the point of capsizing and, if it capsized, this only added to his fun. The Fireball disappeared from view and Lily turned her attention to the GP running down the dam towards the wall, the colourful striped main sail and jib stretched out wide on either side of the boat. Oliver was sailing his boat with John, and, even from where she sat she could see that John was talking animatedly to Oliver, hands gesturing, head bobbing.

Lily's musings were interrupted by Serena and Bea who came to join her, also with tin mugs of tea, and a plate of biscuits. Bea pulled up two more deck chairs while Serena offered Lily a biscuit. She eased herself into one of the chairs and placed the plate of biscuits on the ground next to her.

'Ants Mum, the ants will be all over those biscuits in no time if you leave them there,' Bea said, swooping up the plate and taking it back to the table.

Serena rolled her eyes. 'The lunch went down well, Lily. Many thanks for arranging everything. It was delicious.'

'Pleasure, and thank you for all your help.'

'Not at all.' Serena sipped her tea. 'What a lovely day it is, and so special having all the grandchildren back from university.'

'A pity Ron couldn't make it,' Bea muttered. He had told her on Thursday night he couldn't come after all.

'Yes, work seems to be taking up much of his time these days,' Serena said.

Bea grunted. She glanced down the hill towards the dam, where most of the kids were lying on the grass, chatting to each other. Only Cassia and Jane were missing, Cassia having gone out with Amanda in her Enterprise and Jane with Dominic.

'At least they're all enjoying themselves,' Bea said. 'Thank goodness that nasty incident is behind us now.'

'Yes, although Oliver and Dominic do still go around the farm with guards, and Dominic arranged to have some guards here today, checking the bush in the near vicinity,' Lily said.

Bea glanced into the bush. 'Gosh.'

'Just a precaution,' Serena said. 'Graham, Martin and John also have guards when they are out and about on the farm, although we are thinking this may now be unnecessary.'

'That's good to hear.' Bea helped herself to another biscuit and crunched into it. When she'd finished eating she continued, 'Changing the subject; I think my Jane may have a crush on your Dominic, Lily?'

Lily smiled. 'Mm. I noticed how quick her offer to crew for him was this afternoon.'

'I hope Dominic didn't notice. It's never good to look too keen. I need to speak to her.'

'Daughters never listen to their mothers,' Serena laughed. 'We all loved that delightful American girl, Michelle. It was such a shame they broke up.'

'Yes. But, when she decided she wanted to go back to America, and he did not, it was always going to fizzle out.'

'Sadly, yes. It's pointless pursuing a long-distance relationship.'

'I think our lifestyle is too rough for your average American,' Lily said.

'Rough?' Serena gasped. 'We are the epitome of sophistication.'

'In an African sort of way, which isn't what she was used to.'

Serena smoothed her skirt and patted her hair, but any further discussion on this topic was interrupted by Graham. He'd been napping under a tree by himself since they'd finished lunch and now wandered over to them.

'Ah, here you are. Tea, darling?' Serena said.

'No thanks. I'm going to walk to the dam wall first. I'll have some tea when I return. Do any of you ladies want to join me?'

They looked at each other. 'Lovely idea,' Serena said, pulling herself out of her deck chair.

'I'll stay,' Lily said. 'I want to sort out the food and drinks when Farai returns with them.'

'And I'll stay to help you,' Bea said.

As it turned out, Molly brought all the food and drinks to the dam. Lily and Bea hadn't even noticed she had not been around. 'I snuck back to the house for forty winks, followed by a cup of tea,' Molly said.

'Clever girl,' Bea said. 'Maybe I should have done that too.'

'When I was about to return, Farai pitched up at our house asking if we had some extra butter, Lily, as you'd run out.'

'Oh dear, had I? Sorry about that.'

'Not a problem, but after seeing him, I realized it made sense for me to swing past your house and collect the food and drinks to save him from coming all the way back here with it in the mule cart.'

'Good thinking. I'm sure he was delighted.'

They went to Molly's truck to collect everything.

'Let's leave the cooler boxes in here for someone stronger to lift out,' Bea said, grabbing a couple of Tupperware containers. 'What have you got in these, Lily?'

'Sausage rolls, mini quiches, chicken wings, biltong.... um,'

'Gosh, we're going to have to go on diet after today,' Molly said as she picked up some more containers. 'How's the afternoon gone? Everyone relaxing and enjoying themselves? Any arguments broken out between the cousins?'

'Not that I've noticed. It's been an almost perfect day, as far as I am concerned. I think Oliver will have thoroughly enjoyed it too.'

'It was a good idea having it here. The family gatherings we've had over the years, here at the dam, have always been fun. I've always loved being a part of them, from the very first time I came as a young, pregnant seventeen-year-old child-bride.'

Lily smiled. She loved Molly's candour. She never made any attempt to hide the fact that she and John had had to drop out of their final year of school to get married. At the time, it had caused a great deal of anxiety in Serena's life. Molly's parents, who she'd never even met then, had phoned her out of the blue to tell her their sixteen-year-old daughter was pregnant by her youngest son. Serena had been so shocked, she'd nearly dropped the phone. As someone who had always portrayed herself as a stickler for perfection, it was her worst nightmare. Besides this, society was intolerant of something like this back in 1956. As such, she and Molly's parents met as soon as they could to plan "the best way forward". Their choices were to either send Molly to another country, perhaps England, perhaps South Africa, to have the baby, or otherwise to put her into St Clare's Home for unmarried mothers in Bulawayo. Both options meant she would be out of sight until the baby was born, and then they would put it up for adoption. Molly's parents had travelled nowhere out of Rhodesia, and so they decided St Clare's would be the best option. But these plans never materialised because when John heard what they intended, he flatly refused to allow it to happen. He insisted that he and Molly loved each other and that they must be allowed to marry. Friends and family who were in on "the secret", were shocked (and even a little impressed by his stance) but what surprised them even more, was how easily Serena capitulated and agreed to their marriage. These people muttered to each other that they'd never known before that Serena was such a romantic. She went out of her way to arrange what she hoped would be "the wedding of the year", inviting anyone who was anyone in Bulawayo, and Rhodesia. Some people politely excused themselves, out of principle, but many did attend, and it was a splendid occasion. Serena never regretted her decision. John and Molly's marriage had been a happy one, and their first-born son, William, who would have been given away if their original plans had come to fruition, was a much loved member of the family.

Right now he was the most vocal out of everyone lolling on the lawn in front of where the ladies were arranging the snacks.

Molly glanced at her watch. 'It's almost five o'clock. Let's start the ball rolling and pour ourselves a gin and tonic with a slice of lemon and lots of ice. We can sip these while we finish laying out the food.'

'Great idea,' Bea said.

'Hey boys, come and help me get the cool boxes from the back of my *bakkie*,' Molly yelled to the kids lying on the lawn.

*

The walkers were back. The boats were lying on the shoreline like a pod of beached whales, except for their masts protruding into the sky at various angles. The fire roared in the fire pit, with mainly the young milling around it, chatting while they tossed logs into the flames, and the oldies sat in their deck chairs further away. In September, after months of no rain, the sky was spectacular at sunset because of all the dust in the air. This evening was no exception. The horizon glowed orange, fading into a golden glow further into the sky, with streaks of blue overhead. From time to time people glanced at it. No one wanted to miss the sun setting and the full moon rising.

Cassia was not with her contemporaries at the fire. Instead she was sitting with the oldies, next to Amanda. Lily could hear Amanda discussing with her different aspects about sailing. Although she tried to hide it, both Lily and Serena had noticed that Bea's daughters did not get on with Cassia. Such a shame, when they were all so close in age, and had been the best of friends when they were small. Poor Cassia had been so keen to return to the country of her birth, yet she now found herself an outsider in many ways. Is this what happened when you lived in a different environment for so long? Cassia certainly dressed differently from her cousins. They were all wearing short shorts, t-shirts and slip slops while she was wearing a long, flowing, cream-coloured dress, leather sandals and her wide brimmed straw hat. She'd taken the sandals off and tucked her dress into her knickers earlier to climb into Amanda's boat, but Lily saw this had only induced a few sneering looks between Sarah and Jane.

As if she could read her thoughts and wanted to reassure her that not everything was wrong with her life, Cassia broke Lily's train of thought by saying: 'This really is a perfect place to watch sunsets and moon rises. I see we have a near three sixty degree view from here.'

Lily smiled at her. 'Oh yes, that's why Oliver and I chose this site to build the campsite all those years ago, once the dam had filled.'

'Oh wow, I didn't realise it was you and Oliver who chose this spot.'

'Yes, it was. The dam was always Oliver's pet project, along with your Grandpapa Tim, poor man.' She stared over the water for a while. 'I remember how exciting it was once the wall and spillway had been completed, watching the dam fill, observing how the bays and basins formed. Oliver and I used to ride down here at least once a week to see how it had changed. And once it was full, we'd ride along the shoreline, exploring it. There are lots of lovely places, but this site won our vote because it's elevated, but at the same time, it's close to the water, even if it means a bit of a climb to get here.'

'I can't imagine this area without water now,' Cassia said.

'Yes, it's hard to believe that where we are sitting was once the top of a hill in a dry and arid landscape.'

Their conversation was interrupted by Will. 'Hey *okes*, check, the sun is about to go down.'

Everyone stopped talking to look westward and watch the sun setting. At first it was a bright, glowing mass, too powerful to look at directly, but as it slipped slowly down, the light became filtered by the dust in the air, and they could make out the orange ball sinking silently into the horizon. The breeze died, and no one uttered a word, mesmerised by the sight, captivated by the mysticism of the moment. Only the sound of the crackling fire broke the silence. With no clouds in the sky, varying tones of blue, yellow, orange and cream became more clear, broken by rays of light stretching into the clear evening sky.

'Perfect,' someone muttered.

'Always,' said someone else.

'Look guys, I can see where the moon is about to rise,' Sarah said, pointing in the opposite direction.

Heads swivelled to observe the eastern sky. Earlier, this had been dull compared to the west but now it was changing. As they watched, they saw a brightness growing along the horizon, lightening and brightening with every second until a line of deep orange popped into sight, delineating the earth from the sky. But only for a moment. This line became ever thicker, morphing into a wedge, becoming bigger and rounder and bigger and rounder until a huge, orange, full moon sat on the horizon before moving upwards into the sky.

'That's awesome,' Will said.

'Brilliant,' others agreed.

'Who's for another beer?' John asked.

'Wine for me, please darling,' Molly said.

The mood was broken. The reverie ended, and the revelry started. Oliver and Lily, Serena and Graham left shortly afterwards, but the others remained, lolling around the open fire. The evening was balmy and the food and drinks were plenty. Life was good, and they wanted to draw out the moment. The full moon gradually reduced in size and increased in brightness, rising into the clear night sky, its reflection shining on the rippling surface of the water, creating a glitter path, a long trail of shimmering light.

CHAPTER 9

OCTOBER ARRIVED, bringing sweltering, dusty days followed by still, sultry nights, a reminder of why October is known as "suicide month" in this part of Africa. The students had returned to their respective universities in South Africa, and the scholars were preparing to write their O and A level exams at their local schools. Cassia only taught junior forms at Freedom High, so she didn't have the pressure of preparing any of her pupils for final exams.

On the farm, the spring calves were flourishing, and the newly planted fields of maize and sorghum had sprouted. The Brookes and Craigs were fortunate they could plant their crops early as they could use the dam to irrigate, unlike most farmers in Matabeleland, who had to wait for rain to germinate their seed. Sporadic rainstorms often fell in October and early November, but with intervals of hot, dry weeks in between, it was unwise to plant early without irrigation.

On Sunlands, they grew crops mainly as fodder for their dairy herd, with left-overs being fed to the beef herd, especially the new mothers, as the indigenous grasses had little nourishment.

*

A few weeks after Oliver's party, Dominic drove one of their tractors from Brightside to Sunlands early in the morning, He was towing a trailer to Sunlands with the intention of loading it with hay and lucerne. This was usually a job for one of their tractor drivers, but Dominic enjoyed doing it when he could. He spotted John and Will in the driveway at Graham and Serena's house as he puttered by. He waved at them, parked the tractor and trailer in the road, climbed down from the tractor and walked up the drive to find out what they were up to.

'We're off to Kezi for the day,' John said. 'To the Chester's place. They've sold up and are emigrating to South Africa.'

'Yes, I'd heard.'

'There have been some nasty incidents in that area and they've had enough,' John said.

'They've caught a *skrik*,' Will laughed.

John threw him a bemused look. 'Each to their own, my boy. They believe the grass will be greener down south. They phoned last night to say they're selling their dairy herd in the next few weeks and they've offered us first dibs, which is mighty fine of them.'

'You driving there?' Dominic asked.

'Nah, there's an airstrip nearby, so we're flying. Might as well make use of the pilot in the family, eh?'

Graham walked out the house as he said this. 'Yup, might as well make use of the old bugger while he's still got some flying time left in him.' He had just the one plane now, but he always enjoyed flying family and friends. 'It'll make the trip much easier. We can get there and back by mid-afternoon.' He looked at his watch. 'On that note, we'd better get going. Always best to fly as early as possible, before the air thermals cause problems. We don't want a bumpy ride both ways, do we?'

Graham and John climbed into the cab of John's Mazda *bakkie*, while Will hopped in the back.

'I'll come over and see you when I get back later,' Will said to Dominic. 'We can have a beer, and I'll let you know how many animals we think are worth buying.'

Dominic walked back to his tractor and continued with his chore. He thought no more of them until after lunch, when his mother came to find him in his cottage. She was ashen faced, her hands shaking.

'Something terrible has happened,' she said. A tear rolled down her cheek and her mouth trembled. She put her hands to her face.

Dominic's stomach contracted. 'What, Mum?'

'They were ambushed at the farm in Kezi.'

His stomach tightened further. 'Who?'

'Graham and John and Will.'

There was silence for some moments.

'And?'

'Graham and Mr Chester are dead. They don't know where John and Will are.' Further silence, until Lily sobbed. 'Serena.... Serena told me. Someone phoned her.'

'Where's Dad?'

'In his study. He's talking to Martin on the phone.'

'Martin and Kate are in South Africa, right?'

'Yes, but they'll get back as quickly as they can.'

Dominic leapt up and ran to his parent's house while Lily sank into one of the chairs on his veranda and stared out at the garden, tears running down her cheeks.

When Dominic entered his parent's house, he could hear his father's voice, still talking on the phone, but when he got to the study, Oliver had put the receiver down. He was sitting at his desk, biting his bottom lip, not knowing what to do.

'Bloody hell,' he said when he saw Dominic.

'Mum told me,' Dominic said. 'They're dead?'

'Graham, and the farmer. Ambushed as they were driving from the airstrip to the dairy, a couple of miles away. No one knows where John and Will are. The vehicle was still on the road.'

'When did it happen?'

'They found the bodies about an hour ago. Mrs Chester sent one of their guys to look for them because they hadn't come back to the house for lunch as they'd arranged.'

'She found them?'

'No, no. A driver I believe.'

Dominic looked at his wristwatch. 'They would have arrived in Kezi hours before. I saw them at about six this morning when they were preparing to leave. It would've taken them less than two hours to get there. So the ambush would've happened around eight or nine. Fuck, that's a long time before anyone discovered them. What could have happened to John and Will?'

'They think they've been abducted.'

'No!' Dominic's mind raced as he considered other abductions that had taken place in the last few years; six foreign tourists travelling from the Victoria Falls to Bulawayo in 1982, presumed dead, but their bodies had still not been found; a rancher and his grandson abducted when they visited a dip tank on their farm on New Year's Eve in 1982. One body was found quickly, the other months later, buried in the cattle kraal. The cattle had scuffed the dirt so much, no one noticed the ground had been dug up. As he reflected on these examples, he realized abductions ended badly. He groaned as he thought about John; the most happy-go-lucky member of the family. Everyone loved John. And Will, the Brooke cousin he was the closest to, especially after they'd spent nearly a year together in London. He'd bought an old garage and converted it into an upmarket bachelor pad, and Will had helped him. They'd made a nice chunk of change for their efforts. He couldn't bear to think of his life without Will in it.

'I'm going to drive down there and see if I can help find them,' Dominic said. 'Maybe it's not too late.'

Oliver grimaced. 'I'm not sure if that's wise. The police will look for them?'

'And you think that'll help?'

'Maybe, maybe not. It depends on who is behind this ambush.'

'Exactly. So I won't just sit here and wait. I'm going to go there and see what I can do. I'll take Petros with me. There are a couple of people in town I can call on to help us too... ex-army.'

He picked up the phone to make some calls and found Brian Brooke on the other end of the party line, wanting to speak to them. He appeared to be in a fighting mood too.

'I'll come with you,' Brian said when Dominic told him his plan.

'Thanks man. Bring a weapon. Make sure you're carrying the license for it so the police don't give us trouble. I'll pick you up in about fifteen minutes.'

'You get yourself ready,' Oliver said. 'Don't hang around here making more phone calls. I know a couple of farmers down in the Marula/Figtree area who will probably want to help. They have experience with this sort of thing, plus they know the lie of the land. I'll call them while you get going. I'll tell them you're coming down there.'

Lily had come into the room a few minutes earlier and picked up the gist of their conversation. She knew her son. He wouldn't sit around when one of his best friends was in jeopardy. He would never just wait to hear bad news if he could help. As soon as she comprehended what he was planning, she rushed to the kitchen to prepare what food she could for them in the short time before they left.

She ran out to the garage and handed him a cooler box as he was climbing into his station wagon Land Cruiser. He patted her arm, assuring her he'd be careful, then drove round to the farm fuel tanks to top up the Land Cruiser and fill up some jerry cans with diesel. They needed to be prepared for any event. He had no idea how much driving they might have to do, and he didn't want to be stranded in the middle of the bush with no fuel.

Oliver stood next to the diesel tank, his face stiff with worry. It had been bad enough constantly worrying about him when he was doing his national service during the war, but this was worse. Back then, you understood what the fight was about – blacks and whites fighting each other for control of the country. But he couldn't understand what was going on now. Now, the blacks had control of the country but black people were still killing white people. For what? Publicity? These murders certainly got a lot of attention. Black people were also killing other black people. Why? For retribution? There were rumours of thousands of people being rounded up and killed. They'd had people being rounded up here. What would have happened if he hadn't gone to the scene? If thousands of people were being killed, it wasn't getting any publicity. Those murders got no attention. No one knew anything for sure.

*

Dominic drove down the narrow tar road through the Matobo Hills to the small village of Kezi, winding his way around huge, rounded *dwalas* and jagged *kopjes,* separated by grassy plains. It was late afternoon and he could see there was going to be another magnificent sunset. Under normal circumstances, they would stop to enjoy it. Perhaps climb a *dwala*, have a beer and some biltong while they were up there.

Brian must've been thinking the same thing because he said: 'Last New Year's at Rhodes' grave was a *jawl*, hey?'

It had become a tradition for crowds of people from Bulawayo to go to the site of Rhodes' grave on New Year's Eve. Few went there to pay tribute to Cecil John Rhodes, the man who the country had been named after, initially, but to enjoy the magnificent vista from his gravesite, instead. He had chosen this site well, on the top of one of the biggest rock *dwalas*, with a three hundred and sixty degree view of other massive *dwalas*, scraggy *kopjes,* and grassy plains. The view was even more impressive because there was no sign of any other human activity, just the graves of Rhodes and two other pioneers, Jameson and Coghlan, and a monument containing the remains of the European men who died at the hands of the Ndebele when they were looking for King Lobengula in November 1893. But, other than a cursory glance at the graves and monument, most visitors on New Year's Eve were more interested in sprawling out on the rock hill with their cooler boxes and snacks, soaking in the breath-taking night sky, alive with millions of stars. The party always became more raucous as midnight approached. After seeing the New Year in, the less robust would make their way down the rock to their cars and drive the thirty odd kilometres back to Bulawayo, while those with more stamina remained to watch the first glimpse of the first sun on the first day of the New Year.

'Yes, it was a great party,' Dominic said, rubbing his hands on the steering wheel. 'Will was with us, if you remember. Who would have thought we'd be in this situation now?'

'Fuck, no.' Brian's face tightened.

The Chester's farm was before Kezi, so they decided they would stop there first and find out if there had been any further updates. They felt awkward doing this as they assumed Mrs Chester would be there and they did not want to intrude on her at such a difficult time. But they did not want to receive any bad news in the impersonal environment of the Kezi police station either. As it happened, there were no fresh developments and Mrs Chester appeared touched to see them and receive their condolences. Many of the farming families in the district had converged on her house with plates of food, so Dominic and Brian faced a house full of strangers when they arrived at the Chester's homestead. Some must have known who they were, glancing at them with looks of concern on their faces.

Mrs Chester approached them, pushing her handkerchief into the pocket of her flowing floral dress, running her hand through her short, greying hair.

'We're so sorry,' Dominic said, thinking how strong she was. Her eyes were puffy and her cheeks blotchy, but she was putting on a brave face.

'It's too terrible for words,' she said, 'and we are so worried about your family.'

Dominic's heart contracted. She must've noticed the pained look that crossed his face, because she added. 'No news is good news, hey?'

'I'm not so sure,' Dominic said. 'We've come to see what we can do to help find them.'

A familiar face appeared at Dominic's side. Darvie Peters. Another Kezi farmer, who Dominic had known as a senior when he first attended Plumtree School back in 1968, and then remotely when he was doing his national service. Darvie had been a major in the Rhodesian Light Infantry then.

'Howzit Dom, sorry about the situation your family is in, hey,' he said.

'Thanks. Have you met Brian Brooke?'

'Howzit Brian. No, I don't believe we've met. How do you fit into the Brooke family?'

'I'm Martin's eldest son.'

'Right. Where's your old man now?'

'He and my mother travelled down south last week. They'll get back as quickly as they can.'

'And how is poor Serena?' Mrs Chester asked. 'She and I... we've both... she needs people with her.'

'My Aunt Bea has gone out to the farm to be with her and Aunt Molly, John's wife. And the Craigs are around too.'

'Good to hear this. My kids are in South Africa but they're both flying up here tomorrow, and I'm lucky to have all these kind folk to support me until they get here.' She waved her arm, showing all the people who had gathered there.

'Come, I need to talk to you,' Darvie said, laying a hand on Dominic's shoulder. 'Let's go outside.'

They walked off the veranda and into Mrs Chester's lush garden. Security guards were walking around the perimeter of the garden, next to the fence.

'It's a fucking, fucking shame, hey' Darvie said, taking a box of Madison cigarettes from the top pocket of his shirt. He pulled one out for himself and then offered the pack to Dominic, who took one, even though he hadn't smoked since his army days. But he needed to calm his nerves right now. 'Just when the Chesters decided to throw in the towel and move down south, this has happened to them. Fuck, fuck, fuck.'

'Who's done it?' Brian asked.

'Dissidents, I reckon.'

'But why? Why did they pick on my family and the Chesters?'

'I hate to say it, but it's because they were an easy target. I kept telling Old Man Chester not to drive the same routes, not to tell anyone his movements, not to do anything predictable, and what did he do? Have his cattle ready at a designated place with six of his labour, waiting for them to get there. One of these people, or maybe all of them, could be moles, or intimidated into becoming informants. And then matters get worse because the Brookes arrive in their bloody aeroplane so everyone on the ground can see them flying in and know exactly where they are going. I'm afraid to say they were sitting fucking ducks.'

Dominic dragged hard on his cigarette. 'But why does anyone want to kill them?'

'For the same reason, they have killed all the other white farmers since Independence. So that it makes the news. So that it causes instability. The problem in this country is we have two dominant tribes. Both of them want to be in power, and remember, there's a history of animosity between them. Before the whites came here, the Ndebele were the dominant tribe. Now the Shonas want their turn. And, you know, all the other stuff going on, all the black people being killed, doesn't make the news. Let me tell you, it should...... but it won't. Everything we hear is through word of mouth, whispered by terrified locals who claim to have seen or even witnessed terrible atrocities, like entire families being killed. Bloody hell. It's madness. It's why the Chesters wanted to get the hell out of here. They're old and don't need all this crap in their lives. They got through the war and hoped it would be plain sailing from then onwards, but they discovered it wasn't.'

Dominic said: 'What a tragedy for Mrs Chester.'

Darvie drew once more on his cigarette, then threw the butt into Mrs Chester's flower bed. 'It sure is.'

'We've come here to see how we can help... in finding John and Will.'

Darvie rubbed his chin. 'Listen, I think it's best if you let us get on with it. We've already started, in fact. I just came back here to collect more provisions and ammo. But we know the area, we know the locals. This is not the first time we've done this. We know who we can trust and who the snakes are. You let us get on with it. No disrespect to you or anything. We'll make comms as soon as anything turns up.'

'What are you doing?'

'The usual. Mainly following their spoor at this stage. We know some of the tricks these bastards get up to put us off their tracks.'

'And what about my guard, Petros? He's pretty clued up on tracking. Do you want to use him?'

'Ah, na. We've got enough people right now. And anyway, it's best he stays out of this. If he helps us, the dissidents may target him, and if he helps the dissidents, others may target him. It's a real crappy situation.'

Dominic looked at his watch. 'So, do you think it's okay for us to drive back to Bulawayo tonight, then?'

'*Ja*, I think you'll be safe enough. They've hit once today so they won't do it again as they know the area will be crawling with people looking for them. They won't do anything to draw more attention to themselves for a while.'

'Right then, we'll get back to Bulawayo and stay the night with my sister in town. If you need us, we can drive back here again tomorrow.'

'*Ja* man. There is something you should do while you are here......go to the police station to identify Graham Brooke's body. I don't believe anyone has done this yet, and it's part of the procedure.'

This was the last thing Dominic wanted to do.

'Sorry man, I know it's shit,' Darvie said. 'But you'll have seen enough bodies when you were in the army, hey?'

'Yes. Don't worry, and thanks for everything you're doing now. We won't give up hope.'

A sceptical look flashed across Darvie's face for a moment. 'That's the spirit. None of us are going to give up on them.'

*

They arrived at Amanda's home in the suburb of Ilanda in Bulawayo after ten that night. The drive back had been long and grinding, made more difficult because there seemed to be more traffic on the road. They kept having to slow down and pull off the narrow tar every time another vehicle approached them. It was a relief when they got to their destination and, although Amanda wasn't expecting them, they could see from the many lights on in her house she was still awake. They hooted at the locked gate, even though Kevin was already there, barking and jumping up at them when he recognised who they were.

'Down boy, down,' Dominic said as he stood next to the gate in the headlights of the Land Cruiser so Amanda could see it was him.

The hall door opened, and Amanda appeared.

'Howzit, Sis,' Dominic said. 'Do you mind if Brian Brooke and I doss here tonight, and Petros too?'

Amanda hurried across the drive and when Dominic saw her face in the headlights of the car, his heart sank. He could see she had been crying hard. 'Oh no…,' he spluttered.

'Yes…. John. They, they…. they found him shoved into a ditch.'

'Dead?'

'Shot in the head.'

'And… and Will?'

'Nothing.'

Amanda fumbled to unlock the gate, and when she managed, she pushed it open and collapsed into Dominic's arms, sobbing. She buried her face in his chest. He stroked her back and rubbed her arms as tears streamed down his own cheeks. Brian stood next to them, thumping the bonnet of the vehicle with his fist, again and again, before letting out a loud wail.

Amanda pulled herself together. 'Come, let's go inside. My gardener's name is Dumisani. You'll find him in his house there,' she said to Petros, pointing behind the garage. 'Will you need some food?'

'No, we stopped at the Eskimo Hut and bought some hamburgers,' Dominic said.

Louise stood at the front door. They could see she had been crying as well. She hugged Dominic and Brian, and they made their way through to the sitting room where Dominic went straight to the drinks cabinet and took out four tumblers. He poured a double tot of whisky into each glass and handed them out to the others. They all collapsed into the chairs. There was a numb silence as everyone sipped their whiskies. Louise shuddered as she swallowed. She'd never drunk whisky before.

Dominic broke the silence. 'So, when did they find him?'

'After sunset,' Amanda said.

'Who found him?'

'A group of local farmers.'

'Probably Darvie and them, hey?' Brian said.

'I guess,' Dominic said.

'It's just too awful for words,' Amanda said. 'I can't imagine how terrible poor Molly must be feeling right now. Her husband is dead, her son is missing.'

Brian said: 'And Granny. Bloody hell. Her husband, her son, and probably her grandson. Bastards, bastards, bastards.' He let out another long, low wail, slapping his hand against his leg in frustration.

Louise got up and went to sit next to him, putting her arm around him. 'John was always the best person to be around,' she said. 'He always made everything such fun.'

'That's for sure,' Amanda said. 'Right from when he was a young boy, and we used to do lessons together in the schoolroom at Brightside. His antics used to drive Lily mad, I'm sure.' She took a slug of her whisky and also shuddered. 'Lily and Papa have been at

Serena's house all afternoon, as well as Molly and Molly's parents. Bea and Ron are there now too... so at least they are all together to support each other.'

'I'm not sure anything can lessen the pain we're all feeling right now,' Dominic said. 'So everyone is in the know?'

'The only person who doesn't know yet is Cassia, as the telephone at Freedom High is in the Headmaster's office and he's been out all afternoon. I will go there tomorrow to tell her.'

CHAPTER 10

A GUST OF WIND whirled across the sandy soccer pitch, whipping up dust in its path. Cassia turned her back to it to avoid the dirt blowing into her face. A group of schoolboys were on the pitch, kicking a ball made from plastic bags, stuffed with more plastic bags. I should buy them a soccer ball, she thought, then recalled how Mr Mpofu, the soccer coach, always complained about having to keep the balls locked up, to prevent them from disappearing. This put her off the idea. She didn't want to worry about soccer balls.

The boys stopped kicking the "ball" to each other as Cassia drew close. 'Afternoon, Ma'am,' they chirped in unison.

'Afternoon, boys,' she replied.

They continued playing their game, scuffing their scruffy school shoes in the dirt, their socks around their ankles, their shirts untucked, ties pulled loose.

The breeze brought some relief from the oppressive heat, albeit a temporary reprieve. October was just plain hot in Zimbabwe, and nothing changed this. The weather would only cool down when the rains started falling. Cassia shifted her heavy basket from one hand to the other as she continued her walk to her cottage. The basket was full of books needing to be marked, and she expected a long afternoon. At least the lounge in their small cottage had a ceiling, making it cooler than her stifling classroom, which had no ceiling.

She walked around the building at the far end of the soccer field and noticed a green Datsun Pulsar parked outside her cottage. It was like the one Amanda drove. She increased her pace, wondering if it was Amanda. Surely not? Amanda had never been to Freedom High, or anywhere near the vicinity. Most white people in Bulawayo never ventured into the high-density suburbs. But as she neared the cottage, she saw through the lounge window it was Amanda, sitting with her back to the window. How strange, she thought, but as she entered the room and Amanda turned to face her, she could tell that something was dreadfully wrong. Her heart skipped a beat as thoughts rushed through her mind. Was there a problem with her parents? Her grandmother? Aunt Bea?

'Hello Amanda,' she said, dropping her basket beside the door. She noticed Beryl through the back door, boiling the kettle on the fire they used for cooking out there. Beryl glanced up when she heard Cassia's voice, a frown playing across her forehead.

Amanda remained in her chair. She put one of her hands to her mouth and bit her thumb, trying hard to keep her emotions under control. 'Something terrible has happened.'

'What?'

'Graham, John and Will flew to Kezi yesterday. They were ambushed and....... and.'

Cassia's face drained of colour and she clutched the doorframe as her legs trembled. 'And what?'

'John and Graham were killed. They... they can't find Will.'

Cassia stumbled across the room and collapsed onto the chair opposite Amanda. She opened her mouth to say something, but no words came out. Beryl stood at the back door, looking at Cassia, then

Amanda. She was as shocked as Cassia by what she had heard, despite not knowing any of the people involved.

Cassia broke the silence. 'Who did this?'

'Dissidents, apparently. They think John killed one of them before he was killed because....because they found another body near his.' Cassia stared at her in confused silence. Amanda paused, then began again. 'Graham flew John and Will to Kezi yesterday morning to buy some cattle from a farmer who is leaving the country, a Mr Chester. The ambush took place along the road between the airstrip and where the cattle were being kept. They found Graham and Mr Chester right away. Their bodies were still in the vehicle. Hours later, they discovered John's body, hidden in a ditch, along with one of the dead attackers, hidden by branches and other vegetation. But Will has disappeared.'

'On his own?'

'They don't think so. They believe the attackers kidnapped him. The people searching for him saw four sets of tracks and they assume these were Will's, with three other people. They followed their tracks until they disappeared near a huge *dwala,* but they couldn't find where or if they came off it. It's a massive expanse of rock, apparently. They walked all around the area, but there are lots of other rocky outcrops branching all over the place, making it difficult to find tracks.'

'Maybe they're still on the *dwala* then.'

'They've looked for caves and crannies in the rock where they may have hidden, but can't find any. But those rocks in the Matobo can have holes and passages in them that only the locals know.'

'What about Granny and Molly?'

'They're at Sunlands with my father and Lily, Molly's parents, and Bea. They're all devastated. Dominic drove to Kezi yesterday with Brian when they heard the news. They wanted to help with the search, but the local farmers talked them out of it, said they know the area and local people better. So they stayed at my house last night, although Dominic went back to Kezi this morning to.... to identify John's body and plan to have him and Graham brought back to Bulawayo. I'll go out to Brightside early tomorrow morning. Do you want to come with me? We will bury Graham and John in the family graveyard in the next couple of days. I'll stay out there until after this.'

'Yes please, I need to be there too.'

'Right, so do you want to gather your things and I'll take you to my place for the night?'

Cassia looked at Beryl. 'I must tie up some loose ends before I leave. It'll take a while. Can you drive me to Amanda's house this evening, Beryl?'

'Of course.' Beryl turned to Amanda. 'I am so, so sorry to hear this terrible news.'

'Thank you,' Amanda said. 'It is horrific, made worse by not knowing what's happened to Will... and... and if he's being mistreated.'

Cassia shuddered. 'Don't say that.'

She walked Amanda to her car. The two hugged each other in mutual sympathy, and Cassia sobbed as the enormity of what had happened sank in. They both knew there was nothing they could do to make anything better, but they still spoke for a while, drawing comfort from each other.

When Cassia walked back into the cottage, it surprised her to find Gladmore in the lounge.

'Hi,' he said. 'I was outside helping Beryl with the fire when you got back from school and found your auntie here. I didn't want to disturb you, so remained outside, but I heard everything. *Ngixolisa*. Please, I am very sorry that this has happened to your family.'

'Thank you Gladmore. It's terrible.'

'Ah. Sorry...... sorry.'

'No one knows where my cousin is, but my uncle John is dead. He is my mother's younger brother. He was such a fun man, always joking, always finding the bright side of every situation.' Cassia began to cry again as she recalled how much she had always enjoyed John's company. She pressed the palms of her hands into her eyes, moaning and shaking her head. Beryl and Gladmore looked at each other helplessly. Beryl walked over to Cassia and patted her shoulder, but Cassia moved away and sat down, feeling shaky again. Once she'd regained her composure, she continued. 'They killed my step-grandfather, Graham, too. He's my grandmother's second husband, and also my great uncle, because Granny was first married to his brother. Sorry, this is complicated.' She sniffed and rubbed her nose with the back of her hand. 'None of it is relevant to what happened yesterday.'

'Of course it is,' Beryl said. 'Family histories are always relevant, and make us understand how tragic their passing is.'

'My gran is such a lovely lady. She and I have always been close, right from when I was little. I could always feel her love for Graham.' Cassia broke into sobs again.

'She'll be hurting badly then,' Beryl murmured.

'I cannot imagine how terrible she must be feeling.'

Gladmore cleared his throat. 'Sorry, but I have to say something about what's happened.' Deep lines furrowed his brow. Cassia and Beryl looked at him, surprised at the seriousness of his voice.

'What, Gladmore?' Beryl asked.

'No one here must be told anything about what's happened to Cassia's family.'

'What do you mean? Here at Freedom?' Cassia asked. 'I'll have to tell Mr Sibanda because I must apply for some leave days.'

'I know, but we must not give him any details. You must not tell him anything more than that there has been a death in your family.'

'Why?' Cassia said, still confused.

'In fact, I think Beryl should speak to him tomorrow morning before school starts. She can apply for leave on your behalf. She can say you had to leave in a hurry. If she tells him and he asks her for details, she can say she knows nothing else. It'll be easier for her to lie than for you.'

Beryl's eyes widened. 'But why? What's wrong with him knowing?'

'We need to keep quiet about anything that involves dissident activities, especially as Cassia's cousin has disappeared. We mustn't say anything until we find out if he is still alive.' Cassia and Beryl stared at each other, then back at him. 'There are many sides to what is going on,' he continued, 'and we never know who is on which side. Some people may be connected to the dissidents, some people may be connected to the military, and each side will try to use anything they are told to win favour with whichever side they're on.'

'But Mr Sibanda? Surely not. No ways,' Beryl spluttered. 'He's just a school teacher who's been promoted to headmaster.'

An image of Mr Sibanda, his greying hair, his soft voice, his obsequiousness towards the other teachers flashed through Cassia's mind. She found it hard to believe he might have another agenda.

'Maybe, maybe not,' Gladmore said. 'But people have told me stories about him. All three of us must say as little as possible to anyone here about Cassia's relatives.'

*

Most of the people who worked on Sunlands and Sunbright wanted to attend the double funeral. Like Graham and John, many of them had been born and lived their entire lives on the farm, and it shocked them that their employers were now dead. Besides this, the nature of these deaths also horrified them, especially after their experience a few months before.

Many people also drove out from Bulawayo for the funeral. They drove in convoys from town, cognisant of the fact that dissidents had allegedly perpetrated this tragedy, dissidents who could attack anywhere and whose motives for attacking were still unclear, even though they had killed so many people. But despite these risks, they still wanted to attend the funeral and show their support for the Brooke family. They found it hard to digest the magnitude of the Brookes' loss, especially since it could get worse if Will was found dead too. This thought was in the back of the mourners' minds, like a large pulsating boil waiting to erupt, but no one talked about it at the funeral. Instead, they spoke of hope and of Will's courage and heroism, of his diplomatic character.

Everyone gathered at the graveyard on Brightside, where they had buried members of the Brooke and Craig families for the past eighty years. It was an impressive place, surrounded by a low sandstone wall, topped with a chain fence, and affording a striking view of the surrounding area. The acacia galpinis in full bloom were the most impressive feature at this time of the year; creamy puffs in an otherwise grey landscape, demarcating the river as it meandered across the terrain below. Many mourners hovered outside the walled area at the beginning of the service, but the priest, who had come from Bulawayo, beckoned them in. They arranged themselves in between the headstones of the six old graves, taking shelter from the blistering sun under the two large galpinis that grew in the graveyard, thankful for the shade these trees offered and the sweet scent of their flowers. A light breeze fluttered up the hill, causing some flowers to fall on the mourner's heads like confetti.

If only this was a wedding and not a funeral, Cassia thought. She had never been to a funeral in this graveyard, although she had visited it many times before they left for England, and in recent weeks whenever she'd stayed at the farm. One reason she always made a point of visiting it was she loved the view. Another was that the poignancy of being amongst the graves of her forefathers always struck her. Her great-grandparents, her grandfather, and her great-uncle and great-aunt were all buried here. Whenever she was there, she would recall what she knew about the lives these people had led. She, along with everyone else in the family, knew the story of how Anthony Craig had first climbed this hill back in 1905 and sat on the rock beside which she now stood. While there he decided that this was where he wanted to be buried, but, as a young man in his early thirties, he had no idea that they would bury him there just a few weeks later. His death and funeral had also been in October.

Cassia's attention moved to her grandmother, who she knew was in considerable emotional pain. She was bowed over, leaning on a walking stick, despite usually being upright in stature. This shocked Cassia when she saw her. Her grandmother was still relatively young, and she'd never used a walking stick before. She still looked elegant, though, in her calf length black dress and long black veil. The tranquilizer she had taken earlier may help her remain calm during the service and the wake afterwards, but nothing would ease her pain. Cassia, like everyone there, knew how terrible Molly felt too. She stood next to John's open grave, wearing a pair of large sunglasses, which she had to keep taking off to wipe her eyes.

After the service, the priest invited everyone to the Craigs' house for the wake. He asked those who had come in cars to leave them where they were and walk to the house to avoid causing a dust storm. Dominic had arranged for armed guards to patrol the bush along the route in case anyone was feeling unsafe.

Cassia was walking on her own to the house when someone caught up with her. It surprised her to see this was Beryl.

'Oh wow, I wasn't expecting you to come,' she said.

'I feel so sad for your family. I wanted to come and pay my respects.'

'Well, thank you. I appreciate it, and I'm sure the others will too.' They took a few steps in silence before she said: 'Did you drive here on your own?'

'No, no. I phoned your Aunt Bea's house, not knowing she and your uncle were here already.'

'Yes, my aunt came the day of the tragedy. My gran needs all the support she can get.'

'I'm sure. But anyway, your Aunt Bea has someone staying there at the mo, house-sitting. A Mrs Atkinson. She told me she'd be coming to the funeral and offered to bring me. We came in the convoy and we'll drive back in it later. She's that lady over there. Have you met her?' Beryl pointed towards a stout woman wearing an orange patterned dress ahead of them, talking to the man she was walking with.

'No. I don't recognize her from the back, at any rate.'

Beryl glanced about. 'Any news of your cousin?'

'Nothing.'

'Everyone must be worried sick about him.'

'You can say that again.'

Beryl slowed down and touched Cassia's arm. 'I need to talk to you, but I don't want anyone to hear us.'

Cassia raised an eyebrow. 'Oh? Now?'

'Yes.'

Cassia pointed towards a narrow dirt path heading into the bush. 'Okay. Let's go that way. I've been along that path before. It will lead us back to the Craigs' house, although it's a bit longer.'

They walked in single file along the path for a short while, zigzagging between scrubby thorn bushes and long, dry grass. They were soon out of sight of the others strolling along the road. Cassia noticed a large tree growing near the path, casting a deep shadow around it.

'Let's stop there in the shade,' she said, taking off her straw hat and lifting her long hair off her neck. 'What a relief to get out of the scorching sun.' She looked around for somewhere to sit. There were a couple of round-looking boulders and she lowered herself onto one of them, moving her bottom about to get more comfortable. She twisted her hair into a coil and tucked it back into her hat.

Beryl sat down on another rock, blowing the fringe out of her face and fanning herself with the "Order of Service" she still had.

'So, what do you want to talk to me about?' Cassia asked. Cassia glanced at Beryl and was surprised to see tears shining in her eyes.

Beryl spoke in a whisper. 'It's Gladmore. He left the night you came here.'

'Sorry?'

'He's gone.'

Cassia shifted her weight on the rock. 'What do you mean, gone? Did he tell you where he was going?'

'No. He came to the cottage late that night, after I'd gone to bed. He said he didn't want anyone seeing him there.'

'But lots of people know that you two are an item.'

'He said, if anyone asks about him, I'm to say we've broken up.'

'Have you broken up?'

'No, no. He said he had to go somewhere and the only person I should tell is you.'

'Me?'

'He said that where he's going could be dangerous.'

'Now you're confusing me.'

'Can you promise that you'll do what he requests?'

'What? How can I make promises when I don't know what you're talking about?'

'Just promise, and then I'll tell you.'

'Oh for goodness' sake, okay, I promise.'

Beryl took a big breath. 'Gladmore has snuck off to Kezi.'

'Kezi? But that's where... ?'

'Exactly. You don't remember that his family comes from that district?'

'No. I'd forgotten.'

'It's his rural home. So he's gone there to see if he can find out what's happened to your cousin. This could lead him into great danger.'

'Danger from who?'

'Everyone, as far as I can make out, if he talks to the wrong person. Dissidents may see him as a sell-out and kill him, and the army may think he's collaborating with the dissidents and then they'll kill him.'

Cassia shivered, despite the heat. 'Bloody hell. So why's he doing this, then?'

'I think because he hates what's happening in his home district. People he knows have been killed, and others have become dissidents. According to him, all this is not supposed to be happening.'

'Does he think my cousin could still be alive?'

'He said there is a chance.' Cassia's eyes widened. Seeing this, Beryl quickly continued. 'But of course everything might have changed since I saw him.'

'Oh God, I hope not. We have to pray he's still alive. I can't tell you how much we've all been dreading the news that someone has found his body.'

'I can imagine.' They were both silent for a while until Beryl said: 'There's something else.'

'Yes?'

'Gladmore's going to need to get out of the country if he's involved in releasing your cousin.'

'Really?'

'Yes. He says he'll have to go into exile if this happens. He wants us to get married and go to England.'

'Oh wow.'

'Why are you surprised? You know how much we love each other.'

'Of course.'

'What he's doing is a big deal, though, because it means he may never see this country or his family again.'

'That's awful.'

'Yes.' Beryl rubbed her chin. 'So he's going to need financial help to start off with. He wanted me to ask you if you can help.'

Cassia's head spun. '*Eish*, I don't have much money.'

'He said, if you can't, is there someone in your family you can call on? It'll have to be someone who you can trust.'

Cassia thought about this. 'Yes, Dominic. We can trust him.'

A fly buzzed around them and Beryl flapped it away. 'I hope you're right, because you'll have to tell him everything as soon as possible, so he can have the money ready when we hear from Gladmore.'

'I'll speak to him tonight.'

'Gladmore says there will be other people involved and they will need money too.'

'How many?'

'I don't know.'

'Gees, Beryl, I can't believe we're talking like this. This whole situation is surreal.'

'I know, but if it saves your cousin's life, it'll be worth it.'

'We're talking about facilitating murderers and abductors.'

'Gladmore says the people holding Will may be young men who have become embroiled in a situation not of their making. Some people are retaliating against the men that have wiped out whole families. What did you say that special brigade was called again?'

'Um.... *Varume,* I think they're called.'

'So if the people holding your cousin are retaliating against the *Varume,* they probably don't want to kill him.'

'Hopefully, you're right.'

Cassia shook her head as she heaved herself off the rock. All this was making her feel old and tired, but if Will was still alive, they could not ignore what Beryl was saying. She knew Dominic would do anything he could to help save Will, even if it led him into danger too.

*

As agitated as Cassia and Beryl were, thoughts of abductions and ransoms left their minds as they neared the Craigs' house and came across a man walking along the path towards them. This man had his head down, concentrating on what he was carrying; a flattened piece of cardboard on which he had a chocolate cake with a full Camembert cheese on top of it and an array of other food surrounding it. He was dressed smartly in trousers and a jacket, but his trouser pockets bulged and his jacket was weighed down with bottles in all the pockets. Cassia could make out a bottle of gin in one pocket, and beers and cokes in others. He didn't notice them until they had almost bumped into each other, and when he looked up and saw them, he almost dropped everything.

'What on earth?' Cassia said.

'*Salibonani,*' he muttered, moving swiftly around them and scuttling off.

Cassia rubbed her chin. 'I wonder what he's doing with all that food and drink.'

'Well, he won't go hungry,' Beryl said.

The wake was being held in the Craigs' garden, as it was cooler out there than on the veranda or in the house. Cassia and Beryl made their way through the side gate but as they were walking towards the main throng, they stopped in surprise when they saw what was going on. During the service, the caterers had arranged the refreshments on three trestle tables. Tea and coffee, cups and saucers on the first table, with platters of cakes and scones. Drinks and glasses on the second table, with tubs of iced beers, wine, tonics, sodas, Cokes and Fantas on the ground next to it. Plates of snacks covered the third table. The mourners were meant to help themselves as they mingled with each other on the lawn under the trees. However, this was not going according to plan. Cassia and Beryl watched, agog, as a woman wrapped a pat of butter into a table napkin and shoved it into her pocket, followed by some samosas, scones, and a handful of sausage rolls. She then moved to the tea table, where she pushed some biscuits into her bra. Another lady was doing much the same, except she was filling a bag, and a third had taken off her hat, in which she put a milk tart and some scones.

'Bloody hell...' Cassia said.

'Poor women,' Beryl said. 'They must be starving. Can you imagine what a mess all that food will make?'

'Beryl! Even if they were starving, which I doubt they are, they shouldn't be taking all the food for themselves. There won't be enough for everyone else at this rate.'

Beryl bit her lip. 'I doubt she'll eat it on her own. She'll share it with her poor starving children.'

'For God's sake, Beryl. Stop being so naïve. They can't carry on like this. My gran will go ballistic if she notices it. She will have a complete melt down, no matter how many tranquilizers she's taken. Help me. We've got to take everything inside and then we'll go around serving people. That'll stop them from abusing our hospitality.'

'Um. There's an awful lot of stuff to take in.'

'Has to be done. You carry the platters of food to the kitchen while I look for others to help us. You'll find the kitchen through there.' She pointed to a door on the veranda.

While Beryl began removing the refreshments, Cassia located Amanda standing under a tree with Kate and Louise. She explained to them what was happening.

Kate rolled her eyes and muttered, 'typical,' then said she would look for Sarah and Jane to come and help as well. The others rushed back to the tables to assist Beryl, and they soon cleared the tables, leaving only the bare necessities. Once all the food was in the kitchen, they arranged platters of snacks and cakes, and then they wandered through the crowds, serving people individually, and also offering to refill glasses when they noticed these were empty. This kept them busy for a long time, but somewhere amidst all this, they agreed John would have found these antics amusing. It would have delighted him to see how well occupied they were at his wake.

So it was many hours before Cassia thought about the conversation she had had with Beryl earlier, but her heart sank when she did. Beryl was leaving, and she hugged her as she said goodbye and put her mouth close to Beryl's ear. 'Thanks for all your help today. You've been an absolute gem. I'll talk to Dominic this evening and let you know what he says when I get back to Freedom tomorrow,' she whispered.

Beryl's eyes swam. Besides worrying about Gladmore's safety, she had also discovered that Cassia's family was much less snooty than she'd expected. She felt a genuine sadness that they were going through such a tough time.

CHAPTER 11

THE FOLLOWING DAY, the weather started no differently from most days in October. Hot, dry and dusty with the pastel-pink, cloudless, early-morning sky changing to a hazy blue by mid-morning. Everyone braced themselves for yet another blistering day, but, by late morning, hope built that the hot weather might break. Whisker-thin wisps of condensation were at first unnoticeable in the sky, but as the hours passed, they shifted towards each other, joining together, filling out and puffing up, until they turned into clouds.

'It feels like it could rain,' Oliver said to Lily at lunch. They both looked out of the dining room window at the grey clouds in the distance, hovering above the pastures beyond the house. As if to announce their presence, a long, low rumble of thunder broke the quiet of the dining room. 'Maybe we'll have a proper storm,' Oliver continued. 'What a relief that would be to break this damned dry season.'

'Storms in October are always welcome,' Lily said, but as she said this, her thoughts turned to Will, and she wondered how much he'd appreciate a storm if he was out in the bush somewhere. As a professional hunter, though, at least he knew how to rough it in the

African bush. Her stomach lurched every time she thought about him and what might or might not have happened, but she didn't want to verbalize her fears. Instead, she said: 'Whenever we have rain in October I think of the storm on the day your father died and how it washed away the spoor at the scene of the crime.'

Oliver raised an eyebrow. 'Is that what you think? About something that happened almost eighty years ago and about someone neither of us knew?'

'I often do, especially as... well, you know.'

Oliver lent over and squeezed her hand. His father's murder was a sensitive subject for them because Lily's grandparents had been the chief suspects. They had run away, abandoning their newborn baby, Lily's mother, before justice could take its course, and this had left a cloud over Lily's mother until her dying day.

'I'm sure my mother would have appreciated this. She loved him very much,' Oliver said.

Lily sighed. 'Oh yes.'

She was feeling melancholy and introspective today. Oliver's mother, Isabella, had been dead for over twenty years, but Lily would have done anything for her comforting presence right now. Isabella faced great sadness in her life, first with the death of her child, followed by the unsolved murder of her husband little more than a year later. It had been a terrible time for her, yet she had pulled herself together and lived a long and fulfilling life, leaving a great legacy in her many wonderful paintings. Lily glanced around the dining room, at the banks of paintings of African birds that hung in this room. What an amazing collection they were, painted in the year after her husband's death, to ease the pain this had caused her. How lucky she had been to have had this passion, and how lucky her family were to be the recipients of so much of her work.

Lily's passion was the garden she had created during her married life. Would anyone consider this a legacy when she was dead? She doubted it, but it still brought them much joy. When she married Oliver in 1948, his mother had designed the garden with succulents and indigenous grass. This grass died off every dry season because the only water they had then was drawn from a well. However, when they built the dam and piped water to their home in the first year of their marriage, they had an abundant supply from then onwards, and hence began her passion for gardening. Over the years she had created an oasis of huge shady trees with walkways rambling across lush green lawns and around flowerbeds bursting with a multitude of colourful shrubs, and behind the kitchen she'd established an abundant vegetable garden filled with cabbages, carrots, lettuces, tomatoes, and much more besides. Having the wake in the garden yesterday had been balm for their grieving souls, despite the chaos caused by some of the "mourners". Thank goodness Cassia and her friend had noticed what was going on in time to change things so that everyone still had enough to eat and drink.

The telephone rang in Oliver's study. Out of habit, they both stopped to listen to the ring. Two short rings, followed by one long one – the call was for them.

'I'll get it,' Lily said, placing her napkin on the table and pushing her chair back.

It was Martin, asking if they could come over that afternoon for a "family meeting". This surprised Lily. She could not remember a time he had ever requested this before. He and Oliver shared a cordial relationship, accepting the role each played in the other's life, but they had never been close, like Oliver and John. Martin did not have John's easy-going manner and often appeared cold and aloof.

'Let me check with Oliver,' Lily said. 'Either he or I will phone you back shortly. Who's going to be at this meeting?'

'I hope all of us can be there. Mother, Molly, Bea, you two, Dominic. I'd ask Amanda to be there, too, except I believe she went back to town this morning. I'm guessing she won't come back, what with work and all that.'

'No, she won't, and Dominic isn't around either. He went off this morning and I'm not sure when he'll return.'

'Oh damn. Did he tell you where he's gone?'

'No.'

All she knew was that Dominic had told them that morning he needed to sell some cattle, and this would tie him up for the next few days. Both she and Oliver had noticed, and commented on it to each other later, how tense he'd been when he spoke to them, especially when Oliver asked him how many animals he intended selling. Dominic had cut his father off and said he would decide when he knew what prices he could get. Oliver had not pressed him further, but he and Lily agreed afterwards that this was the first time Dominic had ever sold cattle without first discussing everything with him first. They concluded Will's abduction weighed him down and that he was keeping himself busy so he wouldn't dwell too much on what may have happened.

'Martin calling for a meeting with all of us?' Oliver said when Lily rejoined him in the dining room after ending her phone call with him. 'This sounds rather ominous. I wonder what it's about.'

'Mm. He suggested the Sunlands lot all come here.'

'Oh really?' Oliver pondered this for a minute. 'No. I think it'll be easier if you and I drive over to Sunlands instead. Save them all traipsing here, especially if it's going to rain, and that way we can come home when we've had enough. The last thing I'll want is to entertain anyone who insists on hanging around. We'll take Petros with us and make sure we're home before dark.'

*

They congregated on Martin and Kate's beautiful veranda, overlooking the oxbow lake with a huge acacia galpini tree in the middle of it. The galpini was lovely at this time of the year, covered in creamy, sweet-smelling blossom, but everyone focused on the dark clouds instead.

'Please, please let it rain,' Bea said. 'This relentless heat is getting me down.'

Lily caught Molly's eye, and she wondered if Molly also worried about what a rain storm might mean for poor Will, if he was still out in the elements somewhere.

Kate finished serving the tea and cake, and Martin interrupted the chatter about the impending storm.

'I've called this meeting to discuss what we're going to do in the light of what we've just been through. In fact, I should say what we are still going through.' He took a deep breath. 'I think the time has come for us to ask ourselves why we are still living here and what the best way forward is.'

No one said anything until Oliver eventually broke the silence. 'What do you mean? Are you saying we should ask ourselves why we are still on the farm, or why we are still in this country?'

'Both,' Martin said.

Everyone met this statement with another long silence until, as if a higher presence was listening in on them, lightning cracked, thunder crashed and the rain fell. Soft at first, but increasing in strength until it became a torrent. They stared at the storm, mesmerised by the spectacle, sniffing the petrichor, watching the vegetation bending from the weight of the rain and the puddles forming on the lawn.

After some minutes, it eased enough for Oliver to speak over the noise. 'So you want to leave all this, do you? This excitement. This drama.' He waved his hand to show the wet scene in front of them.

'It's all the other dramas we're tired of,' Martin said.

'But this country is our home. It's the only home any of us know.'

'True.'

'It's the place where my generation and my parent's generation worked so hard to make it what it now is.'

'I have also worked hard here all my adult life, as did John and Graham.'

'Of course. I am aware of this.'

'And for what? John and Graham are now dead. Maybe Will too.'

'Stop it Martin. Don't say that,' Molly hissed.

'Sorry, but we discussed all this earlier.'

'Yes, but not about my boy being...' She swallowed a sob.

'Sorry.' He stared at the cliffs on the other side of the oxbow lake. He exhaled and turned his attention back to Oliver. 'We Brookes discussed what we want to do, Uncle Oliver, and we are unanimous. We want to sell up and leave. This country is doomed.'

As the words left his lips, the sun broke through the clouds, throwing a warm glow across the veranda.

Bea couldn't help herself. 'Lordy,' she said. 'What beautiful light.'

Oliver smiled. 'Yes, it's going to be a lovely evening after that storm. There's nothing like the first rains of the season.'

'Absolutely,' she said.

'I think this talk of impending doom and wanting to leave is a knee jerk reaction after what has happened,' Oliver said. 'All of us are fragile at the moment. We should wait until we are feeling less emotional before we make any life-changing decisions.' He looked at everyone on the veranda.

Bea stirred her tea, then held her cup up to her face, as if to hide behind it. Serena stared at her hands in her lap, twisting her wedding ring on her finger. Molly sniffed and wiped her nose with a tissue.

Only Martin met his gaze, defiant, his mind made up. 'I've made some enquiries, Uncle Oliver. Do you know that for every dollar the government pay us for our land, the British Government will add a dollar? They made this arrangement in the Lancaster House Agreement, signed before Independence.'

'Yes, I know this,' Oliver said.

'And there's a good chance the government will buy our farms for rural development. I've been putting out feelers about this.'

Oliver scowled. 'I wish you'd discussed this with me first. I would have told you I don't want to sell.'

'None of us thought we'd ever want to sell until now. But honestly, Uncle Oliver, what is the point of hanging on? When the war ended and the government talked of reconciliation, we hoped we could be a part of the new Zimbabwe. But now we're seeing what the cost is going to be. How many more lives are we willing to lose? That's what we need to ask ourselves? How many more family members have to die before we accept that this is no longer the place for us?'

'It's true that we're going through a bad time at the moment, but the Ndebele and Shona are in discussions. They are looking for a solution. There is talk of the two political parties uniting.'

'For God's sake, Oliver,' Serena butted in. 'If they unite, it will make things worse because then we'll have a one-party state. There's no saying what they'll do after that when there is no one to check or balance them.'

'They'll do what they want anyway,' Oliver said. 'You know, when you look at the rest of Africa, that "democracy" and "Africa" don't belong in the same sentence. One man, one vote doesn't work in a society where most voters think nothing of selling their vote for little more than a bag of mealie meal.'

'Or a clip around the ear if that doesn't work,' Bea suggested.

'Exactly,' Oliver agreed. 'But honestly. I think we should wait and see how the talks pan out before we turn our backs on everything we have. If we can carry on living our lives the way we have all these years, but without the threat of anyone else being murdered, I don't see why we shouldn't.'

'I'm afraid you're out numbered, Uncle,' Martin said. 'Mother, Bea, Molly and I all want out. We've decided if they make us an excellent offer, we should take it. Obviously we'll divide everything between us shareholders. It should work out well for all of us.'

'And what will you do with the money?'

'Kate and I will move to South Africa, to start with, and then to Australia.'

'How do you then intend getting your money out of the country? All you're allowed to take are your household possessions, a vehicle and one thousand Zimbabwe dollars.'

'That's correct, but there are many ways to move money. I'll tell you about some of them if you decide you want to leave too.'

*

'Can they not sell Sunlands, as they appear so desperate to do this, and we remain with Brightside?' Lily asked Oliver later when they were back at home. She could see how agitated he was by what had transpired at the meeting. He was too old to be packing up and moving elsewhere. Not that it would be much easier for her. The thought of abandoning her beautiful garden filled her with despair, and if this was how she felt, he must feel so much worse. This place was more than his home. It was his life's work.

'It won't work if we just own Brightside,' Oliver said.

'Why not?'

'We'd struggle to make a reasonable living. Brightside alone isn't big enough to graze a decent herd of cattle, and we would no longer have the dam to irrigate any pastures. At the most, we could run about fifty livestock units, which wouldn't bring in enough to live on. If it was four times the size, there could be a chance, but not the size it is now. That's the problem with farming in Matabeleland. If you can't irrigate, small pieces of land are pretty useless.'

Lily mulled this over. In all the years she had lived here, they had always thought of Brightside and Sunlands as one farm. They knew this was not the case on paper, as the two properties were on separate title deeds, but this had never been an issue before, because everything they produced went into one pot. No one had ever talked about selling, so no one had ever worried about who owned what or who lived where. But the fact of the matter was, because the dam was on Sunlands (the property where all the Brookes lived), it was a great deal more valuable than Brightside, where the Craigs lived. The irony was that Oliver had built the dam on Sunlands because that's where the river ran. If it had been on Brightside, they could well have continued to farm this property alone.

'And what about us buying them out?' Lily asked.

'There is no way we could pay them what they would want.'

'I wonder what Dominic will say about all this,' she said. 'And Amanda?'

'I don't believe either of them will want to sell. I wish Dominic had been at the meeting this afternoon. He might have changed everyone's mind, especially as he knows what it's like living elsewhere in the world and how much we'd miss everything we own here. Maybe he could have talked them into not rushing any decision making until we're all feeling a little better.'

CHAPTER 12

DOMINIC HAD ARRANGED to sell five of their prize three-year-old bulls to Bert Goosen, a rancher from the West Nicholson area. He hoped this would raise enough money to pay Gladmore and the abductors, if they made contact with him. He had heard nothing from anyone since Cassia had told him that a rescue plan was afoot. All he understood was that if someone made contact with him, he needed to have money ready. Over the years, Bert had bought numerous bulls from the Craigs, and Dominic knew he was a dependable customer who could quickly produce the cash, unlike some other ranchers. Also, since Bert had been wanting to buy more bulls from them for a while, he quickly agreed when Dominic phoned and offered them to him that morning. Bert suggested he could use his cattle truck and drive to Brightside to collect them early the next morning, but he was surprised when Dominic asked him if he was able to give him the money on his way through Bulawayo, before he went to Brightside, as a special favour. He usually only paid once he'd chosen the animals he wanted, but he knew the Craigs and the Brookes were going through a hard time. Knowing the Craigs' reputation for selling top quality bulls, he agreed to meet Dominic at the Hilltop Motel in Bulawayo the next morning at seven-thirty to give him the money. He also offered to sort out the veterinary permit and police clearance on his way through Bulawayo, much to Dominic's relief. Dominic had enough to worry about without having to deal with all that irritating bureaucracy.

To avoid discussing any of this with his parents, Dominic only told them about the impending sale once he'd made the arrangements with Bert. He didn't want to go into any details, in case he had to sell more animals, so he cut his father off when he tried to get into a discussion about which bulls and how many. All he asked of him was to be around when Bert arrived at Brightside the next morning to help him chose the bulls he wanted. He told his parents he could not hang around as he needed to go to town for a few days. This sudden burst of activity surprised them, but luckily they didn't ask any uncomfortable questions. He knew they would quiz him about all this later, and he just hoped that by then he would have brought Will back safely.

He had told Cassia that his plan was to stay at Amanda's while waiting to hear from Gladmore or someone else. The telephone there was reliable, unlike the party line at Brightside, where, even if it was working, there could be a nosey neighbour listening in on any awkward conversations he might have to have. In addition to this, he also wanted to be in town so that he could act immediately if someone contacted him.

He hated all this secrecy, but he knew he had no other option but to say as little as possible to anyone. He needed to be as ready as he could for any event, and then to wait.

Dominic told Amanda nothing about any of this when she arrived home from work and found him there, but he struggled to hide how tense he felt. He saw her throwing him concerned glances, and he hoped she would put his nervousness down to the murders and the abduction. That was bad enough. He wondered what she'd think if she knew of the latest development. His excuse to her for staying in town was that he would need to deposit the money he'd get for the bulls in the bank, and also that he had other business to attend to. This was plausible enough. He often stayed with her when he had things to do in town. He and Amanda were close, but he did not want to involve her in anything that he was dealing with right now unless he had to.

Evening came, and he had still heard nothing from Gladmore, or Cassia, or Beryl. Dominic sat on Amanda's veranda to keep out of her way. Clouds were coming in from the north, as they often did with impending rain, and from her veranda he noticed a storm brewing. Under normal circumstances he would welcome early rain, to break the intense October heat, but not right now when he might have to drive into the bush. Rain and mud would make this even more difficult.

The phone rang and his heart skipped a beat. Amanda ran into the hall to answer it, and, after concentrating on her first few sentences, he concluded the call was not in connection with his mission.

He stopped listening to the telephone call, until her words, 'Oh wow, that's a bit of a shock...' drew his attention back to her conversation. Silence followed until she said: 'You say all the Brookes want this?'

Silence again, until: 'I'm so sorry. I know this will be the last thing you need...'

And so the conversation continued.

Eventually, she ended the call and came through to the veranda to find him. She collapsed into a chair and stared at Dominic.

'You're never going to believe what's on the cards now?' she said.

'What?' His heart sank again.

'Martin.'

'What about him?' For one moment, he thought he'd been killed too. But no, she looked irritated rather than distraught.

'Martin called a "family meeting" this afternoon.'

'And?'

'All the Brookes want to sell the farm.'

Dominic's mouth opened, then closed. He was speechless, knowing that if the Brookes wanted to sell, this meant selling everything, not just the portion of the farm they lived on.

'Papa is pretty upset,' Amanda said.

'Well, it's a bit of a shocker. All the Brookes want to sell, you say?'

'Yes.'

'Fuck.'

'Papa says Martin has been planning this for some time without ever mentioning a word to him until today.'

'Really?'

'Martin's already approached the government to see if they want to buy.'

'Has he?'

'Papa says he thinks he called the family meeting today, straight after what has happened, because he knows everyone is still reeling from shock and will therefore be more likely to go along with what he wants.'

Dominic rubbed his chin. 'Martin has always been a crafty bastard.'

There was a low rumble of thunder, followed by the ringing of the cow bell on the gate.

Amanda turned her head towards the sitting room. 'Did I hear the gate?' The bell rang again. She looked at her watch. 'Now, who can this be? Are you expecting anyone?'

'Um... Let me see who it is. You stay here. It may rain any minute.'

His legs felt weak as he walked through the house and out of the front door. He saw Cassia standing next to the gate, a Datsun 120Y parked behind her, with the engine turned off but the headlights dimmed.

'Hi,' she said, her voice sounding shaky.

'Hi.'

'I've, um, I've come to ask you if you can help me with the car I'm using, um... it's broken down.'

'Oh?' Dominic peered at the Datsun. With the headlights on, he couldn't see if there was anyone in it. 'Are you alone?'

'Yes.'

Dominic looked at his digital watch, pressing the switch to illuminate the face. It was six fifty-seven now. He murmured that he was figuring out a way to stop Amanda from becoming suspicious.

'I've already worked out what to say,' Cassia whispered back. 'I'll go into the house and inform her that Beryl and I met up at Fritz Drive-In Restaurant to get some take-aways. I'll say I borrowed my friend Dave's car and now it won't start.'

'Um... Is Beryl at Fritz?'

'No, she's at Freedom. But I won't mention that. Instead, I'll tell Amanda I've driven here in Beryl's car to ask you to come back to Fritz with me to see what's wrong with my borrowed car. I'll say Beryl stayed at Fritz to look after this broken-down car.'

'Mm. I doubt she'll buy that one.'

'She'll have to.'

Amanda did indeed raise an eyebrow when Cassia explained all this to her.

'Sorry to barge in on you like this, but you live close to Fritz, and I couldn't think of anyone else to ask,' Cassia said. 'Bloody car,' she added for emphasis.

'Is it a bit of a jalopy?' Amanda asked.

'Yes. Have you cooked yet? What are you having for dinner?' Cassia asked.

'Only chicken curry. I haven't cooked the rice yet.'

Cassia turned to Dominic. 'If we get the car going, would you mind following me back to Freedom in case it fails on me again when I'm driving there? You can have some of our take-away dinner from Fritz instead of Amanda's curry.'

Amanda's eyebrows raised further.

Dominic looked from Cassia to Amanda and to Cassia again. 'I guess,' he said. 'You don't mind, do you Sis?'

'Um, no, of course not. We can't leave Cassia stranded on the side of the road.'

'Exactly,' Dominic said. 'Let's go then, shall we Cass? Don't come out, Sis, in case you get caught in the rain... oh, and don't wait up for me.' The crease between Amanda's eyes deepened when she heard this, causing Dominic to smile, despite his nerves and the sickness in the pit of his stomach. She probably thinks there's something romantic going on between Cassia and me, he thought. Best let her assume this. Judging from the blush on Cassia's cheeks, she must've thought this too. The blush deepened when he squeezed her bare shoulder as they stepped onto the front porch.

He had no idea what lay ahead of him, but he'd made some arrangements, packing in his Land Cruiser, various items he thought he might require. A revolver, a pistol, and a box of ammunition, all concealed under the front seat with the gun permits stored in the glove box, and in the back, under a tarpaulin, he'd packed blankets, spare clothes, a twenty-litre water container, and some dry food. In addition, he'd also put together a compact medical kit containing aspirin, tetracycline ointment, rehydration salts, bandages, plasters, and Dettol. He may not need any of this, but he needed to be prepared.

'Wait for me at the corner of Winnie's Way and Fairbridge,' he said to Cassia as he walked towards the carport where he'd parked his Land Cruiser.

The thunder rumbled, and he peered at the sky. 'Go inside, Sis, in case the heavens open.' Amanda was still standing on the front *stoep*, watching him in confusion. 'I'll lock the gate behind me, and please don't wait up.'

Once he was out of the gate, he felt under the seat for his pistol. He pushed it into the top of his shorts, making sure his shirt hung out over it. He drove to the corner where Cassia had stopped the Datsun, the engine switched off. The enormity of what may be ahead of him was sinking in and he was having misgivings. What if they had set a trap to abduct him too? Or what if the army or police stopped him and accused him of enabling dissidents? His mind raced. Maybe he should have found backup? Maybe he should have brought... He couldn't think what? But, no, he mustn't involve anyone else.

Cassia climbed out of the Datsun, biting her lip. 'Sorry for all that crap about coming back to Freedom with me. I said it to buy you more time if you need it.'

'Ah.'

'If I didn't know Gladmore and his family, I'd say... I'd say... we shouldn't be doing any of this,' she said. 'But, Beryl has convinced me that Gladmore was serious when he said he may be able to help. He's a good man.'

Dominic smiled wryly. 'I'll keep this in mind. So have you heard anything? I'll only have the money tomorrow morning, though, so I hope no one is expecting it tonight.'

'Oh golly. I hope that won't be a problem. But I don't know. All I was told was to drive with you to Fritz. We are to park side by side in the parking places closest to the entrance on Thirteenth Avenue. I have to leave after five minutes and you are to order two hamburgers. You must write your contact telephone number on the boxes they serve the hamburgers in.'

'Bloody hell. Whose number?'

'Well, I guess Amanda's as that's where you're staying.'

'Yup. And then what?'

'I know nothing else, someone wrote this in a message and it was given to Beryl by an *arb* person who waved her down at the school gate when she was on her way to the supermarket this afternoon.'

'That sounds dubious. Someone must've been following her.'

'I know.' Cassia glanced around her now. The road was well lit up with street lights, but she wondered if there was anyone in the shadows watching them. Had anyone followed her here? She hadn't seen a car following her, but she shivered anyway.

Noticing this and feeling the same, Dominic said: 'Let's go and just hope we don't need the money.'

They followed the instructions to the best of their ability. Five minutes after parking the Datsun, Cassia restarted it and drove off, glancing at Dominic as she did so. Dominic slid out of his Land Cruiser and walked across the parking lot. He ordered two hamburgers, feeling vulnerable as he stood in the lit-up serving area, knowing he was being watched. He gleaned some relief from the bustle of the other patrons at the drive-in restaurant, but he'd parked his Land Cruiser in the darkest part of the parking area. The people he'd be meeting must have checked the place out before and that's why they'd told him to park there, he thought. The man serving behind the counter handed him his two hamburgers, each in a cardboard box. He took a biro from the top pocket of his shirt and wrote Amanda's telephone number on both boxes. He then walked to his vehicle and, as he did so, someone else moved towards it too. They arrived at the same time. He couldn't see the man as he was staying in the shadows, but he said: 'You have my hamburgers?'

Dominic handed over the two boxes. The man took them, then turned around and walked off down Thirteenth Avenue, his back to Dominic. Dominic wanted to call out, 'What's going to happen next?' but of course he couldn't, so he climbed back into his Land Cruiser. He waited a while and when he realised there would be no further communication, he reversed out of his parking place and drove out of the exit into Thirteenth Avenue and in the opposite direction from the way the man had walked. At least there had been no mention of needing the money, but now the action was over, he regretted not buying something to eat for himself also. He decided to stop at his favourite drive-in restaurant again, the Eskimo Hut, where he bought a hot dog and a double malt. While waiting for his order, he was relieved to see no familiar faces in the car park. He was too nervous to chat to anyone, but he hoped the tasty fast food would help calm his frayed nerves.

*

The heavens opened as he approached Amanda's house and the rain soaked him as he opened the gate and then closed it once he'd driven in. He pushed the pistol back under the seat and made sure the Land Cruiser was securely locked when he got out. Amanda and Louise were watching television when he entered the house.

'You're back earlier than I expected,' Amanda called as he dropped his keys in the bowl on the hall table.

'Yes, her car wasn't as bad as she made out, so there was no need for me to follow her all the way back to Freedom as she thought I might.'

'What was the matter with it?'

'Er... one terminal on the battery had fallen off, so all I had to do was put it back and tighten it.'

'She dragged you out on a stormy night just to do that? I would've thought she could see something as obvious as that for herself.'

'Yup. I don't think she knows anything about car engines.'

'Are you hungry? I can warm you up some curry, although I didn't cook any extra rice.'

'No thanks. I had a hot dog. I'm pretty tired so I'll hit the hay. Night ladies.' He was afraid they would notice how nervous he was still if he stayed up and watched telly with them.

*

Amanda and Louise always left the house at seven in the morning. Dominic lay in his bed listening to them pottering about, waiting for them to leave, praying the telephone would not ring. He couldn't relax until he heard them open the front door and walk to their car, greeting the gardener, Dumisani, as they did so. Dominic heard the car start and the bell on the gate tinkle as Dumisani opened it for them, then closed it after they'd driven out. Only then did he leap out of bed, dress, and rush off to the Hilltop Motel. Bert was already there waiting for him, sitting on the veranda having a cup of coffee. He'd left his farm at four am, he told Dominic. Dominic forced himself to appear relaxed as he sat down and had a cup of coffee with Bert, all the time praying no one was trying to get hold of him while he was there, away from Amanda's telephone. When they finished their coffees, they strolled back to Bert's cattle lorry and climbed into the cab to count the money. Bert had come up with the idea of counting the money there as it was high enough that, if anyone wandered through the hotel car park, they wouldn't be able to see what they were doing. Dominic briefly discussed the bulls, and explained that his father would be at Sunbright to choose the five he wanted with him. After saying their goodbyes, Dominic slid out of the cab and walked back to his Land Cruiser as nonchalantly as he could. Now he had the money, he could return to Amanda's telephone as fast as possible.

He rushed into the house and discovered Agnes in the kitchen, doing the washing up.

'Morning Agnes, has anyone telephoned this morning?'

'Ah, no Boss. Not since I've been at work.'

Relieved that he had not missed a call, he made himself another cup of coffee, wondering if he was going to have a long and stressful wait. He wished he could talk to someone about what was happening, but there was no one he could talk to except Cassia, and she'd be at work now. She must be feeling equally nervous, he believed, maybe even more so, as she wouldn't even know what had transpired last night. It would shock her, as much as it had him, if he told her how all their subterfuge had amounted to so little.

His stomach tightened when the phone rang at nine o'clock. He ran to answer it.

'I want to speak to Craig,' a gruff-sounding voice said.

'Speaking.'

'Have you got four thousand dollars?'

'Ah. Yes.'

'Bring this in a bag to the flower market in Fife Street. Stand on the left-hand side of the men's toilet. Make sure you are alone. Be there at eleven o'clock.' The phone went dead before Dominic had time to utter another word.

He arrived at the flower market at ten forty-five and found a shady parking place half way up the block, opposite the fountain in front of the city hall. To calm himself, he stared at the majestic city hall building with its tall, white columns and stone engraving above the massive wooden entrance, surrounded by well-kept, shady gardens. The flower market, on the pavement between the municipal gardens and the street, was as bustling as ever with what looked like tourists, wandering up and down, more interested in the carvings and curios than the flowers. His hands were sweaty again and his stomach turned as he glanced towards the toilets at the end of the block. There was an elderly man selling baskets on the left-hand side of the door to the gents. Was this the man he was supposed to be meeting?

At two minutes to eleven Dominic climbed out of his Land Cruiser, the bag over his shoulder, and walked up the pavement, passing all the people selling curios, until he got to the basket seller next to the toilets. This man's aging eyes lit up as Dominic glanced at his display of baskets.

The man held up one woven straw basket. 'Do you know how much?' he said.

This was the standard question anyone selling anything on the streets in Zimbabwe asked, but Dominic still wondered if this was his way of initiating a conversation.

'Er... no,' Dominic said.

'Only one dollar-fifty,' the basket-seller said.

'Um...' Dominic said.

The basket seller held up a second basket. 'This one is the same price.'

'I don't want a basket,' Dominic said.

'I can give you a good price. You can have both of them for just two dollars.'

Dominic knew now that this was not some coded message.

'No thanks, I am not here to buy baskets.'

He turned to face the street and break contact with the ever-hopeful basket-seller, who was refusing to take no for an answer. As he was wondering how far he could move away from him, someone else slunk up to him and said in a low voice: 'Be outside the Southern Sun Hotel at eleven forty-five. Walk there. Leave your car here. Make sure you are alone.' This man slipped away and disappeared into the throng of tourists and flower and curio sellers. It happened so fast Dominic registered little more than that he was wearing a faded black t-shirt and jeans.

He looked at his watch. What was he going to do for forty-five minutes? It would only take him ten minutes to walk to the hotel from where he was. Should he go to the restaurant at the top of Haddon and Sly Department Store, over the road from where he was standing outside the municipality? He could have a milk shake, like he and Will had done countless times when they were growing up. But no. There were bound to be friends of his mother's there, enjoying a cup of tea after having had their hair done or completing their grocery shop in the supermarket on the ground floor. He didn't want to meet any of them and feel obliged to engage in small talk, especially because he believed someone would likely be observing him. His nerves were too fraught for chitter-chatter. Then he thought of the Grass Hut restaurant on the opposite side of the street from Haddon and Sly. It was dark inside, with small, intimate booths, frequented mainly by tourists and expats. There was little chance he'd know anyone there.

The elderly basket-seller appeared at his side with yet another basket and Dominic relented and bought it before setting off for the Grass Hut. He handed it to a beggar who was sitting on the pavement on his way.

He ducked into the Grass Hut and made for a booth at the far end of the restaurant, facing the door. He ordered a cup of coffee. As he drank this he scanned the restaurant, wondering if someone inside was watching him. The Grass Hut only had customers of European origin, and he concluded that none of them would be involved in his drama. But maybe there was someone waiting outside, watching out for him? He concluded there was. All this sneaking around and telling him to move from one place to another must surely be to check him out, to make sure he was alone. As he was thinking this, two men walked in and appeared to scrutinize the patrons in the dim restaurant before sitting at a booth near the door. Dominic felt his stomach turn. He struggled to drink his coffee after this but attempted to keep his nerves in check. He glanced at his watch again. If he walked slowly down Ninth Avenue, he would get to the Southern Sun Hotel at the designated time, but he decided he'd prefer to walk fast, so he remained in his booth for a further five minutes.

He did not look behind him as he strode from the Grass Hut to the Southern Sun Hotel, the strap of the bag over his left shoulder and slung across his chest with the bag secure under his right arm. When he got to the Southern Sun he faltered, not knowing whether to stand at the top of the steps leading into the hotel, or remain on the pavement. Several people milled around the entrance and he was about to walk up the steps when someone nudged him and said: 'Wait at the garage kiosk next door.'

With this, a taxi pulled up next to him, and the man who had spoken to him jumped into the passenger seat. The taxi disappeared around the corner into George Silundika Street. Dominic turned around and walked back towards the garage. As he did this, he considered the taxi and the person who'd spoken to him. The taxi had been a standard Datsun 1200 Rixi Tixi Taxi, like a good many other taxis in Bulawayo, and it had been a different man from the one at the flower market. These people were certainly covering their tracks, he thought.

He got to the kiosk and as he did this, a Skyline Taxi drove into the garage forecourt and stopped right next to where he was standing. 'Give me the bag,' a man hissed through the passenger seat window. Dominic handed it over and the taxi shot off, disappearing down Tenth Avenue.

The man serving at the kiosk stood wide-eyed behind his counter.

'Are you alright, Boss?' he asked. 'Did that man steal your bag?'

'No, no, all is well.' Dominic said. He did not want him to become suspicious and tell anyone what he had seen. 'We are colleagues,' he added, but even as he spoke he wondered what on earth he'd done. The money was gone, and he had no idea what would happen next.

He felt deflated and stupid as he walked back to where his Land Cruiser was parked near the flower-sellers. All he could do was go back to Amanda's and wait and hope that they had not taken advantage of him.

CHAPTER 13

THE SOUND OF A CAR turning into the driveway alerted Oliver of Martin's arrival. He placed his hands on his desk and pulled himself out of his office chair, then hobbled onto the veranda to wait for Martin to come through. After some minutes he did, carrying his briefcase, looking efficient, but his voice sounded edgy when he greeted Oliver. And so it should, Oliver thought, after the way he's treated us, bamboozling everyone into doing what he wants. If only Dominic was here. Two against one is more effective with any argument. Oliver knew Dominic shared his views on Zimbabwe – that the bad times would come and go, but, despite this, they would still have a more fulfilling life here than anywhere they may move to; here, in the country of their birth, the country they had always called home. The years Dominic spent travelling had convinced him of this. Oliver did sometimes wonder if Dominic was as keen on the farming aspect of their lives as he was. He assumed it may be the bush and outdoor living that attracted him more, but he wouldn't delve into this right now.

There were more pressing issues to deal with. Martin appeared to have done a good job convincing his mother, his sister and his sister-in-law that they should sell up. Encouraging them to agree with him when they were still reeling from what had happened just a few days ago. Clever Martin. Calculating Martin. Oliver suspected he'd wanted to sell everything and leave the country for years, and he was now using this opportunity, when things were so bad, to push his agenda. Martin had never been as attached to the farm or his family as Oliver, Dominic or John had always been.

'Afternoon, Martin,' Oliver said in a clipped voice. 'Can I offer you a cup of tea?'

'Yes, please. I'm parched after a long morning in town.'

'Would you like a sandwich too?'

'No, don't worry.'

Oliver walked the short distance to the door leading into the kitchen, where he found Prince standing at the sink washing up after lunch. 'Will you make us a pot of tea, please Prince, with two cups on the tray.'

'*Yebo*,' Prince said, taking the dish towel from over his shoulder and drying his hands before turning the kettle on.

'*Siyabonga*.'

Oliver shuffled back to where Martin was now sitting in one of the comfortable armchairs on their veranda. He had set his briefcase on the coffee table in front of him and pulled out a sheaf of papers. 'The government have shown great interest in buying our properties,' he said, once Oliver had settled into the armchair opposite him.

Oliver could feel a hot flush rising from his neck to his cheeks. He wanted to curse and swear at Martin but after some moments of hesitation while he regained his composure, he said: 'Quite frankly Martin, I am shocked you are presenting me with this today. I haven't even had twenty-four hours to digest what you threw at us yesterday, and now you're telling me you already have a buyer lined up. I find your actions underhand and devious. It shows me that you have been planning this for a long time, and the death of your brother and stepfather has provided you with the perfect excuse to convince the others to go along with you.'

Prince interrupted Oliver by setting the tea tray on the table in front of Martin.

'Let me pour,' Martin said, taking this opportunity to halt Oliver's tirade. He took his time, then sipped his tea. 'Ah, just what I need.' He glanced at Oliver's tight face. 'I'm sorry you see things this way, Uncle Oliver.'

Oliver set his teacup down on its saucer. 'Well, how else am I supposed to see it? As I said yesterday, we should let the dust settle after the tragic events of the past few days before making any major life-changing decisions.' His eyes shifted from Martin to scan Lily's magnificent garden beyond the veranda. He knew she would be heartbroken if they were to leave after all the years it had taken her to create it.

'I've made no secret in thinking we white people don't have a long-term future in Africa,' Martin said. 'The blacks don't want us here. They will only ever use us. That's why they're still murdering us. It would be much better for all of us to move to somewhere like Australia where we can build ourselves a more secure future.'

'I'm sure the indigenous Australians don't want whites there either.'

'Well, they have no choice, do they? They're out-numbered, thanks to the way non-whites have been treated in the past. It's a shame the Aussie government changed their White Australia Policy. That kept the non-white population in check, didn't it?'

Oliver took some time swallowing the retort he wanted to make to these crass comments. However, he didn't want to divert their conversation to Australian politics, so eventually he said: 'This difficult time we're having in Matabeleland won't last forever. It will get better, you know, especially if we all learn to work together.'

'I know it will, but I don't want to wait for it to "get better", only to have another bad time come along further down the line. Because that's how it will always be here. You build something up, and someone will come along, wanting to take it away from you. It's better to get out now, while we can.' Martin was not looking at Oliver while he spoke. Instead, he was shuffling through the papers he held in his hand. 'Ah. This is what I wanted to show you.' He handed Oliver a wad of papers stapled together. 'Look at this. The government say they will give us an average of fifteen dollars per acre. That's pretty damned good when you compare it to what buyers have paid other people for their farms. If I remember rightly, the Beamishes got way less per acre when they sold to Siphas Ngwenya back in 1980.'

'Yes. That's because the Beamishes didn't build a dam.'

'True, and that's why the government is so interested in buying our place. They can use the dam for irrigation. It will help the black people farm this area themselves.'

'You shouldn't have been doing all this behind our backs,' Oliver said, paging through the papers. 'Did you ever bother mentioning any of this to Graham or John?'

'No, but please stop going on about it, Uncle Oliver. Someone needed to start the ball rolling.' He put down his teacup, collected his briefcase, and stood up. 'I'll leave you now to read through this and we can complete everything at a later date. Don't worry about seeing me out.'

Oliver was so furious with him, he had no intention of doing this, or of reading the document Martin left with him. Once the sound of Martin's footfall had faded in the hall, he reclined in his chair, lacing his fingers together and twirling his thumbs as he contemplated their conversation. The idea of being made to do something so transformative against his will was something he loathed. He admitted that there had always been a possibility of it occurring, with two families jointly owning the same properties in the name of one company. They were lucky that, in the eighty years since his father and uncle had bought the farms, no one had ever wanted to sell up before. Even during the Independence War, they had resisted the temptation to leave, determined to hold out. When the war ended and the new Prime Minister offered a hand of reconciliation to the white community, they were determined to forge on. It was most unfortunate that this window of reconciliation seemed to have soured now, for reasons he could not understand. All he knew was that they were facing another real setback, with both white and black people being killed indiscriminately, but he still believed they could see this through, too, despite what had happened to two, maybe three members of his family.

He had inherited his stoicism from his mother. He considered her now, and his Aunt Celia, his mother's sister. At first, their husbands had lived near town, in a house called "Sunrising". They had formed a mining and exploration company and, on one of their many expeditions, looking for unknown places to mine, they had passed through this very area. He exhaled as he looked out at the view he had of the farm from his veranda, knowing how different it was now from what it had been like then. He gazed beyond the garden to the open fields, fenced and gated, thick with the nutritious pastures they had planted to supplement the poor indigenous grass. The weaner heifers were grazing in the field nearest the house, and the next field was empty, to allow the grass to seed and the seeds to fall and germinate. That's how he'd always farmed, planning everything, caring for everything. He'd spent his life doing this and it had resulted in enhancing what would otherwise still be a dusty, unproductive slice of arid African bush. He had hoped he would end his days as they had started, right here.

Oliver's mind turned to the main caveats that put him in the position he now found himself – being outvoted by his family. His first major setback was that his father had died so young, and his mother had never remarried, making him an only child. His aunt, on the other hand, had had three children. This meant they outnumbered him right from an early age. Thankfully one of those children, his cousin Patricia, had packed up and moved to Australia with her family years ago, and none of her offspring had ever had any interest in returning. So at least they were all out of the picture. However, his cousin Tim had had four children, while he had only had two. Thank God Graham and Serena had had no children together, and one of Tim's four children, Cassia's mother, had left and gone to live in England, otherwise the 'Brooke' side of the partnership would be even more weighted. As it stood now, there was just him, Amanda and Dominic on the 'Craig' side, with the 'Brookes' comprising Serena, Martin, Molly (who took over John's vote) and Bea.

Oliver considered these four 'Brookes' and wondered if he could convince any of them to change their minds about agreeing to sell up. Serena? Maybe once she had recovered from the terrible events of this week, but he couldn't talk to her about it now when everything was still so raw. He must say the same about Molly. The situation was even worse for her. No, he could not try to change either of their minds. Bloody, bloody Martin, striking when they were at their most vulnerable. His thoughts turned to Bea. Bea lived in town, but she loved the farm. Whenever possible, she came out to stay with her mother. She always insisted how lucky they were to have the farm. She frequently mentioned their fortunate situation of having so many family members living close by, unlike other Rhodesian families who had scattered worldwide.

And it was the farm that kept so many of the Craigs and Brookes here.

Mm, he thought, if he reminded Bea of this, perhaps she would change her mind. In this case, Martin would be outnumbered, not him.

Oliver looked at his watch. It was three-fifteen. There was enough time to drive into town and speak to Bea, before Martin went any further with his plans. They could stay the night with Amanda and return tomorrow.

He ignored Martin's irritating document on the table as he eased himself out of his chair and went to his office to phone Amanda.

*

When Oliver and Lily reached Amanda's house at dusk, they found Dominic, Bea and Ron sitting on the veranda. Oliver had asked Amanda to invite Ron and Bea for supper when he'd phoned her earlier. He hadn't told her why, but he was relieved to see they were there already.

'Howzit,' Dominic said, standing up and greeting his parents, ignoring the suspicious look his mother gave him as he bent to hug her. 'Everything go okay with Bert this morning when he collected the bulls?' he asked his father.

'We disagreed over Beethoven. Bert wanted to buy him, even though I mentioned we were keeping him for our own breeding purposes. He eventually got the message.'

'He knows a quality bull when he sees it, and of course he will always try his luck. Can I pour you both a drink? Bea, Ron, are you ready for a top-up?'

Amanda had gone off to the kitchen to talk to Agnes about dinner but returned minutes later. Oliver had asked her to be around when he began his discussion with Ron and Bea.

'Good to be with you,' Bea said. 'I was so pleased when Amanda phoned earlier to say you were coming in from the farm tonight and asked us to join you for dinner. It's four days now since the ambush and I'm still feeling as raw as if it happened yesterday. However, I find I'm better when I'm surrounded by other people.'

'Me too,' Lily said.

'Here's to the memory of Graham, John and... um,' Ron reddened as he held up his glass, knowing what a blunder it would have been to drink to Will's memory. 'It's a bloody depressing time right now. This time last week we had no idea what we were in for, did we? How's Serena?'

'Not good. She's staying with Martin and Kate,' Lily said. 'I'll pop over and see her again tomorrow when we get back to the farm.'

'And Molly?'

'Her parents are still with her, so that helps,' Lily said.

They all sipped their drinks, each considering the terrible happenings earlier that week and the heartbreak it had caused. Serena and Molly in particular, because they had each lost the person they lived with. And as for Will's abduction, they couldn't even begin to contemplate what they would do if he was found dead too.

Oliver cleared his throat. 'Because of what we're going through, I believe Martin's sudden announcement that we should sell the farm is wrong.'

'Yes, Bea told me you didn't approve of his proposal,' Ron said.

'It will be so disruptive to all of us. Surely it's better to wait until we are all thinking straight again.'

'I agree. He could have waited before he made this suggestion, but now that he has, I think it's the best thing to do.'

Oliver turned to Bea. 'Do you really agree with this, Bea? It's your childhood home and to this day, you spend as many weekends and holidays out there as you can.'

Before she replied, Ron butted in. 'For many years, it's been a strain having to arrange trips out there around guards and weapons and convoys. During the Independence War we all worried that *gooks* would kill us. Many farmers were. Well, that should all be over now, but nah-ha, the situation has got worse. Admit Oliver, since the first stirrings of nationalism in the early sixties, farmers have been, and continue to be, a soft target. First, the *gooks* were the enemy. They killed farmers because it was easy to do so, and now, well, farmers appear to be pawns in the current troubles.'

Dominic said: 'This is true, but what's happening now won't continue forever.'

Ron said: 'I know, but something else will come up, maybe in years or decades to come, but I guarantee, it will be the farmers who'll take most of the flack again.'

'Think about it, Uncle Oliver,' Bea said. 'You could use the money you get to buy yourself a lovely home here in Bulawayo. There are some beautiful places on the market right now with so many people leaving, aren't there Amanda?'

'Yes, there are.'

'You see. You would be comfortable and secure.'

Oliver stared at her, his lips clamped together in a tight line. The idea of living in town horrified him.

Amanda could see her father's distress. 'The thing is,' she said, 'we cannot replicate in town the lifestyle we all enjoy on the farm. I've lived in town since I married Edward in 1961, but I still much prefer being on the farm, and especially when there are lots of other family members there, too, like at Papa's birthday recently. I believe you feel the same way, Bea.'

'Oh yes, I do.'

'Exactly,' Oliver said. 'The farm is the glue that has held us together all these years. Think how other Rhodesian, now Zimbabwean, families have disintegrated and scattered to all the corners of the world, while most of us are still here, congregating on the farm for family events and holidays. They are special times.'

'When you say our families have remained intact, you're forgetting Valerie,' Bea said, 'moving to the UK all those years ago.'

'Well, Val always was different, and Martin, too, to a lesser degree. But the rest of us have stayed, and look, Cassia has even returned. I doubt the draw would have been as strong if it wasn't for the farm.'

'I guess you're right,' Bea said.

The ringing cow bell on the front gate interrupted their conversation. Amanda glanced at her watch. 'Who on earth could be coming here now? Let me find out.'

'No, no, I'll go,' Dominic said, jumping up and almost running into the sitting room.

'He seems rather jumpy,' Bea said when they heard the front door slam behind him.

'You can't blame him,' Lily said. 'We're all out of sorts.'

'True,' Bea said.

'He and Will were... I mean are... very close,' Lily said.

'That's why we shouldn't be discussing anything as drastic as selling the farm right now,' Oliver said.

'You know what? I agree with you, Uncle Oliver,' Bea said. 'We should at least wait a while and then revisit the idea. There's no need to be doing anything right now.'

'Well, thank you. So can we tell Martin this? He thinks all the Brookes are behind his plan to sell.'

'Hey, hey, steady on,' Ron said, thumping his beer glass on the coffee table. 'We'd agreed it was a good idea, Bea.'

'I know Ron, but Uncle Oliver is right. None of us is in the right state of mind to make such a huge decision. There's no harm in waiting.'

'Bloody hell!' Ron said. He stood up and looked at his watch. 'In retrospect, I don't feel like dinner here tonight after all. Sorry Amanda.'

Bea flushed.

Amanda stood up too. 'It's okay Ron, one of us can drive Bea home after dinner.'

'Good, So I'll be off then.' He almost bumped into Dominic as he strode through to the sitting room.

'What's up with him?' Dominic asked as he reappeared on the veranda again.

'Don't ask,' Bea said.

'I hope you don't mind Sis, but it's Cassia and her friend, Beryl, at the gate. They've invited me to go out with them.' He ignored the surprised look on all their faces.

'For God's sake I'm trying to have a family discussion here,' Oliver said.

Cassia popped out onto the veranda from behind Dominic. 'Hi all. We wanted to say thank you to Dominic for sorting out the car yesterday evening. I felt stupid when it turned out to be something so easy to fix. Sorry, I didn't realise you were all here, otherwise we'd have come later.'

'Would you two like to join us for dinner?' Amanda asked. 'It's only lasagne and salad and there's more than enough, especially now that Ron's not joining us.'

Cassia and Dominic glanced at each other. 'Ah, maybe we'll just grab a bite elsewhere,' Dominic said.

'Beryl's shy amongst strangers,' Cassia explained.

'Okay... well, that's fine. I can put the leftovers in the fridge for tomorrow,' Amanda said.

'Right, thanks. I'll grab a beer for the road and then we'll be off. Don't stay up for us,' Dominic said.

Oliver waited until he was gone and then said: 'This is why we shouldn't be making any irreversible decisions right now. Just look at this evening. Ron storms off. Cassia arrives unexpectedly and Dominic rushes off with her. Everyone is behaving strangely. We need to let things settle down.'

'You have convinced me, Uncle Oliver. I'll phone Martin in the morning and tell him. Sorry about Ron, but, as you know, he can be hot-headed at the best of times. Don't mind him.'

Lily leant forward and touched Bea's arm. 'Thank you.'

CHAPTER 14

CASSIA AND BERYL had come to see Dominic to find out what was happening, but none of them wanted to discuss anything outside Amanda's gate. For all they knew, there could be someone hiding in the dark, watching them.

'Let's go to the Eskimo Hut,' Dominic suggested. 'We can order something to eat and have it in the car while we talk.'

'Sounds like a good plan,' Cassia agreed.

'I'll take my Land Cruiser and you girls can follow me. I'll see you there.'

On arriving at the Eskimo Hut, he parked in the section of the car park overlooking the Academy of Music, the darkest spot he could find. Beryl drew up next to him in her Datsun. She and Cassia hopped out, locked the doors and climbed into the back seat of Dominic's vehicle. After asking them what they wanted – cheeseburgers, chips and cokes – he walked over to the hatch to place the order. Yet again, he was glad he couldn't recognize anyone in the car park he knew, but he felt vulnerable standing in the lighted area waiting for their orders. He glanced at the other cars in the car park again, hoping no one had followed them. The run-around he'd gone through that morning had frayed his nerves and left him feeling foolish and more agitated than ever. How stupid, or desperate, was he to have handed over thousands of dollars to complete strangers? What if he never heard from them again and they found Will dead? He thought he would have a complete melt down if that happened.

The girls were equally nervous. When he returned to the car and handed them their food and drinks, Beryl burst into tears.

'So sorry. It's just that I haven't heard a thing from Gladmore since he disappeared five nights ago,' she sobbed, removing the paper serviette wrapped around the hamburger and blowing her nose.

'That's why we came to see you this evening,' Cassia said, 'to find out what's been happening.'

Dominic drained the beer he'd brought with him and opened the second one. 'I'm afraid not what I expected. I'm beginning to lose hope.' He told them about the events of that morning. The girls listened in stunned silence.

'It sounds like they were playing with you, making you go here, there and everywhere,' Cassia said.

'I'm hoping they were checking me out, making sure I was on my own, and I wasn't leading them into trouble,' Dominic said.

'I think you're right about that,' Beryl said. 'The situation will be very dangerous for them.'

'It's dangerous for all three of us, too,' Dominic said. 'I was okay about everything this morning, but now I'm starting to wonder. It's been...' he glanced at his watch, 'almost nine hours since I handed over the money... and not another peep. Maybe they've taken it and done a runner.'

'No! Gladmore would never do anything like that,' Beryl said.

'But he's not the only one involved. Maybe he doesn't have a say in what's happening.'

'He will see you right, I'm... I'm, well, I'm sure of it,' Beryl stuttered, her eyes swimming with tears again.

None of them knew what else to say about the predicament they were in, so they sat in silence, eating their cheeseburgers. They could hear a violin playing from the depths of the Academy of Music.

'Someone must be having a late music lesson,' Cassia said. 'I wish it wasn't a violin. It sounds so... so mournful.'

'I can't go back to Amanda's until everyone there has gone to bed,' Dominic said. 'They're already giving me side-long glances, and they're soon going to quiz me hard. When I first saw you this evening, I hoped you had an update for me.'

'I wish,' Beryl said.

None of them had an appetite, but they continued to force their burgers down for want of anything better to do.

'You know what?' Cassia said when she'd finished hers. 'Let's go to Talkies Nightclub down the road. That would be better than hanging around here. We can listen to the music, take our minds off this dreadful situation, have a couple of drinks to calm our nerves.'

Beryl took the last swig of her coke. 'Yes, we can't do anything constructive anyway, can we?'

'Not right now,' Dominic said, setting his empty beer bottle on the centre console between the front seats. 'We'll go in two cars, so you girls can leave to go back to Freedom from there. I'll follow you this time.' They fumbled in the dark to open the back doors of Dominic's Land Cruiser, then slid out and hopped into Beryl's Datsun.

They were soon at the Talk of the Town nightclub. Dominic paid their entrance fees to the sour-looking woman in the hatch at the door, and the bouncer stamped each of their arms with a smudgy mark as they walked in. Coloured lights flashed from a disco at the far end of the smoke-filled room, and a bright strobe light shone at a glass disco ball hanging above the dance floor, showering the dancers in shards of brightness, as they jived to the Bee Gees' hit, "Staying Alive".

Dominic turned around and looked at the girls. 'Bloody hell,' he yelled. 'If our situation wasn't so serious, I'd say that song was a joke, hey?' The girls nodded in agreement, feeling some relief when the Bee Gees song merged into Wham's "Wake me up before you Go Go".

'At least the music is livelier than that violin,' Cassia shouted.

Dominic made a move towards the bar and the girls followed. The nightclub was so full it took some pushing to get to the bar area.

'What do you want to drink?' Dominic yelled.

'Vodka tonic for both of us,' Cassia mouthed back. She and Beryl shoved their way to a space beyond the bar and stood watching the surrounding revelry until Dominic returned with their drinks. He also had a packet of Madison cigarettes and, although none of them smoked, they each took one when he offered them. Dominic looked about the place and spotted the Davidsons and Fletchers with some other people he didn't know at a booth nearby. As he was thinking how he could avoid them, Davo noticed him and stood up to beckon them over. Their party shuffled around in their booth as Pete also indicated that they should come and sit with them. There was nothing for it but to join them but, to their relief, the loud music drowned out any talk as they didn't want to get into a conversation with any of them. The time passed, drinking, smoking and swaying to the music, with a few grunts and nods at the others in their booth. These people went to dance from time to time, but Dominic and the girls sat where they were, even when Davo tried to cajole Beryl into a dance. She shook her head so hard he quickly got the message. Dominic could imagine that Davo would have a lot to say about "that chick" next time they met. However, they managed to forget their troubles for a few hours and it surprised Dominic to see it was after ten o'clock when he looked at his watch. He indicated to the girls that they should leave, yelling good bye to his friends.

Once they were back on the street, with the music a dull thud from behind the thick walls, Dominic suggested maybe he should follow them back to Freedom, after all.

'No, don't,' Beryl said.

'But I'd prefer to. Maybe there's been some development since you've been away and Gladmore has left a clue there.'

Beryl's face lit up for a moment in the hopes that this may have happened, before reality returned and she said: 'I doubt it. It's not a good idea for you to come back to the school with us. Gladmore told me there are eyes and ears there. It could raise suspicions if you're seen driving in with us. We'll go back alone, and if we hear anything, we'll let you know as soon as we can.'

'Alright then, and I'll do the same. Let's just hope something happens soon. This suspense is doing my head in.'

*

As it turned out, Dominic only had to wait a few more hours. He spent a restless night, tossing and turning in Karen's narrow bed, so he was only dozing when Amanda came rushing into the bedroom at dawn.

'Wake up, come quick. You won't believe what's happened,' she cried, shoving his shoulder. He groaned, confused for a moment. 'Come quick,' she repeated.

'What?' He sat up, now alert, his heart thumping.

'The deputy headmaster of Saint Benedict's School near Mbala Mbala is on the phone. They have Will.'

'What!'

'Will, they've found him. You're wanted on the phone.'

'Who... who's on the phone?'

'I've just told you. The deputy headmaster of Saint Benedict's School near Mbala Mbala. Will's there and he asked this man to

171

phone you. Quick, get dressed, he's waiting. Use the phone in my bedroom. I'll go tell Papa and Lily. Oh my God... I can't believe this... what a relief.'

Dominic pulled on a pair of boxer shorts as he was making for the door. He stumbled down the passage to the phone in his sister's room and snatched up the receiver from where it lay on her bedside table.

'Hello.' He could feel his heart beating against his chest.

'Good morning, is this Dominic Craig?'

'Um ... yes.'

'I'm Ted Squires, deputy head of Saint Benedict's School.'

'Um...'

'Sorry to wake you so early, but we have William Brooke here.'

'But... how?'

'He made his way to the school. I believe he walked.'

'Gees...'

'We know Mr Brooke is the abductee we read about in The Chronicle the other day, and he's confirmed this.'

'Yes. Yes, he is. How is he?' As Dominic spoke he glanced up to see his parents stumbling into the bedroom, tying their dressing gown belts, looks of shock and concern on their faces. Amanda and Louise were also in the room, tears streaming down their cheeks.

'Well, I'd be lying if I said he is one hundred percent,' the deputy head told Dominic, 'but I think he'll be fine once he's over the shock of being released in such an odd way.'

'How was he released?'

'Tossed out of a car on the side of the road in the early hours of the morning, blindfolded, with his hands tied. But Mr Craig, can you come down here now, and I'll tell you everything I know?'

'Yes, yes. Umm... It'll take me about... about an hour or more to get there, I guess.'

'Come as quickly as you can. We'll keep Will safe here in the meantime. Do you know how to get here?'

'I've seen the turn off, opposite the road to Zvishavane.'

'Correct. Just follow your nose and you'll arrive at the school. Ask the security guard at the gate to tell you where my house is. It's easy enough to find.'

'Okay, thanks. I'll be as quick as I can.'

He put the receiver back on its cradle, his hand trembling. The others were standing at the bottom of the bed, staring at him.

'Is he alright?' his father asked.

'I think so.'

His mother burst into tears. 'Happy tears,' she spluttered as she sat down on the bed.

Dominic explained to them what he'd been told. 'He's at Saint Benedict's School in Mbala Mbala. His abductors tossed him out of a car sometime last night and he found his way there. He's asked me to fetch him.'

'You'll have to let the police know,' his father said.

Dominic's heart sank. 'Do I?'

'Of course. The police will have opened a docket. They'll have to be told about this latest development. I'd say, if he's in Mbala Mbala, it'll be the jurisdiction of the Filabusi Police. Do you want me to come with you?'

'No. It could be a very long day. Thanks anyway Dad.'

'You get yourself ready,' Oliver said. 'We'll let everyone on the farm know, if they don't already.'

'Right. I need to get to Mbala Mbala as soon as possible.' He ran down the passage to the room he'd been sleeping in, while Amanda went to the kitchen to make him something to eat and drink. When Dominic came through five minutes later, his family were discussing who would phone who and in what order.

Amanda handed him a cooler box and a pack of sandwiches wrapped in tin foil. 'I've put some bottles of water and cokes in the cooler box.'

'Thanks.'

'Try to keep in touch, if possible.'

'I will. Maybe you could phone Darvie in Kezi and tell him what's happened. Dad has his number. He'll want to know, I'm sure.'

'Will do. Thank God we can give everyone good news.'

As Dominic drove from Bulawayo to Mbala Mbala, a myriad of thoughts raced through his head regarding what he would say to the police. He considered the details he had noticed; the fearful look on Beryl's face when she first told him what Gladmore was intending on doing, her and Cassia's discomfort and distrust with everyone at Freedom High School in case they were informants, the way the people yesterday had sent him from here to there while they checked him out. All this convinced him he must tell the police as little as possible. He would act as dumb as he could and pray they never linked him to Gladmore. If they ever did, he would deny any knowledge of him. He'd never met the guy anyway, so it wouldn't be too hard.

By the time Dominic arrived at the school and found the relevant house, Will had had a shower and changed into a pair of brown checked shorts and a paisley button-up shirt lent to him by the deputy head. He was sitting in a chair in the Squires' sitting room, a mug in his hands, but he scrambled to his feet when Dominic entered the room. Dominic didn't even notice the Squires as he crossed the room in three quick strides, relieved to see that at least Will looked strong physically. However, when Dominic reached out to hug him, he collapsed against him and Dominic had to hold him up as they hugged each other tighter than they'd ever hugged anyone before.

Dominic's eyes shone with tears. He sniffed and rubbed his eyes with the balls of his hands when they let go of each other.

'You okay?' Dominic said.

'I've been better. It was pretty shitty.' He glanced at Mrs Squires. 'Sorry.'

'Not at all,' she said. She turned to Dominic. 'Will has had some toast with Bovril and two cups of tea. Can I get you anything?'

'Yes please, I'd kill for a cup of coffee.'

'Would you like some coffee too Will?'

'Yes please.'

Mr Squires cleared his throat. 'I took the liberty of phoning the police in Filabusi to report that we have Will. I thought we better not dilly dally on that front.'

A shadow crossed Dominic's face. 'I suppose that was the right thing to do.'

Mr Squires fiddled with the pens in the top pocket of his beige safari suit. 'Unfortunately, they don't have transport available to come and speak to Will here. So they asked if you could take him there.'

'Yes. I can do that.'

'I'll have to come, too, as will Tapson, the security guard who found Will wandering around the school at dawn. We'll have to give our statements. Being a Saturday, we have cricket matches, but I've let the headmaster know I won't be available to umpire the under fourteen match against Falcon College today. Tapson is waiting for us at the gate.'

'Is it okay if we finish our coffee first?'

'Take your time,' Mr Squires said. 'I'll leave you two boys to talk a bit before we leave.'

Dominic turned to Will after Mr Squires had closed the door behind him.

'I can't tell you how happy I am to see you.'

Will swallowed hard. 'Fuck, me too. How's my mum and Tom?'

'They'll be better now that you're back.'

'I nearly freaked out and lost it when they killed my old man. Fuck, I was so mad.'

'So what happened? How did you end up here?'

'It's all a bit of a blur. After the um, the... the attack... we... we walked a long way through scrubby bush. When night was falling, we climbed a *kopje*. I think we stayed that first night under an overhanging rock half way up and remained there for all the next day. They tied me to a tree, and they went off, leaving one person to guard me, but he kept his distance. That night we walked for many hours again, and ended up climbing to the top of another *gomo*, heaven only knows where. They tied me to a tree again. Someone would bring me food and water twice a day. I talked to them a bit, but they mainly kept out of sight. The days and nights became a blur until, last night, I guess, they untied me and we climbed down from the *gomo* and trekked through the bush until we got to a dust road. A truck was waiting, and they shoved me into the back. It had a canopy. They kept my hands tied and pulled a sack over my head. After driving for what seemed like a long time the vehicle stopped and they threw me out. They didn't hang around, but at least the person who had been guarding me in the back loosened the ties around my wrists before he tossed me out, so I got free pretty damned quick and pulled the sack off my head.'

'Thank God,'

'Yes. Check my ankles and wrists. From being tied up for so long.' Will showed Dominic the red burn marks. 'I must've stank like crazy when I got here. After my shower, the old lady, Mrs Squires, gave me some Dettol to bathe my feet in and rub on my wrists, but I don't think I'll be able to wear anything except slip slops for the next few weeks.' He kicked off the red Bata slops Mr Squires had given him and held up his feet for Dominic to inspect. 'Walking for so long barefoot has left them pretty beaten up. They insisted I take off my shoes right away, and we all walked in our bare feet. They were pretty damned good at covering their spoor.'

There was a knock at the door and Mr Squires reappeared. 'We'd better get going boys. Are you ready?'

'I suppose,' Dominic said.

They arrived at the Filabusi police station half an hour later. Mr Squires and Tapson sat on a wooden bench pushed against a wall in the charge office while Will and Dominic stood at the counter. Dominic was worried at how frail Will now appeared. He stood close to him in case he needed help. There was no one else in the charge office so the policeman on duty, a Constable Sithole, could attend to them straight away. He took his time writing Will's details – his full name, place of birth, date of birth, home address, national identity number and occupation. Constable Sithole's face showed no emotion as Will gave his statement, although a second policeman, who had been sitting on a stool reading "The Chronicle", looked up from the newspaper as Will's story unfolded.

'Where was the ambush?' Constable Sithole asked when Will finished talking.

'On the Chester's Farm near Kezi.'

'Was a police report made at the Kezi police station?'

'Yes,' Dominic said.

Constable Sithole glanced at his colleague, then wrote this down. 'How many people attacked you?'

'I can't say for sure. You'll have to liaise with the Kezi police about this, as the attackers took me from the scene.'

'How many people were they?'

'Three, I think.'

'Did you know any of them?'

'No.' Will said.

'Can you describe what they looked like?'

'Not really. All I can say is they were all dark in complexion with short, black hair, and they were young.'

'How young?'

'Around my age, I'd say.' He then repeated his version of the events of the last week, as Constable Sithole wrote it down. This took a long time with Constable Sithole stopping and asking Will to repeat himself many times. Dominic glanced at his watch in frustration. He wanted to get Will back to Bulawayo and take him to a doctor, but he knew the process would be no quicker if he tried chivvying Constable Sithole along.

'Exactly where did you... um... alight from the truck?' Constable Sithole asked when they reached the part where Will was thrown onto the side of the road.

'It was somewhere along the Mbala Mbala, Zvishavane Road.' Will bent down and picked up the sack he'd brought with him. 'This was over my head. By the time I got it off, they had driven away but as it got light, I recognized the Mbala Mbala rock hills in the west so knew where I was. I've been on the road before, so I walked along the road towards the rock hills.'

Constable Sithole took the sack, saying he would need it for evidence. He wrote down everything Will had said and then asked: 'What type of truck was it?'

'It was a Peugeot 404 truck with a canopy on the back.'

'Colour?'

'I have no idea. It was dark when they put me in it.'

Sithole wrote this down. 'Can you give me the registration number?'

'No.'

Constable Sithole's face remained expressionless.

'What time did they drop you from the truck?'

'You mean threw me out of the truck? I don't have a watch so cannot give you a time, but I'm guessing it was somewhere around four in the morning.'

Constable Sithole filled in this detail. 'And you say you walked to Saint Benedict's school?'

'Yes.'

'Why?'

'Because it was the closest place, I knew to walk to, although I'd never been there before so wasn't sure… The security guard,' Will pointed to where Tapson was sitting on the bench near the entrance, 'spotted me wandering around the school grounds and took me to the deputy headmaster's house.' Again Will waved towards the bench where the two men sat.

'What time was this?'

'I can't say, but it was light by then.'

'The security guard brought him to my house at five thirty-five am,' Mr Squires called from the bench.

After signing his statement, Will went to sit down, and the constable turned to Dominic. When he finished providing his personal details, he explained how he had been staying in Bulawayo with his sister. She had woken him early this morning to tell him that Mr Squires wanted to speak to him. He said this was the first he knew Will was safe. He signed his statement, and Constable Sithole then called the security guard. Yet again he started by asking for all his personal details. The guard had little else to say, but it still took a while to give his statement, and then Constable Sithole went through the whole rigmarole again with Mr Squires. It was well after midday by the time they were told they could leave.

'Thank God that's over,' Will said as Dominic drove his Land Cruiser around the dirt roundabout in front of the police station, surrounded by whitewashed rocks. The Zimbabwean and police flags flew proudly on flag poles in the middle of this roundabout.

'I'll never for the life of me understood the need to whitewash perfectly decent rocks,' Mr Squires muttered from the back seat, where he and Tapson were sitting.

'A hang-over from colonialism,' Dominic said.

When they returned to Saint Benedict's School, Mr Squires asked them if they would like "a bite to eat" before heading back to Bulawayo. 'Thank you, but don't worry,' Dominic said. 'My sister packed some sandwiches for us.'

Will said nothing for a long time as they drove back to Bulawayo. Dominic glanced at him from time to time, worried, but Will just stared through the front windscreen at the tar road in front of them, his hands grasped around a bottle of coke, taking the occasional sip, his face blank.

'It was really weird,' he eventually said.

'What?'

'At first I thought they were going to kill me too.'

'Fuck man, it must've been shit.'

'Old man Chester and Graham were in the front of the Land Rover when they ambushed us. The *gooks* were on either side of the road and they... Graham and Mr Chester were both shot multiple times. The Land Rover crashed off the road. Dad and I were in the back. I ducked straight away, but Dad grabbed that small pistol he always carried in his shorts, you remember?'

'Yes.'

'Well, he started shooting at them and killed one of them before they killed him. He dropped almost on top of me, and he died straight away, lying over me, blood dripping everywhere...' His voice broke. He swallowed a sob.

'I'm sorry.'

Will paused for a long time, controlling his emotions. 'But, you know what, because of what he did, they didn't shoot me too.

My old man saved me because if they'd seen me straight away, they'd have shot me too.'

He took another slug of his coke and they drove on in silence.

'What happened next was they started arguing with each other,' Will began again. 'I could pick up one was Shona because he spoke in Shona and broken Ndebele. I think Dad must've shot the ringleader because the Shona guy was freaking out, yelling and shouting at them to drop their guns, and he shot one of them. Fuck man, it was crazy because the next thing I knew one of them then shot him, the Shona guy, and there I was, lying in the back of the truck with Dad on top of me. Things calmed down a bit after they'd killed the Shona guy, and they began talking about what to do. They were talking in Ndebele but I could pick up what they were saying. They were worried that they'd killed this Shona guy. I thought they were going to fuck off without noticing me, but then one of them came up to the Land Rover and saw me and, I think, because I spoke to him in fluent Ndebele, he didn't kill me. I dunno. Maybe they thought I'd be a bargaining chip. Maybe they'd had enough of killing that day...'

'I thought all the dissidents were Ndebele,' Dominic said.

'Me too, but I could have sworn two of them were Shonas, and the Ndebele thought they'd fucked up when both the Shonas ended up dead. They were panicking a lot. They carried my dad and the guy they'd shot away off and hid them in a ditch and covered them with branches and leaves and whatever else they could find lying around.'

'Why did they do this?'

'Dunno. Maybe to confuse everything.'

'But it helped you, eh?'

'I guess. For most of the time I was with them, I still thought they would kill me at some stage. I kept waiting for it to happen, but they stayed away from me, except to give me food and water, until I ended up on the fucking road to Zvishavane, of all places. How weird was that?'

'Really weird. It's the last thing I would have expected,' Dominic said. He resolved not to say anything to Will just yet about his involvement in any of this. Will had enough on his shoulders without having to think that anyone else may have put their lives at risk to save him.

However, Will shattered this resolve when he said, 'But how come these people knew you?' Dominic's eyes shifted towards him. He was pulling something out of Mr Squire's paisley shirt pocket. It was a scrappy piece of paper. 'They gave me this. They said I had to phone you to fetch me, and to give you this piece of paper.'

'To me? Who gave it to you?'

'The person who was guarding me in the back of the truck. He pushed it into my shorts pocket last night when they were driving off with me. He said I had to give it to you, no one else. I didn't think much of it at the time, but now I'm wondering how the fuck he knew your name.'

'What's written on that paper?'

'It says "GLAD MORE DUCK INN DECEMBER", all written in capital letters, with the word "in" spelt wrong. Do you have any idea what it means?'

'I haven't the foggiest. Is there anything else written on the paper?'

Will turned it over. 'Nah, just that.'

'Do you mind not saying anything about it to anyone else? I'll think it over and try to work out what it's about. But I don't want my name being mentioned in connection with this.'

'Yeah, sure.' Will handed him the scrap of paper and Dominic pushed it into his short's pocket. He'd read it again later and try to fathom out what it meant.

To take his mind off it, Dominic said: 'The day of the attack, Brian and I drove down to Kezi, in case there was something we could do to help. I ended up having to identify Graham's body, and your dad's.'

'Shit man.' Will rubbed his eyes. 'What's happening about the funerals? Were they waiting for mine too?'

'The opposite, actually. Your Mum and Gran insisted on burying your dad and Graham as soon as possible. They said it showed how confident they were you would be coming back alive.'

'Really, huh? They were more confident than me then. So where are Dad and Graham buried? In the family graveyard?'

'Yes.'

Will swallowed hard and wiped his nose with the back of his hand. 'Fuck these people, man, doing this to our family.'

'But at least you're back. This has done a lot to restore some of my faith.'

Will was quiet after this and before long, he'd fallen asleep, his head resting on the door. Dominic's thoughts turned to the message on the paper. He took the paper from his pocket and glanced at it again, his eyes darting between the words and the road. Was the "Glad more" part something to do with their Gladmore? And yes, the word "in" was misspelled, showing that the person who wrote it was not a strong speller. Otherwise, it could've been gibberish.

As confused as ever, he pushed it back into his pocket.

CHAPTER 15

DOMINIC AND WILL drove up to Amanda's gate and saw, from all the cars squeezed in her driveway, that the whole family had gathered there, no doubt to wait for them to get back from Mbala Mbala. Molly and Tom came running through Amanda's front door moments after they arrived, followed by the others. Will climbed out of the passenger seat and pushed the gate open, and then his self-control melted away. He rushed across the driveway and into his mother's waiting arms, as if he was a little boy again.

'My baby, my baby,' Molly sobbed, hugging him tight for a few moments, before pushing him away to inspect him, then pulling him into her arms again. 'I always knew you'd come back to us.' She clung to him, and he clung to her, the tears flowing down both their faces. Tom stood next to them, also crying, and when Molly noticed him, she pulled him into their ruck.

Dominic's vision blurred. He knew they would be feeling the loss of their husband and father deeply, despite their relief that Will was back. He parked his Land Cruiser next to his parent's Peugeot and turned off the ignition, waiting for emotions to die down.

This took a while, but they were eventually all gathered on Amanda's front veranda. Bea had brought two bottles of champagne and insisted they each have a glass to celebrate. Oliver made a short toast and, as they lifted their glasses, each one of them buried the foreboding they had felt deep down that Will's abduction would not end well. In the last few years, they all knew about other people who had been abducted and found dead, days or months or even years later. They all knew that the dissidents, who they believed were responsible, would not have wanted a white person with them. It would have been difficult to keep him hidden in the rural areas around Kezi, and some people may well have informed on them if they'd seen Will. So, their easiest option would have been to kill him and dispose of his body down a mine shaft or an ant bear hole, and then get as far away from the scene of the crime as possible. These dark thoughts had gone through their minds in the five days Will was missing. Now that he was back, they wondered why his situation had ended differently and why the dissidents had released him, but it was not a topic they wanted to discuss yet. Maybe later, but for now, it was best to celebrate their good fortune and not question why.

Only Dominic's brow furrowed as he raised his glass to toast Will's safe return.

Even Martin appeared more easy-going than usual. 'Thank God,' he said. 'We can now pick up the pieces and move on with what we need to do.'

Amanda knew what he meant, but did not want to reopen the argument about selling the farm, so, to change the subject, she said: 'We need to sit down and phone all our close friends and tell them the happy news. So many people have contacted us asking about you, Will. Do you want to let people know, or can Bea and I do it?'

'I'd rather you did it. All I want is to get home, have a good meal, and then go to sleep in my pit. I am totally fucking shattered. Sorry Mum.'

'Don't worry, sweetheart,' Molly said. 'Granny and Grandad are at the farm, waiting for us, and Granny will be cooking your favourite steak, egg and chips. I'm sure you need some sustenance after what you've been through.'

'We'd better all drive back to the farm in convoy,' Martin said, reverting to type. 'The last thing we need is another mishap on the way.'

'I'll make my own way home, Martin,' Dominic said. 'There are a few things I need to do before I leave town.'

Lily's face fluttered with worry. 'You'll be back before dark, won't you?'

'Yes, Mum, but don't worry. I can take care of myself.'

*

Dominic drove to Freedom High as soon as the others had left for the farm. Cassia and Beryl needed to be informed about what had happened as soon as possible. He hoped they could make sense of the note Will had given him. He assumed mid-afternoon was a good time to visit them at Freedom as they wouldn't be teaching.

Beryl snatched the piece of paper from Dominic's hand when he removed it from his pocket after telling them about it. She stared at the scrappy piece of paper for some time, her lips twitching as she read. She looked at him, frowning, as confused as he and Will were about what it meant.

'I'm pretty sure it's Gladmore's handwriting, but as for the rest, I do not know.' She scratched the back of her head, and pulled at her pony tail, reading the words again. Shaking her head, she passed it to Cassia.

Cassia read it out loud: ' "GLAD MORE DUCK INN DECEMBER". Wow, what on earth is he trying to tell us, or should I say you, Beryl?'

'Well, I'd say he included the "December" part because he knows we will be tied up here at Freedom until then,' Beryl said. 'We won't be able to go anywhere until school breaks up.'

'True.'

'Weird that he spelt the word "in" wrong though, with a double n. But I guess English isn't his first language, so he gets spellings confused from time to time.'

'Yes, that's probably it,' Cassia said. 'Obviously the "Glad More" part is to tell us it's from him, and he's written it as two words so no one else will get it.'

'Yes. But as for the mention of a duck, I have no idea. I've never known him to talk about ducks before.'

'When he told you he was leaving, did he mention how he'd get hold of you again?' Dominic asked.

'All he said was that he'd get word to me as to where he'd be. To be honest, he left in such a hurry, and he was so unsure of how things would turn out, he didn't say much about it. He just said he'd make sure we'd meet up.'

'We need to visit his mother again,' Cassia said. 'There's a chance she can help.'

Beryl flashed her a worried look. 'But we can't tell her about any of this.'

'Of course not. But think about it, it would look rather odd if you didn't show any concern that he's disappeared. It's the correct thing to do, Beryl, to visit his mother and tell her how worried you are that he's missing. There would be nothing suspicious about you asking her if she has any idea where he might have gone. No one would find this odd.'

'True. Let's go there this weekend.'

'It can't be much fun for you girls,' Dominic said, 'always wondering who is eyeing you with suspicion, having to think about how they may interpret your every move.'

187

'It's awful,' Beryl said. 'I never imagined it would be like this. Every time I see Mr Sibanda, I cringe inwardly.'

'Me too,' Cassia said. 'And because of this, we've both decided we're going to resign our posts here at Freedom. Unfortunately, we can't do this until the beginning of next term, as we have to give a term's notice. If either of us also left suddenly, without giving notice, it would give the spies Gladmore alluded to reason to question why. And even when we resign, we've decided we'll hand in our resignations separately, with a week or two in between.'

*

Dominic drove home thinking how fortunate he was that no one he knew had ever knowingly set out to harm him severely. True, there was animosity in his extended family right now – he foresaw some tense times ahead – and in the course of his life he had fallen out with various friends and girlfriends, but the events of the last week were more sinister than anything he had ever known.

Even worse than when he was in the army. That had been a straight forward conflict – them against us. So different from what was happening now. None of it made sense. From the attacks, to the murders, to the abduction, to Gladmore becoming involved and then needing to flee, to the girls having to watch their backs. It was impossible to understand why this was happening.

It made him wonder if Martin was right when he said they should sell everything and get the hell out of the country. But even as he thought this, he knew he couldn't. For one, his father would never speak to him again, and for another, he had hated living elsewhere in the world when he'd tried it after the army. He had missed the bush and the wildlife. The harsh, beautiful African bush, filled with hundreds of species of birds and animals, was in his blood, and it would be for the rest of his life.

*

That evening, his father came to visit him at his cottage. They sat on the veranda, enjoying the balmy evening, each drinking a cold beer. Oliver told him how he'd convinced Bea that selling the farm was not a good idea right now, and he hoped that Will's safe reappearance would make Martin agree with this too. Dominic smiled to himself while he listened to his father talking about factions and how devious Martin had been, trying to convince everyone they should sell up at such a stressful time. True, it was devious of him, but Oliver hadn't been even-handed, either, to go straight off afterwards and convince Bea otherwise. But he wouldn't point this out to his father. He'd always known that Bea loved the farm as much as his parents did.

Bea found any excuse to come out to the farm, and the following weekend was no exception. Serena wanted to move back into her own home and Bea offered to stay with her for a while, knowing how difficult she was finding everything without Graham.

When Oliver heard Bea was staying with Serena, he decided this would be an excellent opportunity to have another family gathering, this time to explain to Martin that the vote had now swung in favour of them not selling up. He suggested having this gathering at Serena's house as an evening braai. This would be less formal than the meeting Martin had had, and a pleasant way to pass an evening too. Oliver asked Amanda to come out to the farm also, to give him extra back up.

The Craigs brought all the meat for the braai, as they always had plenty of beef and lamb in their deepfreeze, and each family made a salad. It was another balmy evening at the beginning of November, and they relaxed near the stone braai area Graham had built years ago. Coloured lights, strung between the trees, cast a golden glow over the garden, and the scent of damp lawn and flowering shrubs mingled with the smell of smoke and meat barbequing. Serena and Lily sat in metal garden chairs, chatting to

Molly and her parents, while the others hung around the fire, helping with the braaing. Oliver decided this would be the perfect time to mention to Martin and Kate that the vote about selling the farm had now swung in his favour.

He cleared his throat and took a sip of his beer. 'Since you came to tell me about how far you'd gone with your plans to sell the farm, Martin, a lot of water has passed under the bridge, eh?'

Martin slapped Will on the back. 'Yes. Thank God it's ended so well.'

'Exactly. And it just goes to show, all is not lost for us. I was talking to Bea about it, and she agrees; we shouldn't sell everything right now.'

Martin glanced at Bea, who was standing nearby, arranging the plates and knives and forks on the stone table next to the braai. 'Really Bea? You told me it would be better to sell, that this would give us all more freedom to choose what we want to do.'

'I did, but on consideration, I've changed my mind. It's a huge thing you're asking, Mart. You know how much I love it out here, and I'm sure Mum will change her mind too once she's come to terms with Graham's passing. She's lived here for over fifty years. This farm is as much a part of her identity as it's Olivers's, and all of ours. We need to go through everything rationally, which we can, now that Will is home safely.'

Martin sipped his beer and flipped the lamb chops closest to him. 'Well, I wish you'd said this the last time we spoke Bea.'

'For goodness' sake, Mart. None of us was in the right state of mind to understand the implications of what you were suggesting.'

Dominic eyed Martin. He seemed way too calm for his liking. Did he have another trick up his sleeve?

Sure enough, Martin produced it. 'Well, it's a shame you think like this now, because, to be honest, I'm not sure we can back track.'

'What do you mean, Martin?' Oliver asked, his voice tight.

'Did you read those papers I gave you the other day?'

'Ah, no, I haven't had time to look at them yet.'

'Mm. Well, if you had, you'd have seen that the government is more than keen to buy this place.'

'So what? We can tell them we've changed our minds.'

'That won't be a good idea.'

'Why not?'

'We are all aware that land is a big issue in this country. The government wants to buy farms from white farmers. They see land ownership as empowering for black people. The government wants blacks to have access to more land, better land. This place ticks all their boxes, and now I've alerted them to the fact that we are thinking of selling...'

'You mean "you",' Oliver chipped in. 'You are thinking of selling. Not "we".'

Martin held his breath for a moment, then continued. 'Now that they know that our place is up for sale, they want it.'

'Well, they're not going to just grab it from us. The Lancaster House Agreement stops them from doing this.'

'For now. But only until 1990. After that they can do what they want, and I'm afraid to say they want this place. It would be stupid of us not to take up their offer now, while it's given in good faith. They're offering us a bloody good price.'

Bea bit her finger nail. 'You say the government has made us an excellent offer, Mart?'

'Yes. I can go through the details with you tomorrow.'

Dominic looked at his father's face. He could see that he was furious with the way this conversation had turned. Martin had a point, and Dominic could see that Oliver knew this. His heart went out to his father, being out manoeuvred by Martin and the state of affairs in the country he loved so much.

'When did you get the government involved, Martin?' Dominic asked.

'A while ago. I put it to them, to test the waters, so to speak.'

'Telling none of us?'

Martin took another swig of his beer and then poured the rest onto the flames that had licked up in front of him. 'Well, I admit, I jumped the gun a bit, but I didn't know the government would be so keen to buy.'

Dominic was doubtful. His father was right. Martin was devious.

'So all I can say is, you all need to read the document I gave Oliver, and then we can work out what we're going to do with all the money we get from the sale. Kate and I intend moving to beautiful Cape Town until Harry finishes varsity, and then we'll head to Australia. Life will be so much easier there.'

'And how do you intend getting your money out of the country?' Oliver asked.

'I've come up with a brilliant plan,' Martin said, his eyes dancing from one of them to the next.

Oliver raised an eyebrow. 'And what, pray, is your plan?'

Martin began removing the meat closest to him and putting it on the platter Bea was holding. 'I will tell you, as long as it goes no further than here. You can't go around telling anyone what we're up to. Maybe you can do something similar when you decide to leave, too.'

'Maybe. So spit it out. What?'

'I'm going to buy gold.'

'Gold?' Oliver spluttered. 'What on earth are you going to do with a lot of gold?'

'Make tools, Uncle Oliver. Hammers, screwdrivers, spanners, etcetera, and then I'll get them dipped in zinc so they look like ordinary workshop tools.'

'Workshop tools?'

'Exactly. I intend taking these tools out of the country by registering them as my personal tools for the part-time jobs I'll be doing in Messina.'

'Messina?' Oliver was struggling to follow.

'Just over the border from Beit Bridge, in South Africa.'

'Of course I know where Messina is,' Oliver spat.

'True. Well, I've already lined up several part-time jobs there as a mechanic. I intend finding other jobs further afield, in Louis Trichardt and Pietersburg. Every time I cross the border to do a job, I'll take my tools with me. Then I'll leave them behind and bring back proper tools in their place.'

The braai area was quiet while everyone digested what they had heard.

'Whoa, that's pretty clever,' Bea eventually said. 'Who gave you this idea?'

'You've never met him. But he's been doing it for a while and it works really well. He's got thousands out this way.'

Amanda said: 'A friend of mine has been buying precious stones. Diamonds, emeralds and the like. She has jewellery made using them and takes the stones out that way.'

Martin nodded. 'Yes. I've heard of lots of people doing that, and we've already bought some stones too. Haven't you noticed Kate's new ring?'

'Nope.' Bea and Amanda said, together.

Kate held up her hand for them to inspect it.

'However, my plan with the workshop tools is better, on the whole, for the sums of money we're talking about,' Martin said.

'And what about those of us who are not planning on leaving? We will need money to live on,' Oliver said.

'Keep your share of the money in your bank account here, although my advice to you is to get as much money out of the country as you can. Things are only going to go one way in this country, and that's down, down, down.'

The furrow between Oliver's eyes deepened. 'I'm afraid I still can't see how it's going to work. It's not as if you can withdraw sizeable sums of money without the bank becoming suspicious.'

'Correct. However, if it's withdrawn slowly, it won't raise suspicions. I've already started. If you check my bank account now, you'll see I have almost nothing in it. I've been buying gold and precious stones for a while. Besides this, I've also developed a relationship with a miner and he's put me in touch with a toolmaker. Both dependable white guys who are happy to help me out, for a fee, of course.'

Oliver picked up the platter of meat. 'Let's eat,' he said, although this conversation had made him lose his appetite.

CHAPTER 16

THAT WEEKEND, the girls paid their visit to Ma Moyo.

They felt Gladmore's absence badly as they drew up to his house and remembered the last time they'd come, and he'd been waiting in the street to welcome them. Later, they realised he did this mainly because his mother was difficult, and he wanted them to feel at ease. It was still a thoughtful gesture on his part, though. Beryl looked at Cassia, her eyes shiny with unshed tears.

Cassia reached over and patted her arm, which was still gripping the steering wheel as she gazed through the windscreen. 'Don't you sometimes wish Gladmore hadn't involved himself in my family's problems, and the two of you could get on with your lives?'

'I thought so at first, but now I've changed my mind. As much as I worry about him, I believe there have been things happening in his home area which he can't accept. I think that saving your cousin was his way of righting, in a small way, the many wrongs that he has found out about. Plus, he'll be helping some of his friends too.'

'Mm. It's all so complicated. I felt uncomfortable when Mr Sibanda came to the cottage to see us. He was definitely trying to get information out of us. Thank goodness Gladmore warned us about him.'

'Yup.'

Cassia was staring at the house, and she saw the fabric in the front window twitching. 'Someone has seen we're here. I guess we'd better go in.'

Beryl checked all the doors and boot of her Datsun 120 Y, then followed Cassia through the small gate and up to the front door. The dirt in the yard, which was neatly swept the last time they were there, was now splattered with dark purple stains from the ripe mulberries that had fallen from the tree and been trampled on.

Cassia knocked on the front door. They waited a while and when no one opened it, she knocked again. They stood on the front step for a few more minutes, but the door remained closed. 'Shall we go round the back?' Cassia mouthed, pointing towards the rear of the house.

Beryl shook her head. All they could do was leave, hoping they would have better luck the next time they came. They retreated through the small gate but, as Beryl was unlocking the passenger door to let Cassia into the car, she noticed Ma Moyo turning the corner and walking down the street towards them, deep in conversation with another woman. Both women were balancing plastic bowls on their heads and looking down at where they were walking. Ma Moyo glanced up and saw them, and an odd expression crossed her face.

Beryl took a deep breath. 'Hello Ma Moyo. I hope you don't mind us dropping in like this, but we didn't know how else to get hold of you.'

Ma Moyo took the bowl off her head and straightened her headscarf. The girls noticed the bowl was full of neatly folded pieces of material. 'Hello Beryl.' She turned to the other woman. 'This is

Beryl and her friend Cassia. They both live in England, but they teach at Freedom High at the moment. This is Mrs Ncube.'

The girls smiled at Mrs Ncube.

'*Salibonani*,' she said with a curtsey.

They stood in silence, with no one knowing what to say next. Beryl cleared her throat.

'Would you like to come in for a cup of tea?' Ma Moyo asked.

'That would be lovely.' Beryl delved into her bag and brought out a packet of lemon creams. 'I've brought you a packet of your favourite biscuits again.'

'Thank you.' Ma Moyo said goodbye to Mrs Ncube, picked up the bowl and, balancing it on her hip this time, she pushed the small gate open. She unlocked the front door and invited the girls to take a seat in the lounge, saying she would find Precious to make some tea. While she was gone, the girls regarded the room. Nothing had changed, but they missed the comforting presence of Gladmore. They wondered where Innocent was. Ma Moyo was gone for what seemed like a long time, but eventually the inter-leading door opened and she returned, carrying a tray. Precious followed with the now empty plastic bowl and a tin jug. She nodded at the girls and then knelt in front of each of them, placing the bowl on the floor and pouring water over their hands, as she had done the last time they'd visited. After serving them all a mug of sweet, milky tea and a lemon cream biscuit, she left the room without having said a word. Again, the girls found this ritual discomforting but realised now it was normal behaviour in the Moyo household.

Beryl nibbled her lemon cream. 'We're sorry to impose on you like this, Ma Moyo, but we're anxious about Gladmore. He hasn't been at work for over two weeks. Have you any idea where he may have gone?'

Ma Moyo dipped her lemon cream into her mug, then bit off the soggy piece before taking a sip of her tea. She finished her mouthful before saying: 'The headmaster, Mr Sibanda, came here last week to ask me the same question.'

A frown crinkled Beryl's brow, and Cassia clasped both hands around her mug. 'Mr Abednico Sibanda came here?'

'Yes. He also asked me if I knew of Gladmore's whereabouts, but I told him I did not.'

Beryl sucked in her cheeks, disappointed that Ma Moyo didn't know where Gladmore was, but relieved she hadn't been able to help Mr Sibanda either, or at least she claimed she hadn't helped. She hoped this was true.

Ma Moyo scratched her head beneath her headscarf. It puffed in and out as her fingers rubbed back and forth underneath it. The silence drew out again.

Eventually Beryl asked: 'Do you think Innocent or Precious know where Gladmore is?'

'Innocent is no longer here, either. Precious does not know where they are. I have asked her.'

'Oh, wow. When did Innocent leave?'

'It seems at the same time as Gladmore. When I woke up in the morning, they were both gone.' Mrs Moyo finished her tea and put the mug on the table in front of her.

'You must be worried also,' Beryl said.

'No. They have done this before. Gladmore is my first born and Innocent is my second born. Precious has another father. The father of Gladmore and Innocent is from Botswana. I think they will be with him. They went to him in the 1970s so he could help them with their further education. I believe they will have gone to him now.'

Beryl stared at Mrs Moyo, wide-eyed. 'I didn't know Gladmore's father came from Botswana. He told me he was brought up in Kezi district.'

'Kezi is my home district and Precious's father is from there as well. Her father is late now, but my mother and other family members still live there. I live here in Bulawayo because the father of Gladmore and Innocent bought this house for his two sons when they came back from Botswana to live in Bulawayo in 1980.'

'Gladmore has the surname "Moyo", like you. Is that the surname of his father?'

'No, his father's name is "Ontiretse". When they are with their father in Botswana, they use his name. When they are in Zimbabwe, they use my name. They don't talk about Botswana now they are living in Zimbabwe.'

'I see,' said Beryl, although she did not.

Ma Moyo explained further: 'When I was a young girl, I used to walk from Kezi to Selibi in Botswana. There was a copper mine there and I could earn money at the mine, sewing. That is where I met the father of Gladmore and Innocent. He was learning to be a mechanic at the mine. He became a very skilled mechanic.'

'You walked to this mine? Wasn't it a very long way to walk?'

'It is near the border with Zimbabwe. I used to walk there with other girls, and some men who worked at the mine. They did piece work.'

'Is Gladmore and Innocent's father still there, at the mine?'

'Not any more. As I said before, Gladmore and Innocent went to their father in the 1970s and did their further learning in Botswana. In Gaborone. They only returned to Zimbabwe in 1980, after Independence, when they thought things would be prosperous here. Their father left the mine at the same time and went to Maun to work as a mechanic, fixing engines for the safari camps.'

'Maun? Where is that?'

'It is in northern Botswana, near the Okavango Delta. It is where Mr Ontiretse's mother comes from.'

'So is he still in Maun?'

'Maybe.'

Beryl rummaged around in her bag and brought out a piece of paper and a pen. She held it out to Ma Moyo. 'Please, can you write down the name of their father for me, and his address if you know it?'

'I don't know where he lives or works.'

'Okay, then just his name, please.'

Ma Moyo wrote down his name, after which she appeared to have nothing else to tell them. She fidgeted with her scarf again.

'If we hear from Gladmore, we will let you know,' Beryl said, standing up. Cassia followed her lead.

'Thank you,' Ma Moyo said.

She remained seated while the girls let themselves out. They hoped Ma Moyo was right about Gladmore having gone to his father in Maun. He must surely be safer there.

CHAPTER 17

THEY SIGNED the agreement of sale for the purchase of the farms by the government in early-November and the painful process of packing up eighty years of work, memories, and personal possessions began. What to keep? What to throw away? How best to remove everything?

Besides this, they also had to decide where they would live once they moved off the farm.

Only Martin and Kate appeared to find all this easy. They rented a house in the Bulawayo suburb of Fortune's Gate, and Kate moved there immediately. The government had already selected Philip Jones from Harare to oversee the dairy, even though the takeover was scheduled for the end of March. Martin promptly invited the Jones family to move to the farm, expressing the importance of Philip becoming familiar with the job. Martin went as far as offering to pay Philip a salary until the end of March, when the government would take over paying him. This surprised everyone until they figured out it was yet another smart move by Martin. With Philip employed there, Martin would be relieved of his responsibilities in managing the dairy, thus giving him more time to focus on his own goals. The Joneses moved into Sunlands House in late-November. Martin had been commuting to the farm before the Joneses arrived, but his time there decreased significantly after this. On the occasions when he did need to stay the night, he used his mother's house.

Bea invited her mother to live in the cottage on her and Ron's Hillside property, and Serena accepted. Once they settled this arrangement, Bea began spending a significant amount of time on the farm. This time, her focus was on helping Serena sort out her possessions, pack, and transport them into town.

Until she got her share of the farm sale, Molly planned to move in with her parents in Matsheumshlope, another suburb in Bulawayo. She wanted to externalize a significant portion of her money, with Martin's help, and move to Pietermaritzburg in Natal, where Tom would be attending university the next year. She hoped Will would move to Natal with them, but for now, he said he could not make his mind up about what he wanted to do or where he wanted to live.

Will had still not come to terms with the ordeal he had been through, nor his father's death.

The Craigs were slower than the Brookes with their decision making and packing. Amanda suggested her parents buy a house in Bulawayo. They said they could not do this until their share of the farm sale came through, so she invited them to live with her until then. However, Oliver and Lily found it hard to move on from their home and the farm. Amanda's house in town lacked sufficient storage space, so they opted not to pack up hastily and leave, unlike the Brookes. They decided they wouldn't budge until the end of March when it was absolutely necessary.

Dominic also chose to delay things for as long as he could.

Everything appeared to be going smoothly for the Brooke contingent until Bea returned to her home in town a day earlier than expected and found Ron in their marital bed with his secretary. On reflection, Bea wasn't that shocked about this. Ron had so often made the excuse that he was "working late", it surprised her, in hindsight, that she had not become suspicious. Everyone said she was too soft-hearted to suspect her husband of cheating on her, but in fact, she realised it was because she didn't really care that much for him any more. Somewhere in the twenty-plus years they had been married, they had stopped enjoying each other's company. It hurt her, though, that he obviously relished the company of his secretary, to be romping around naked with her at four o'clock in the afternoon when most people she knew were enjoying a simple cup of tea.

Ron told her this was not the case and there was nothing serious between them, but Bea would have none of it. She intended finding a good divorce lawyer as soon as possible.

However, she couldn't help wishing the breakdown of her marriage hadn't happened right then, when she was half way through helping her mother pack up her life on the farm. Their guest cottage was already brim full with Serena's furniture, and now she and Ron would have to sell the property and divide up their own furniture as well. She planned to get more out of this divorce than Ron, as she was the "injured party", and it would be difficult to move all her possessions, plus her mother's, and to where? She had no idea. Like Oliver and Lily, she would have to wait until she received her share of the farm sale before she could buy herself a decent house in Bulawayo.

After she found out about Ron, she often wished they were not selling the farm after all. She would have happily moved straight out there and lived with her mother once she and Ron were divorced. She loved being on the farm. She and her mother got on well, and they could have comfortably rattled around in Sunlands Cottage, which was big enough for the two of them. But this was not to be. At the same time, she felt relieved that she had discovered Ron's cheating ways before receiving any money from the sale of the farm. Otherwise, he would have found a way to get his dirty hands on some of it. He would not be entitled to any of it in a divorce settlement, as it was her inheritance, but, being the sharp accountant he was, and being the naïve person she was, he would no doubt have syphoned a great deal of it away from her if they were still married. No wonder he had been so angry when she'd changed her mind about wanting to sell up.

After the blow-up with Ron, and once the dust had settled, they decided he would stay at their house in Hillside and Bea would stay back at the farm until they sold the Hillside house and they had both found themselves somewhere else to live.

Sarah and Jane began looking for a place to rent so they could move away from their father as soon as possible.

Sunlands Cottage was now only half full of furniture, but there was enough there for Serena and Bea to live comfortably enough. Serena was still struggling to come to terms with Graham's death. The enormity of selling the farm and giving up her life there was sinking in, so she was thankful to have Bea with her for the next few months. She intended to make the most of this time, instead of rushing to leave the farm, as they had been doing.

Molly came to the same decision. Why pack up and leave so quickly? Just because Martin and Kate had, did not mean she must, too, especially now that the Jones's had moved into Sunlands House, Serena and Bea were still in Sunlands Cottage, and the Craigs were nearby. She knew this would make Will happy. He wanted her to remain at the farm for as long as possible.

*

Cassia and Beryl made plans to go to the farm on their next free weekend. Like Bea, Cassia was always looking for excuses to spend time there, and the excuse she told herself this time was that they needed to tell Dominic what they had learnt from Gladmore's mother. Cassia phoned Serena from the office at Freedom to ask if they could stay the weekend with her.

'Oh dear, darling. That will be a bit awkward as I have so little furniture now, and Bea is sleeping in the only other bed here. It won't be much fun for you and your friend to sleep on the floor.'

'We can cope with that, Granny.' She didn't tell Serena that Beryl slept on the floor out of choice, anyway.

'No, no. Let me check with Lily if you can stay at Brightside with them. Just to sleep there, Cassia, darling. You're welcome to spend the rest of your time here.'

They arrived at the farm early Friday afternoon, having left Freedom as soon as school ended, and popped in to visit Serena, before heading on to the Craigs'. Serena invited them in for a cup of tea and Cassia eagerly agreed. She wanted to see what the cottage looked like now that they had removed so much of the furniture. After tea, she wandered around and saw that despite the minimal furnishings and few paintings, the place was still as beautiful as before. A feeling of sadness washed over her as she realised that soon she would no longer be able to come here. She expected she'd feel the same way multiple times over the weekend, and on future visits, until the government assumed control of the farm.

'Bea will be sorry to have missed you, but she's gone to have tea with Molly and her parents this afternoon.' Serena said. 'However, we've all been invited to Brightside for dinner tonight, and tomorrow night we're having a braai here, so you'll see lots of her. Nothing much has changed. We are always interacting with each other like as per normal, except, of course, Martin and Kate are no longer here.'

'What are the new manager and his family like?'

'Philip and Marian Jones. I have to be honest, we were all rather surprised when we heard that the government had employed a white man to manage the dairy. I thought they wanted to advance black people. However, who am I to question the way the government runs their newly gained farms?'

Cassia noticed Beryl's face tighten. 'Have they settled in okay, Granny?' she quickly asked, preventing Beryl from lecturing her grandmother on race, segregation or unequal opportunities.

'They're getting there. They're younger than Kate and Martin, and they've got two dear little girls who are still at school in Harare. Marian and the girls only came down for the weekend, then they returned to Harare until the end of the term. They'll be going to Whitestone School next year.' Serena turned to Beryl. 'Whitestone is a lovely private junior school in Bulawayo. Most people avoid government schools now,' she said, making Cassia's heart quicken again. Thankfully, Serena did not give Beryl time to question this statement as she went straight on with 'I think I'll ask Philip to join us at the braai tomorrow night, as he's on his own. That'll give you two girls an opportunity to meet him.'

To Cassia's relief, Beryl said nothing about Serena's remarks when they drove to Brightside later that afternoon. Instead, Beryl commented on what they saw on the way. The dairy, the cattle sheds, the workshops, the pastures with cattle grazing on them. She appeared to be impressed. 'I did not know the farm was so developed. What's going to happen to all the animals?'

'The government has bought almost everything, lock, stock and barrel,' Cassia said, swallowing a lump in her throat.

They found Lily in the garden, wearing a large sunhat and holding a pair of secateurs. She straightened up and blew a stray lock of hair from her face when she saw them. She kissed each girl on both cheeks, holding her hat on the back of her head, then led them through the front door into the hall. As had been the case when they first walked into Sunlands Cottage, the smell of creosote and the cool, muted ambiance created by the thatched roof enveloped them as soon as they entered. Unlike Sunlands Cottage, though, this house was still full of beautiful antique furniture and paintings covered all the walls. Beryl had seen none of this when she'd come for the funeral, and her eyes were on stalks now. Lily guided them through the hall and onto the deep veranda, with comfortable armchairs arranged around a coffee table and surrounded by a vast array of clay pots filled with ferns and other indoor plants.

'Can I get you two girls a cup of tea before I show you to your room?' Lily asked.

'No thanks Lily, we had at Granny's.'

Lily led them down the veranda to the stable door at the far end. The top half was already open and latched against the wall, so she pulled open the bottom half and they walked into a bright and airy bedroom.

'This is your room for the weekend. The bathroom is through there. Relax and make yourselves at home. I know Dominic is looking forward to seeing you, but he's out and about on the farm right now. Hopefully, he'll come back soon. In the meantime, I need to finish what I was doing in the garden, so I'll leave you two girls to fend for yourselves. I hope you don't mind. I'm propagating as many plants as I can to take to our new home when we move.'

'Wow, what a place,' Beryl said, once Lily had left them. 'I thought your Gran's cottage was lovely, but this……. it's amazing.'

Cassia was again thankful for Beryl's positive response to everything she was seeing. 'Yes, it is. This house, and Sunlands House, are the biggest and oldest houses on the farm, and both are equally impressive. Molly's place is great, too, as is Granny's cottage, which you saw earlier. They were all built years ago, and all have a history of their own.' She exhaled. 'Oliver's mother did most of the paintings you see in all these houses and many reflect this history.'

'Oh wow.' Beryl studied the painting above her bed.

Cassia walked to the window and stared out of it at Lily's productive vegetable garden.

'I can see why you're sad they've sold it,' Beryl said.

It amazed Cassia that Beryl's radical stance had softened so much. A few months ago, she would have given Cassia a lecture about the evils of exploitation and colonialism after seeing how they lived on the farm. In fact, a few months ago, she would not have even come to the farm with Cassia.

'Yes,' Cassia said. 'I am quite heartbroken about it. I've always loved it here. Let's just hope the government look after the place as well as my family has over the last eighty years.'

'I'm sure they will. It's their country now.'

Cassia sighed and picked up her hat. 'Let's go for a walk. Hopefully, Dom will have returned when we get back.'

They wandered through the garden to the gate leading onto the paddock in front of the house. They walked across the paddock, avoiding the cattle grazing there as Beryl said she feared them, climbed through the fence on the other side, and made their way to the graveyard. The fresh piles of soil on the two new graves gave them a start when they first saw them.

'So sad,' Cassia muttered. 'I guess someone will have to arrange for headstones to be put on these new graves sometime soon, before they have to leave.'

They climbed the rock next to the oldest grave, the grave where Anthony Craig had been buried in 1905, and sat there, staring at the view from this elevated position. They could see dust billowing into the air from a vehicle driving along a dirt road in the distance. It was getting closer and after some time Cassia recognized who it was.

'It's Dominic with his dog, Luna. Let's make our way back to the house so we can talk to him before dinner.'

Fifteen minutes later, they arrived at the gate to his cottage and spotted him sitting on his veranda, throwing pellets on the lawn to his pet duiker. Luna was watching with much interest, keen to eat the pellets and chase the duiker away.

'Don't you dare,' Dominic growled, before noticing the girls at the gate. He waved at them, and they waved back. He showed with his hand that they should open the gate and walk along the hedge towards the cottage. They did as indicated, but the duiker saw them and skipped away, jumping over the fence and out of the garden.

'Never mind. I'll give him some more pellets when he comes back later,' Dominic said.

'He's so sweet,' Beryl said. 'What's his name?'

'Grey. I've had him for a few years, so he's pretty tame, and not in the least bit worried about Luna. Mum told me you were coming to stay for the weekend. How's everything?'

The girls seated themselves in the metal chairs on the veranda. 'We're okay, thanks,' Cassia said.

'Can I get you something to drink? I'm going to pour myself a glass of cold water.'

'Yes please, that would be great,' Cassia said.

'Me too,' Beryl agreed.

He returned with the water, and the girls launched into the story about their latest visit to Gladmore's mother.

'So Gladmore's father is from Botswana,' Dominic said when they'd finished. 'I think his mother could be right in thinking he's gone there. He would have struggled to cope, but if he's got family in Botswana, he'll find everything much easier.'

'I've still been sick with worry,' Beryl said. 'What if Mr Sibanda knows he did his teaching degree there? Then he may also assume he's gone back.'

'I doubt anyone from this country will go there to harm him. I've never been to Botswana, but it's a bloody big country. You say his father has moved to Maun?'

'Yes. Let's hope his mother didn't tell Mr Sibanda that. He did his degree in Gaborone, apparently, so if Mr Sibanda considers this, he may decide that that is where he's gone.'

'Exactly,' Cassia said. 'But his mother did say she hadn't told Mr Sibanda anything.'

'Forget about Mr Sibanda,' Dominic said. 'I don't think he's a threat to Gladmore if he isn't in the country. What we need to be concentrating on is how do we find him? We're just making assumptions, and none of them relate to the note I was given, do they?'

Beryl bit her thumb and furrows appeared between her eyebrows. This was not what she wanted to hear. 'No.' but then her face softened. 'Unless he's in Maun with his father?' she suggested.

'But Maun is a very long way from here and I, for one, don't know anyone there. Do you?'

'Of course not.'

'It's a bloody long way to go on the off chance that he'll be standing at the "welcome to Maun" sign, waiting for us.'

Neither girl responded to his joke, shaking their heads instead.

'Sorry Beryl, but I can't be optimistic about finding him at this stage. I haven't heard a peep from anyone in connection with Gladmore.'

'Neither have we.'

'Will and I had to go to Kezi, as he had to give another police statement there, but of course, we mentioned nothing to do with Gladmore. Will wouldn't have said anything, anyway, as he doesn't know about him, but at least the police didn't ask me any awkward questions. I was a little worried that they might.'

'That's a relief,' Beryl said.

'Yes. But I've been thinking since then that maybe we should tell Will about Gladmore's involvement in his release. It may help him accept what he's been through. He's still feeling pretty low about everything and often feels bad that he was the only one who survived. Maybe if he knows there were people working to save him, and putting their own lives at risk, he may come to terms with it more.' He paused for a moment. 'But I wanted to run this by you first.'

They discussed the pros and cons of telling Will, and decided it would be best to tell him.

'After dinner tonight, then. I'll invite the three of you back here for a night cap, and we can reveal everything to him then.'

Will was utterly shocked when they told him their story. He had never met Beryl before, and he hadn't got to know Cassia properly since she'd returned. Yet here they were, explaining how they had helped Beryl's boyfriend save his life.

'Fuck man.... excuse the language.... but I can't believe what I'm hearing. Why did this Gladmore guy do this if it was so dangerous for him?'

'He left in such a hurry, he didn't make his motives clear,' Beryl said. 'All I picked up from him was that there had been some horrific things happening in that area, and people he knew had become inadvertently involved.'

A more cynical thought snagged Will's mind. 'Was Gladmore not just using my abduction as an escape route out of Africa, and a way of making money to help him along the way?'

Beryl's eyes narrowed. 'If that was the case, why were you released? They didn't have to do that. They already had the money.'

'True.'

'He and I have known each other for over a year now, and planned to marry a long time ago. He had no reason to find an escape route, because he already had one through me....' She dropped her voice to a whisper. 'If.... if we ever meet up again.'

'It's okay, Beryl,' Cassia said. The last thing she wanted was for Beryl to revert to her judgemental attitude about their "racist mentality".

'Yes, let's not start making accusations,' Dominic threw Will a warning look.

'Ag, sorry man. I'm just trying to get my head around all this. No wonder they knew your name, Dom. I wondered, even though you blew me off when I asked.'

'I couldn't say anything about it then. I hope you understand.'

'Yes, I do. As for that scrap of paper they told me to give you. Do you think that was a message from this Gladmore guy?'

'We assume so, but we still can't work out what it means.'

'What did it say again?'

'GLAD MORE DUCK INN DECEMBER,' Beryl said. 'He spelt the "in" part wrong with a double n. Have you got a bit of paper, Dominic? I'll write it down as he wrote it, with all the words in capital letters.'

Dominic walked to his writing desk and found a piece of paper and a pencil. Beryl wrote the five words on the paper and handed to Will.

He read it a couple of times. 'Fuck man, December makes sense, and now the Glad More part does too. But the mention of ducks is weird.'

'Yup,' Beryl said. 'I can't remember him ever talking about ducks before.'

'We even went to see Gladmore's mother to ask her if she knew where he might have gone,' Cassia said, 'without telling her about anything to do with you.'

'Did she have any idea where he may be?'

212

'She thinks he might be in Botswana, because his father is from there. Neither Beryl nor I knew this before. We thought his whole family came from Kezi, but it turns out his mother used to walk from Kezi to a mine on the border, where she met the father. He's subsequently moved to Maun where he's.......'

'Hey man, listen,' Will interrupted, staring at the note, and then looking up at the three of them. 'I've been to Botswana. A group of us *okes* went to the Okavango Swamps in 1980.'

'I remember when you did that,' Dominic said.

'*Ja*. We stayed in Maun, and there was a bar there called The Duck Inn.'

The room fell silent.

Dominic eventually broke the quiet. 'Bloody hell,' he said.

'So when he wrote "Inn" he wasn't just struggling with his English,' Cassia murmured.

'I don't know what you're talking about,' Will said, to Cassia, 'but I bet my bottom dollar he was referring to the Duck Inn. He wants you to meet him at the Duck Inn in December. When in December?'

'It'll be after schools break up, which is soon,' Beryl said. 'He'll know this. He'll be expecting me then. How far away is Maun from here?'

'It's a fair distance. Somewhere around a thousand kilometres, I'd say. Maybe more. And no, that Datsun 120Y of yours won't get you there. The roads are pretty fucked,' Will laughed.

'I'll take you,' Dominic said. 'Now we have something more positive to go on. It will be worth the effort. We can all go. I've always wanted to see the Okavango Delta, anyway. We can drive there in my Land Cruiser.'

'Now we're talking,' Will said. 'Those wheels will get us there easily, and it'll be good to get away from the general depression and packing up going on here.'

*

Will's demeanour improved significantly after he'd found out how and why he'd been saved. Although he knew he could tell no one about Gladmore, the weight he'd been carrying on his shoulders eased significantly once he knew about him; knowing how lucky he was that his cousin, Cassia, had a friend, who had a boyfriend, who came from the place where the tragedy had occurred. In fact, where a great deal more tragedy had occurred, if the rumours they heard were to be believed.

For the rest of the weekend, he spent a great deal of time in Cassia and Beryl's company, getting to know them better. He took them sailing on the dam, and he took them game viewing in the more remote areas on the farm, but the trip they enjoyed the most was when he took them to see the murals on the walls of the farm chapel. Will asked Lily to come with them, so she could tell them the history behind the project, as she had been involved, in a small way, with it.

'The King and Queen of England toured Rhodesia in 1947,' she told them. 'I'm talking about the present Queen's parents, plus Princess Margaret and her. Part of their tour included visiting the Matobo Hills. My father was the Assistant District Commissioner, and he was on the organizing committee when they came to the Matobo. I can't tell you the effort everyone went to, preparing for the Royal family.

'But that's by the by. Everyone first attended a tea party for the Royal Family and, at this tea, Oliver's mother, Isabella, presented them with a painting she had done of the Matobo Hills. There was an Anglican priest at the tea party, too, the Reverend Ned Patterson, who was also an artist, and he and Isabella were introduced to each other. He was the headmaster of a mission school nearby, Cyrene Mission, and he told Isabella that he had been encouraging the school children at the Mission to paint murals on the walls of the mission chapel. The idea of this intrigued Isabella, and she asked him if she could visit the mission at a later date to see what these children had done. Well, when she saw their murals she was determined to do the same thing here, and voila, here you see the result.' Lily moved her hand in a sweeping gesture, indicating all the walls in the chapel.

They moved around the chapel, staring in wonder at the murals. Every one of them stretched from the roof to the floor, simply drawn and painted in flat, bright colours. They depicted bible stories, but the scenes were African.

'They are stunning,' Beryl said.

'Aren't they?' Cassia agreed.

'You need to go out to Cyrene Mission, if you get a chance, and see the murals there. They're only on the inside walls of this chapel, whereas at Cyrene, they're painted on the inside and outside of the chapel. They could do that there because that chapel has a wrap-around veranda. We don't have a veranda here, so we could only paint them inside.'

'I'm still blown away by them,' Beryl said.

Lily walked up to a mural near the door. 'This is my effort, for what it's worth. Moses in the bulrushes.' She laughed softly. 'I don't have much artistic talent, but Isabella talked me into it, and once I started, I found it quite easy, mainly because I didn't have to put much detail into the painting.'

'It's impressive, Lily,' Cassia said.

'That's because of its size. But come and look at this one.' Lily wandered over to the side of the altar. 'This is the one Isabella did. Even though she tried to keep it simple, her talent shines through.'

They had to agree with her.

Lily pointed to another mural. 'This one was done by the headmaster at the time, Toby Tate.' She turned to Beryl. 'He was a coloured man who Isabella met in 1905 when he was a child and living in some huts with his African mother and European father. She ended up doing what she could for him for the rest of her life.'

Cassia could see that Beryl was having difficulty processing this information, but Lily moved on before she could comment.

'The school children did all the other murals. Many of them still live and work here on the farm. Oh dear, I hope the government looks after all of them, and all of this now that it's going to belong to them.'

'I'm sure they will,' Beryl said.

CHAPTER 18

THEY LEFT for Botswana the day after the school term ended, just as dawn was breaking. According to Dominic, they could reach Maun in one day in his Land Cruiser if they left early and minimized unnecessary stops.

Cassia sat next to Beryl in the back seat, gazing out of her window as the sun rose and the sky transformed from dark grey to yellow grey to blue grey. As they drove through the tiny village of Figtree and on to the equally small village of Marula, she spotted the huge, grey, lichen covered rock *dwalas* of the western Matobo Hills in the far distance, separated from the tar road by miles and miles of scrubby, thorny bush. The morning light made them look incredibly impressive. She knew Kezi was located beyond these *dwalas,* not too far away. What secrets lay hidden within those hills? If they could speak, what would they disclose about the circulating rumours? Would they confirm the atrocities the people in this area had witnessed? Could they explain why?

As they neared the small town, memories of their school days in Plumtree flooded back to Will and Dominic. This was the first time they'd come this way since Independence. Dominic had enrolled in the school a few years before Will, prior to the war escalating, so he and his classmates were spared the war-related challenges faced by Will's year and the following years.

'In the last few years I was at Plumtree School, all of us schoolboys used to travel to school and back by train,' Will said. 'It was less dangerous than travelling by road. We had soldiers escorting us. When Dom was there, most of the *okes* used to come with their folks, hey Dom?'

'Sometimes we caught the train, sometimes our parents brought us.'

'The things we got up to on those train journeys,' Will said. 'Shit! Some boys used to get so pissed, they struggled to walk from the station to the school.'

This shocked the girls. They could imagine none of their pupils at Freedom arriving at school drunk. Coming late and leaving early were the extent of any wayward behaviour.

While driving through Plumtree town, Will pointed out some water towers that guerrillas had mortared during their lessons. He told the girls how the teachers made them sit under their desks, in case the school came under attack as well.

'As if sitting under our desks would keep us safe,' he laughed. 'But we weren't worried about an imminent attack. We were all put on the next train and sent back to Bulawayo for the weekend, so it ended up being a gas, having an unexpected exeat weekend.'

After passing through Plumtree, they made their way towards the border post, pointing out the place along the road where they had to run to for their school cross countries.

'Teachers were stationed along the way, carrying guns, just in case,' Will said. 'I doubt any of them would have been much use if the *gooks* had attacked us.'

They passed through both border posts in less than an hour and after driving a few kilometres along the road to Francistown, they turned off and headed towards the road to Maun. What struck them the most about Botswana, besides it being more dry and arid than Zimbabwe, was the litter. It seemed to be everywhere; lying along the roadside, stuck to the fences, blowing about open spaces. They weren't used to this in Zimbabwe, which was much cleaner than Botswana appeared to be, or at least this part of the country.

The journey to Maun was long, slow, and boring. The only memorable moments on their journey were passing the outskirts of Nata and, hours later, seeing tall palm trees in the semi-desert landscape. Before these palm trees, dotted about, the only vegetation they'd seen were scrubby bushes and the odd outcrop of stunted acacia trees.

'They're called ilala palms, or ivory palms,' Will said. 'The Okavango delta is full of them. They're called this because the fruit looks like ivory. They germinate in the stomachs of elephants.'

Just then, they noticed a solitary male elephant by the roadside.

'Oh my God, stop. I've never seen an elephant before,' Beryl cried.

'And it's the first time I've seen an ellie since I've been back,' Cassia said.

Out of habit, Dominic checked his rear-view mirror to make sure there weren't any vehicles coming up behind them, even though they had not seen any other vehicles on the road. He pulled over so they could take their time looking at the elephant, but he kept the engine running, in case the elephant decided he didn't like them there. This also turned out to be an unnecessary precaution. The elephant ignored them as he continued wrapping his trunk around the branches of a small acacia tree, tearing them off and shoving them into his mouth.

'What about the thorns?' Cassia whispered.

'Ag, they eat thorny vegetation all the time,' Will said.

They arrived in Maun at dusk, as the setting sun was changing the colour of the sky again, this time from hazy blue to creamy gold and deep orange, the closer it came to the horizon. Will directed them to the campsite he had stayed in the last time he'd been there, and they spent some time unpacking the car and erecting their tents. Girls in one tent, boys in the other. Cassia smiled to herself as she unrolled the thin foam mats they'd brought to sleep on, wondering if Beryl would have preferred her grass sleeping mat.

Beryl wasn't thinking about what she would sleep on. She was keener to find the Duck Inn right away. The others persuaded her otherwise. They did not know if it would be open, or if they'd even find Gladmore there. They convinced her it would be better to get there during the day, when they would have time to have a good look about.

At ten o'clock the next morning, when they arrived there, the first person they saw was Gladmore, standing near the entrance. He held a tray in his hands and wore an apron around his waist.

Beryl was about to throw herself at him, but he stepped back. 'I'm working as a part-time waiter and I'm not allowed to hug the patrons,' he said with a half-smile.

'Of course. Oh my God, I am so happy to see you,' she said, her eyes shining.

'Me too,' Cassia murmured. She sniffed and wiped her nose. 'This is Will, who you… um… and this is Dominic.'

'Howzit,' Will took Gladmore's hand in a firm grip and shook it vigorously, staring at him, struggling to read him.

'Good to meet you,' Gladmore said.

'Likewise,' Will said.

Gladmore turned towards Dominic. 'So you're Dominic? I am glad to meet you too. I worried you may not have understood my message as I wrote it in such a hurry.'

'You were right to worry,' Beryl laughed. 'We had no idea what you were telling us. I couldn't understand why you were mentioning ducks.'

Gladmore laughed, too, but then his brow furrowed. 'But you didn't discuss it with anyone else, did you?'

'No, of course not.'

'Thankfully Will has been here before so he knew about this place,' Cassia waved her hand, indicating the building they were standing in front of, 'but the rest of us had never heard of it.'

She glanced around her. The Duck Inn was little more than a semi-open shed with a corrugated iron roof and low walls along the front to prevent the goats roaming in from the dusty car park. There was a bar counter at the back of the building and tables and chairs were in front of it. A few punters were now sitting there. Her eyebrows knitted together when she saw them.

'Could anyone be watching us, Gladmore?'

'No, no. We're all safe.'

'What happened to the other people who... who held me?' Will asked.

'They are not here.' Noticing the blank looks on all their faces, he started again. 'They did not come to Maun with me. They travelled to Gaborone to look for work, or maybe elsewhere, if they were unsuccessful there. My brother has contacted me to tell me he is in Gaborone, but not with the others.'

'What time do you finish?' Beryl asked.

'I have an eight-hour shift. I finish at six.'

Beryl glanced at her watch. 'Six o'clock? Oh no, that's still ages away.'

'Sorry, but I had to get a job here. I couldn't just hang around waiting to see if you'd come.'

'We understand,' Dominic said. 'Where are you staying?'

'At my father's house.'

'Right. We're at the campsite. We'll have something to eat and drink now and then come back later when you've finished your shift.'

Gladmore showed them to a table and handed a menu to each of them. The Duck Inn became busier as noon approached, and he did not speak to them again.

When they'd finished their meal, they went off to look around the town. They found a place offering *mokoro* trips into the Delta, and Will suggested they go on one. Beryl said she would only go if Gladmore could join them, which meant they would have to wait to ask him before they could confirm their booking.

They wandered around the town, noticing how dusty and dry Maun was. It had wide sandy roads with lots of goats and cows milling about. The buildings were mostly small, squat, bungalows, dotted around in a disorderly fashion and there was very little vegetation besides some grizzly thorn trees, stunted by lack of rain and goats nibbling on them all the time. They discussed how different Maun was from Bulawayo, with its grid-like central business district of tarred, tree-lined streets, and buildings of various architectural styles, and its leafy, residential suburbs systematically branching off from the city centre. None of them had ever seen a cow or a goat on any of the roads in Bulawayo.

They soon realised there was not a great deal to do in Maun, so Dominic suggested that Beryl and Cassia run back to the Duck Inn and ask Gladmore if he would like to join them on their *mokoro* trip. Once they knew what he wanted to do, they could make their booking and set off the next day, instead of hanging around in Maun for another day. The girls returned, saying Gladmore could not go with them and that Beryl would stay with him at his father's place while they were away.

They picked Gladmore up from the Duck Inn when he eventually knocked off and drove to his father's house a few kilometres out of the town. Dominic had to put his Land Cruiser into four-wheel drive as they struggled to get through the thick sand on the dirt road. Gladmore pointed out landmarks along the way so they could find their way back to the campsite later; a large baobab tree here, an old car door there, a sign saying "Bus Stop" nailed to a mopane tree further along. They were grateful for these landmarks because everything appeared indistinguishable; just sand, scrub, and small bungalows now and then, with very little else.

Gladmore's father's house was smaller than Ma Moyo's house in Makokoba Township in Bulawayo, but similar in that it was situated in the middle of a well swept, bare, dirt yard, with a toilet and an outside kitchen at the back.

Mr Ontiretse was not there. Gladmore explained he had gone to Xaxaba Camp in the Delta to work on some boat engines there.

Talk of water and boats intrigued Cassia when everything they'd seen so far was so waterless. She could not fathom what this famous "Delta" would be like, as there was no evidence of it in Maun. The only hint of anything to do with water was a wide, dry, river bed. Certainly not a swamp or a delta. She asked Gladmore how his father had got to the camp and when he told her by motor boat, it seemed quite bizarre when their surroundings were so lacking in water.

They'd bought some grilled chicken from a road side shack to eat with Gladmore at his father's house, but when they produced this, he told them he'd eaten dinner earlier. This was a part of his wage packet. However, he had a couple of beers with them while they ate, but the conversation remained superficial. They all wanted to ask him how he had saved Will, but no one knew how to broach the subject.

Will tried. 'I couldn't believe what I was hearing when Beryl and Cassia told me about you, and how you'd gone off to see how you could help me,' he said.

'I'm sure,' Gladmore responded.

'All I can say is, thank you, thank you. I was so afraid they would kill me. My mind was numb, but I still never stopped being afraid.'

'They treated you alright?'

'Yes, as far as possible.'

'It was an advantage you spoke Ndebele to them.' Gladmore twisted the beer bottle in his hands, then took a slug. He dropped his voice to a whisper. 'They were afraid, too, you understand. They were being forced.'

'Forced... Forced by who?'

Gladmore said nothing. The silence expanded as Gladmore stared at the floor in front of him. Eventually he said: 'Many people they know have been killed. They knew this could happen to them, too, if they did not follow orders. One reason they could save you was because both the leaders of your attack were killed.' His voice was so quiet they struggled to hear what he was saying. Another long silence, then he looked up at Beryl. 'But I must thank you for bringing Beryl here. I was worried that you would not get my message, and I'd have to find another way to contact her. Now she and I can make plans for our future. I am looking forward to seeing what her England is like.' His voice dropped to a whisper again. 'Thank you also for the money. We needed it when we first got here.'

Will sensed this was their cue to drop the subject of his abduction. Having thought he wanted to find out more details, he realised now that he did not. He wanted to forget those horrific few days. Of course, he knew he would not, but talking about it would not help either.

'Pleasure, man,' he said. 'It was a good excuse to come here with Dominic and Cassia, too, as they've never been to Botswana. I'm just sorry you are not coming with us into the Delta.'

'But you have a guide?'

'Yes, we have two. I was talking about... well not guiding us...
but you coming as one of our party.'

A smile spread across Gladmore's face. 'No. Beryl and I need
to discuss what we are going to do. We need to make plans. But I'm
sure you will enjoy yourselves.'

Beryl had brought her bags to Gladmore's father's house to
stay there as the others planned to leave early for the Delta the next
day.

*

The Okavango Delta surpassed Cassia's wildest expectations,
especially after the two days they'd spent in such an otherwise dry
and arid country.

The Delta is an unspoiled water wilderness, created by the
Okavango River spreading into the Kalahari Desert, in the shape of
a fan, forming a network of waterways meandering across sprawling
grassy plains. Crystal clear water flows gently between curved sandy
islands, covered in high papyrus reeds and soft grass, separated by
canals and lagoons.

Cassia and Dominic shared one *mokoro*, with Dominic sitting
behind Cassia, and their guide, Metse, standing at the back, using his
pole to manoeuvre the *mokoro* along the waterways. Will shared his
mokoro with a German tourist by the name of Helmut, with a guide,
Kana, poling them. They were on a low budget trip, which meant
they had to provide their own food and camping gear, and they would
be setting up camp wherever they found themselves at the end of
each day. There was not much to buy in the way of food in Maun,
especially vegetables, but Will knew this from his previous trip, so
he'd brought a cabbage, onions and carrots from Bulawayo, hidden
under their kit in the Land Cruiser, in case anyone had wanted to
confiscate their vegetables on the way to Maun. They'd also brought
packets of biscuits, tins of Colcom hams, and tinned tomatoes and
baked beans from Zimbabwe. In Maun they'd found some eggs and

fresh rolls, and, at a bungalow with a hand written sign stating it was a "Butchery", they'd bought some dodgy looking beef steaks. However, they cooked them over an open fire on their first night and, wedged in a roll with fried onion and an egg, they were delicious. They erected their tents close to the fire, while Metse and Kana upturned their *mokoros* and slept underneath them.

Helmut spoke little English, but they did work out that he had come to the Okavango from South West Africa, which he managed to convey to them was well worth a visit, despite the war in the north. They said no thank you to this, they'd had enough of wars in African countries. Helmut had brought a lot of Swiss chocolate, which melted just a few hours into their excursion, so they ate all of it on their first night. He also had several bottles of schnapps, which he was happy to share with them too. This made a pleasant change from the warm water and warm beer they were drinking otherwise.

Besides being mesmerised by her surroundings, Dominic and Will's knowledge and interest in everything around them impressed Cassia. As far as she could make out, they knew a great deal about almost every bird, animal and tree they came across and, if they weren't sure about anything, they'd find what they wanted to know in the assortment of books they'd brought with them.

They were forever hollering across the water at each other.

'Look, there's a group of sitatunga', one of them would call to the other, pointing at a type of antelope Cassia had never heard of before, wading through the reeds in the distance, or

'Hey, that's a juvenile carmine bee-eater,' as a bird swished in the sky above them, or

'That combretum is as big as any you'd see at Mana Pools,' as they stared into the branches of one of the few large trees they came across, besides the ilala palms.

All she could identify were the most obvious species; crocodile, hippo, elephant and the like. She felt stupid compared to them, and attempted to learn what she could. Besides the sitatunga, she soon learnt to identify another type of antelope she'd also never seen or heard of before, the lechwe. It looked similar to, but bigger than, the impala which she'd seen plenty of on the farm.

On the first night, she lay alone in her tent, wedged between Helmut's tent and the tent Dominic and Will were sharing, listening to their muffled banter as they commented on the noises of the night; hyena cackling, lion roaring, jackal crying, hippos honking, fish plopping, elephant rumbling, night jars calling. The sounds came from far off, but before they retired, they washed up and cleared away everything they had used for supper so as not to attract any animals into their camp.

However, on the second night, while they were still sitting around the fire after supper, a pride of lion came uncomfortably close and refused to be scared off, despite being shouted at and having burning logs from the fire thrown at them.

'With these lions lurking nearby, you *okes* better sleep in a tent tonight,' Will advised Metse and Kana. They said they'd be fine under the *mokoros,* but Will would not take no for an answer. 'I can go into Helmut's tent. Hope you don't mind, bud, and Dom can share Cassia's tent, so our tent is free for you *okes* to sleep in. You'll be much safer in there.'

The guides reluctantly agreed, and they tentatively shifted sleeping bags from one tent to another tent, all the time keeping a watchful eye out for the lion.

Will's recommendation ended up being a wise one. The lions moved into their camp soon after they had all zipped themselves into their respective tents, sniffing around the fire, panting and groaning as they padded about. Cassia had never been so scared in her life, knowing they were so close, with only the thin canvas the tent was made from separating her from them. Sensing her fear, Dominic pulled her against him and held his hand over her mouth. He put his mouth to her ear and whispered 'Sshhh, and don't move,' as quietly as he could.

Sleep eluded them for most of the night, with the lions lying so near their tents. Things got worse when one of them started roaring in the early hours of the morning, the powerful sound piercing their eardrums like nothing they'd ever known before. Thankfully, the lions must have wandered off before dawn because when the guides unzipped their tent at first light, there was no sign of the animals, just a lot of spoor. The guides built up the fire and told everyone to stay close together in case the lions were still nearby, but by the time they climbed into the *mokoros* and drifted off a few hours later, they had not seen any sign of them again.

Whenever Cassia thought about that night in years to come, she thanked those lions for bringing her and Dominic together. At first she felt threatened by their proximity, but when Dominic pushed his body up against hers and tucked her head into the warm crevice between his head and his chest, she began to relax and feel safer. It amazed her when his breathing settled into a steady rhythm sometime before dawn and she realised he had fallen asleep. She did not get a wink of sleep, but she still found herself filled with excited energy the next day when they were again floating down canals and across lagoons. The previous night had changed the dynamic of their relationship and Dominic now kept teasing her, flicking water at her, digging his toe into her hip, pulling her plaited hair which hung down her back; anything to show her he was as aware of her as she was of him. She loved every minute of it.

The next night was the last night of their trip and, as if there was an outside influence helping to solidify their newfound closeness, they shared her tent again, this time because of the rain. They first noticed the storm clouds building up in the distance when they were setting up their camp at sunset. Before then, they had counted themselves lucky that they had had no rain, because it was

228

the rainy season and they expected thunder storms most nights. They hoped their luck would continue, but knew before they retired to their tents, this would not be the case. The first drops splattered off their tents when they were still washing up after supper and, as with most African storms, it soon turned into a torrent. Everyone rushed about putting things away, but it soon became apparent that Dominic and Will's tent did not keep the rain out. Water came pouring in along the seams and through the zip, and it soaked most of their kit in the tent within minutes.

'Can I sleep in your tent again, Cass? And Will'll have to share with you, Helmut,' Dominic said.

They all agreed this was the best plan, as it would have been a very long and cold night for Will and Dominic if they'd stayed in their own tent.

Dominic's clothes were soaked by the time he clambered into Cassia's tent. He peeled them off and unzipped her sleeping bag, climbing in and pulling it over the two of them.

The rain stopped a short time before dawn but, despite having abandoned the least waterproof tent, the only people who remained dry after the deluge were the guides. They had spent the night under their *mokoros* again. They had also had the good sense to store fire wood underneath them too. Will woke first and walked over to the *mokoros* to collect some wood to stoke the fire and when he saw the guides, warm and snug underneath their canoes, he let out a hoot of laughter. So different from him with his wet t-shirt clinging to his chest and his arms and legs covered in goose bumps.

He re-laid the fire with dry wood but, with the sand still wet, acrid smelling smoke soon wafted through their sodden campsite. He put the kettle on for tea and everyone else emerged from their beds and huddled around the fire and they were soon drinking mugs of hot tea and warming up. It didn't take long once the sun had risen, before they were wishing they could feel cool again.

They arrived back in Maun later that afternoon, sunburnt, dirty and smelly, and their first stop was the campsite to use the ablutions. Cassia had loved their *mokoro* trip, but she had still wished at the end of every day that she could have had a refreshing shower and the use of a proper latrine, so it was bliss to do this now. When they'd finished, they went to the Duck Inn to buy something cold to drink and hot to eat, and to let Gladmore know they were back. They walked into the place, expecting to find him there, and were surprised to discover that he was nowhere about.

'He handed in his notice two days ago,' the barman told them as he slid three bottles of ice-cold beers across the counter towards them. 'Do you want a glass?'

'No thanks,' Will said, taking a long slug from a bottle.

They drank their beers, digesting this information.

'Did Beryl say anything to you about resigning?' Dominic asked Cassia.

'Not a squeak,' she said, wiping beer froth off her top lip.

At that moment, she was more concerned about having a good meal than the whereabouts of Beryl and Gladmore. However, it was a surprise to her when they got to his father's house later and Beryl told her she was going to stay on in Maun with Gladmore. Beryl explained they planned to marry as soon as their paperwork was in order, and then they would fly to the UK together.

Cassia's mind skipped over these details. 'What about Freedom High? You're supposed to come back, hand in your notice and work off your notice period. Aren't you going to do that?'

'No.'

'But Beryl, I don't want to be there without you. We decided we both needed to work a term's notice, so as not to make Mr Sibanda suspicious.'

Beryl shrugged her shoulders. 'Gladmore thinks he will not link us to Will's abduction and release, so his family will be safe from any recriminations.'

Cassia wasn't happy about this development.

'Don't look so worried, Cassia,' Beryl said. 'You'll be fine there without us. You enjoy teaching the children, you're friendly enough with a number of the other teachers, and you've got lots of family nearby.'

'And what about your stuff? Your car?'

'You're welcome to use the car for as long as you want, and, when you don't need it anymore, would you mind selling it and giving the money to Ma Moyo? The same with the rest of my things. Take what you want and give the rest to Precious.'

'Are you going to tell them you've... you've gone off to England together. They'll be a bit surprised when I pitch up with money and all your possessions, Beryl.'

'Yes, I will write to them and let them know,' Gladmore said, 'although I won't tell them the reason for our hasty departure, and please don't either. We have to stick to our rule about not talking to anyone else about our involvement with Will.' Gladmore looked at them all. Noticing Cassia biting her lip, he stepped forward and pulled her towards him in a big bear hug. 'You only have to watch out for Mr Abednico Sibanda and Miss Edna Mpala at Freedom.'

She pulled away from him, surprised. 'Miss Mpala who teaches in the classroom next door to mine?'

'Yes, her.'

'Oh, wow. No wonder Mr Sibanda never reprimands her for arriving at school late.'

Gladmore gave her a weak smile. 'I don't think there are any other informants on the staff there. I know the others like you and are happy that you are on the staff.'

'But it'll still be lonely without the two of you.'

'You can come out to the farm every weekend,' Dominic said. 'My parents will love having you there.'

She turned her gaze towards him, noticing straight away that he had said "my parents" rather than "I". Was he going to be disappearing too? Was their newfound closeness over?

'Thanks,' she said

'And our Gran, too, of course,' Will said.

She nodded. 'Of course.'

After saying their goodbyes to Gladmore and Beryl, they returned to the campsite, where Cassia soon became even more apprehensive about Dominic. He drove up to one of the simple thatched shelters, open on all sides and with concrete floors, dotted about the camping ground. 'I propose we sleep here,' he said. 'I doubt there will be any wild animals threatening us so close to the town, and it'll mean we can get up and leave early tomorrow morning without having the hassle of taking down our tents.'

'Great idea,' Will agreed.

Cassia said nothing as she climbed out of the Land Cruiser.

They returned to the Duck Inn later for an early dinner, and when they got back to the campsite afterwards, they spread their thin mattresses on the concrete floor, with Cassia in the middle, 'just in case,' Dominic said. Once they'd all climbed into their sleeping bags Cassia lay on her mattress between them for a long time, listening to the sound of their even breathing, conceding that the previous two nights she and Dominic had spent together in her tent had not meant as much to him as they had to her. She resolved she would come to terms with this and do everything possible to ensure they remain good friends. She relished his company and found him very appealing, but she did not want to impose herself on him if he did not feel the same way.

CHAPTER 19

THE FOLLOWING DAY, as they drove back from Botswana, Cassia sat alone in the back seat of the Land Cruiser, contemplating her situation.

Despite Gladmore's reassurances, she remained sceptical about forming deeper friendships with any of her colleagues at Freedom. Gladmore had said that he suspected only Mr Sibanda and Edna Mpala of spying on the staff, but his use of the phrase "thought" left her feeling uneasy about his certainty. Knowing what Mr Sibanda and Edna were up to had shattered her innate trust in her colleagues, and it would take a while for it to be rebuilt, longer than one term, for sure.

Without Beryl, she expected she'd be lonely living in the cottage. The start of their co-habitation had been rocky, but things had improved as the months went by, with Beryl sometimes ignoring, sometimes appreciating, the slight improvements she'd introduced to make the cottage more comfortable. They'd spent many evenings by the fire they made regularly outside their kitchen, first with Gladmore, and then just the two of them once he'd left, talking about different aspects of their lives. Beryl's perspective on white Zimbabweans had changed from critical to sympathetic after the murders and abduction of Cassia's relatives. She now understood that the privileged status she once attributed to all white Zimbabweans came at a high price. The irony was that the tragic events of the last few months had caused Cassia to distrust many of her colleagues, but it had brought her closer to Beryl and Gladmore. She was sad that Gladmore could not come back, and understood that Beryl wanted to be with him, but she knew she would miss them both.

Things were no easier on the family front. While she was devoted to her Gran and Aunt Bea, they were both going through the most significant crises of their lives, and they did not need to be worrying about her. It was a shame she couldn't turn to her first cousins for companionship instead. They'd been such a tight gang when they were little, along with Amanda's girls, Karen and Louise. What fun they'd had together, yet most of them now had very little time for her. She glanced at Will and Dominic as they sat in front of her on the drive back from Botswana. Neither of them had been part of that gang when she'd been small, as they were older and considered her and the others childish, but she was grateful they were such good friends with her now. She supposed this was in part because they appreciated what she'd done to help Will. Would the others be more accepting of her if they knew too? Probably not, she guessed. Brian, Harry, and Tom had already shifted their focus to their new lives in South Africa, while Sarah and Jane still exhibited a clear dislike towards her. She suspected that her closeness to their mother, Bea, had something to do with it, but this was strange because she was close Amanda, too, yet her girls didn't ostracize her the way Sarah and Jane did.

The trip to Botswana with Dominic and Will had made things worse. Sarah and Jane had barely been able to hide their surprise when they heard about it, furious that they had not been invited to go too.

All these thoughts snagged at her mind and, without realising it, she let out a long sigh. Will was driving, but Dominic turned around in the passenger seat to see what the matter was. 'Are you okay? What's the big sigh for?' he asked.

'Oh, sorry. I didn't mean it.' She paused, a faint glow spreading across her cheeks. Dominic continued to stare at her, so she began again. 'Well, I'm wondering what I should do when we get back to Bulawayo. With Beryl not there, I'm not that keen on staying at the cottage at Freedom until the school term starts. But I don't have anywhere else to go.'

'What do you mean? There's all of us you can stay with.'

'*Ja*, man,' Will said, glancing at her in the rear-view mirror.

She did not want to burden either of them with her concerns; they had enough to worry about as it was, trying to figure out what they would do and where they would live once they had moved off the farm.

As if he could read her mind, a shadow crossed Dominic's face. 'Unfortunately, everything is a bit of a mess right now, with all of us having to pack up and leave the farm.'

'Exactly. I have my return ticket to England booked for August, and I can't afford to change it. Otherwise, it would probably be best for me to go back there.'

'Do you want to go back to England right now?'

'No.' Her eyes slid from his face to the scenery flashing past them outside. Trees, rocky outcrops, tall, green grass, the Matobo Hills in the background far away. The evening light was spreading over everything, casting a yellow glow. She loved it. The last thing she wanted was to leave Africa, despite everything that had happened. However, what could she do? There was nowhere she felt she really belonged.

Dominic turned to face the front again. He said nothing more on the subject until they were driving into Bulawayo, when he twisted around to face her again. 'I think you should come back to Brightside and stay there until the new term starts. It'll cheer my parents up, having you about the place, and I'd like it too.'

A half smile played across her lips. 'Thanks.' After a pause she added: 'But surely they don't need me descending on them unannounced?'

'They're used to having people descend on them unannounced. It happens all the time on the farm. In fact, I'd say they'll be half expecting you, and I'm sure Amanda and the girls will come out and stay soon too. It'll be good for them to have the place full and busy right now.'

'That sounds like a plan, man,' Will agreed, giving her a broad smile in the rear-view mirror. 'My ma told me Sarah, Jane and Richard will stay with us over the Christmas holidays, as there's no room for them at Granny's cottage, so we can all have a *jawl* together. You'll have a much better time on the farm than if you went to stay with Brian and Harry and their folks in Fortune's Gate.'

'Yup,' Cassia said, not wanting to burst their bubbles, or to mention that out of all her relatives, that branch of the Brooke family had been the least welcoming.

*

Will's prediction that they'd have a *jawl* did not come true. Instead, an air of gloom hung over everyone on the farm and no one could shake it. Dominic and Will did not hang around long enough to even try. Shortly after returning from Botswana, Will decided he would work a season with Pro Hunters Africa, the company whose clients he often hunted with. Pro Hunters Africa had a lease on one of the Matetsi hunting concessions near the Victoria Falls. Pro Hunters Africa told him their camp needed an upgrade before the hunting season began, and Will asked them if they would consider allowing him do this. He had enjoyed the time he'd helped Dominic convert an old garage in London into a bachelor flat and had learnt a fair amount about renovating at the same time. Pro Hunters agreed, and Will asked Dominic if he wanted to join him. Dominic jumped at the chance as he was finding himself becoming more and more depressed on the farm as they wound down all their activities there.

No one could blame him. Many people on the farm were miserable. It was difficult to decide who was the unhappiest.

First there was Oliver, who could not come to terms with moving into town, despite Amanda finding several houses which she thought would suit them. With the exodus of people leaving the country, there were many beautiful properties on the market, but none of these interested him. All he wanted to do was sit on his veranda, looking out at the view, mulling over the life he'd led there. What was most concerning was he seemed to be visibly aging, adding to Lily's already high stress levels.

Bea and her daughters were no happier than Oliver, but for different reasons. After Bea's initial stoic attitude about the end of her marriage, hurt and bitterness had now set in. She struggled to hide her emotions, and when her daughters noticed how sad she was, they became even angrier with their father than they had been when they first heard about his affair. The legalities of the divorce were making the Pierces' plight worse, as they became ever more lengthy and acrimonious. In the meantime, Bea did not want to make an offer on any of the houses she'd looked at until they had finalised everything. This, in turn, frustrated Serena, who was now feeling unsettled in her half empty cottage. She was already struggling to face her first Christmas without Graham, and Bea's deadlocked divorce was making the situation worse.

Then there was Molly, also dreading her first Christmas without John, remembering all the many festive "festive seasons" they'd enjoyed together. She kept breaking down in tears, and no one could do anything to make her feel better.

None of this made for a happy environment, but at least Dominic was correct when he said his parents would appreciate having Cassia around. She was grateful and made herself useful to both of them.

To Oliver, she became a sounding board for his musings. This happened by chance on the first morning she was back from Botswana when she joined him for a cup of coffee on the veranda. Lily had left some old photograph albums on the coffee table and she flicked through one of them, asking Oliver about the photographs she was looking at. She encouraged him to tell her stories relating to the photographs and, from then onwards, they did this every day. She knew some of the stories he told her, others she had never heard before, but she found all of them fascinating, and she looked forward to their sessions more and more.

To Lily, Cassia became a dispassionate judge of what possessions needed to be kept and what needed to be thrown away. Whenever Lily entered one of the many rooms in their house, her heart sank at the thought of packing it up, until Cassia stepped in and suggested what she should keep and what she should throw away. Sometimes this was tricky for Cassia. She felt bad when she described something as "dated" and noticed a look of surprise flash across Lily's face, but when she apologized Lily would say: 'No, no, you're right. I need someone with no personal attachment to point this out to me.'

However, Cassia found that the more Oliver told her about their long life on the farm, the less dispassionate she became about their possessions and the less she wanted to throw away. She mastered this new urge to keep everything by focusing on what they could give to the farm workers. She felt uneasy about how much they all had, compared to these people, and so she always looked out for things around the house they could give them, knowing how much they appreciated, however small.

'Much better than lugging everything into town where it'll just continue gathering dust,' she said to Lily.

'You're right,' Lily said, vowing to set aside one of the guest bedrooms to store whatever she was going to give away.

'That's one thing I love about Africa,' Cassia told Lily. 'There will always be someone who will appreciate the possessions you no longer want or have a need for. In England, we just take them down to the tip, but here, you can give them to someone and know they will treasure them for many years to come.'

'Sad, but true. I'll give away whatever I can. Oliver and I feel bad enough that we're leaving them without jobs. Oliver is having a particularly hard time with this. Many of the people have worked and lived here their whole lives and the old-timers are just as unhappy that we have sold the farm as Oliver is.'

'But won't the government keep them on?'

'Only the young ones. The older ones have been told they will need to go.'

'But to where?'

'That's the problem. They'll have to go back to their families in the rural areas, but many of them don't want to do that. They have made this farm their home. It's all very sad.'

*

Early most mornings, when Cassia knew Sarah and Jane would still be in bed at Molly's house, she would drive Oliver's old series 2 Land Rover across to Sunlands Cottage to have a cup of tea with her gran. Sometimes Bea would join them, most often she would still be in bed too. Cassia did not mind. She loved spending quality time with her gran, and she also knew that Serena needed everyone's support to get through her first Christmas without Graham.

One morning, Serena was waiting for her on the terrace outside her front door.

'I've decided to give you your Christmas present early,' she said. 'Follow me.'

They walked to the garage where her Mercedes and Graham's short-wheel-base Pajero were parked. 'I'd like you to have Graham's Pajero.'

Cassia stared at it, speechless.

'I've been wondering what to do with it,' Serena said, 'and then it suddenly struck me. Out of all my grandchildren, you are the one in most need of a car.'

'But Granny, you can't. I've got my friend Beryl's car, which I can use for the time being.'

'That little Datsun? No, you need a car of your own.'

'But what will all my cousins think?'

Serena raised an eyebrow. 'Does it matter what they think? Surely I can do what I want with my possessions?'

'*Eish*. They're already... well... they think I'm...' Cassia did not know how to talk to her gran about her relationship with her cousins.

'Stop, Cassia dear. You can't expect everyone to like you, and their feelings won't change if you have Graham's car. I've got plenty to give everyone, but I know your need for a vehicle is greater than anyone else in this family right now, so have it, enjoy it, and remember my darling Graham fondly by it. He always made a dashing picture when he was driving around in it.' Her eyes swam as she recalled this. She took a dainty handkerchief from her pocket and pressed it to her eyes.

Cassia wrapped her arms around Serena. 'Oh Granny, I will. Thank you very much. I can't tell you how grateful I am.'

'My pleasure, darling. Hop in and see how it feels behind the wheel.'

Cassia did so, unwinding the window so she could continue talking to Serena. 'You're right, Granny. I can't use Beryl's car indefinitely. She wants me to sell it and give the money to her boyfriend's family. I'm sure they are wondering when I'm going to do this as they'll be needing that money. I've been worrying about how I'll get around when I'm back at Freedom if I don't have Beryl's car. So you have really helped me out.'

'When we've finished our coffee, you drive Oliver's old Land Rover back to Brightside while I drive the Pajero. I would offer to take the Land Rover, except I find the steering so difficult. You'll find this vehicle a dream to drive with its power steering.'

They walked back into the house and settled in Serena's dining room to have tea and toast. 'I've decided I only want to stay at Freedom during the week nights once the school term starts,' Cassia confided in Serena. 'I'm still not sure where I'll go on my weekends off, though.'

Serena had no answer as she didn't know where she would end up either. She frowned. 'All this is such an upheaval, isn't it?'

'It is,' Cassia said. 'But I know what. One weekend, you and I can go out to the Matobo Hills together in Graham's car. We'll stay in a cottage at Maleme Dam. We can lie on the rocks and watch the lizards.'

A smile spread across Serena's face. 'That sounds lovely.'

Cassia smiled back, hiding her concerns. That's one weekend taken care of, she thought, but what about the rest?

*

They spent Christmas Day at the dam, but even then the atmosphere was subdued with the conversations revolving around selling boats and to which farm workers they should give the deck chairs and tables they had there. No one was interested in making Christmas Day special, so they all just brought steaks to eat. They cooked these on the fire and ate with their plates on their laps, sitting on the deck

241

chairs they were soon to give away. A far cry from the previous Christmas Days when the different family households each took it in turns to host the Christmas meal. They'd always made these into formal affairs, with everyone seated at long tables, laid in conventional Christmas style with white table cloths, red napkins, red candles and drift wood centre pieces adorned with sparkly decorations and miniature Christmas trees. Everyone had always dressed formally also, and they'd eaten traditional Christmas fare, with the only exceptions being churkey instead of turkey and marula jelly instead of cranberry jelly.

That they were going to so little effort this time was a stark reminder of how much their lives had changed.

Despite the lack of ceremony, the whole family was there except Martin, Kate and their younger son, Harry, who were spending Christmas in Cape Town. Brian had returned to be the farm. He was not taking the transition from their old farm life as well as the rest of his immediate family.

After the meal, the sailors made for their boats, knowing this would be one of the last times they would sail on the dam.

'Come sail with me in my Fireball?' Dominic said to Cassia as he was about to walk down the hill to his boat.

This both pleased and surprised her. She had noticed Jane hovering around Dominic for most of the day, telling him about the townhouse at Ascot Mews she and Sarah were renting in the new year. They were planning a house warming party which Cassia overheard Jane asking Dominic to attend. Jane had not extended the invitation to her.

'I'd love to go for a sail,' Cassia said to Dominic, 'although I've never been on a trapeze before.' The one and only time she'd sailed with him, they'd gone out in his father's old GP.

'Well, there's only a gentle breeze right now, so you may not need to,' Dominic said. 'But you'll learn soon enough, if the wind picks up.'

Jane pretended she didn't mind he hadn't asked her. Instead she turned to Will: 'Hey, Will. Let's also go for a sail. Can we use your Enterprise, Amanda?'

'I was thinking of sailing too. Three of us in the Enterprise will work, though.'

'Sure thing,' Will said.

The breeze dropped soon after the boats left the jetty, extinguishing any thoughts of an exciting sail. The windless sails flapped and the boats drifted, but Cassia didn't mind this because it gave her and Dominic a chance to chat while they waited for another gust.

'Sorry, I have seen so little of you since we got back from Botswana,' Dominic said. 'But I'm grateful that you've been staying at my parents' and helping them both so much.'

'I'm the one who's grateful to have somewhere to stay.'

'Well, from what I can gather, they both enjoy having you around.'

'I can see how difficult they are finding having to leave the farm.'

'Yes. They hate the idea of living in town, and they're not the only ones. That's one of the reasons I'm away so much. I'm really struggling to come to terms with losing all we've had here. I hope that if I can find somewhere or something to do, it'll sort my head out. I'm not in a good space at the moment.'

'You haven't had any luck with finding anything yet?'

'No, although I am enjoying helping Will renovate the camp in Matetsi. I did something similar for two years when I was in London; buying a dilapidated old garage in Chiswick and turning it into a bachelor flat. It's much easier doing that sort of thing here, though. I had to do all the manual labour myself in the UK. At least I had Will helping me, and we did pretty well out of it financially.'

'Yup, I can imagine. If you'd employed contractors to help you with the heavy work in the UK you wouldn't have made any profit.'

'Exactly.'

As they were talking, Dominic was eyeing the water, watching as it rippled. The breeze fluttered about them, and the sails began to flap.

'Great, we can get going again,' he said. 'Pull in your jib sheet, Cass, and clip on your harness. I think you may have to learn to go out on that trapeze after all.'

CHAPTER 20

JANUARY TURNED into February, and the day drew nearer for them to leave the farm forever.

The money came through from the sale of the farm and Bea found a charming house to buy in the suburb of Khumalo, close enough to Amanda that they could pop in on each other often, and big enough to section off a part as a "granny flat" for Serena. A lovely swimming pool and entertainment area, set in a lush garden, made possible by an excellent borehole, enhanced the property. Serena eyed the entertainment area, with its impressive braai, doubtfully and wondered who would be responsible for the braaing. The men in her life had always done this, but now they did not have a man in their house, except Richard, and she couldn't imagine him staying home long enough to help braai anything. At least they had Frank as their gardener and he could lay the fires.

Molly moved in with her parents and intended to stay there until Martin had transferred enough money out of the country for her to purchase a house in South Africa. Martin had already successfully deposited over fifty thousand dollars of his own money in South Africa, using his "golden tools" scheme. He offered to move money for Molly, too, and she gave him the first tranche to move soon after she received her portion from the farm sale.

As he embarked on the process, he doubled what he'd move this time with his own money, thinking he might as well transfer as much as he could in one hit.

He knew the format well now. He bought gold from his "friendly" gold miner and took it to a person who made the "tools" for him. At each stage, they meticulously weighed the gold, and he also discussed with the toolmaker what tools to make (hammers and spanners were the best) and how much the chrome coating would add to the overall weight. Confident in the smooth process, as always, he reached out to his contact in South Africa while waiting for the tools to be fabricated. It took a week this time, longer than on the previous occasions, but he saw no reason to be concerned as he had given the toolmaker more gold this time.

He collected the tools as soon as they were ready and added some real ones to his tool bag, to make it look more authentic. Early the following morning he left for South Africa, allowing him to reach Beit Bridge before the border post became crowded. Kate had joined him on his previous trips, but this time she did not, and he missed having her with him when he was dealing with the customs and immigration officials on both sides of the border. He always found this part of the process nerve wracking, in case an extra vigilant customs official decided to examine his tools. He was confident that, even if this happened, it would be almost impossible for anyone to tell the real tools from the ones made from gold, but this did not stop him from worrying. No customs officials had ever shown any interest in his tools, and he breathed a sigh of relief this time when the security guard lifted the boom on the South African side of the border and waved him through. He had successfully negotiated the border yet again.

He did not like to stop unnecessarily en route with so much of value in his car, so a couple of hours later he was driving over the impressive mountain range before Louis Trichardt, with the picturesque town nestling in the foothills and spilling onto the flat plains beyond. This part of the journey was always his favourite. The thickly wooded mountains, often shrouded in cloud, provided an interesting change from the rest of the scenery on his journey, which consisted mostly of undulating, dry terrain with few interesting features.

Louis Trichardt was where his journey ended as his gold buying contact was based there. He went straight to his warehouse to hand over the tools and again felt a flood of relief, this time because he no longer had the responsibility of keeping them safe. It was the gold buyer's job now. The two of them weighed the tools, as they always did, discussed the weight of the chrome plate and how much money Martin would receive for the gold, and then Martin gave him the bank details of all the banks the money needed to be deposited into, and how much into each account. This time, there would be six bank accounts. Firstly, the gold miner. Secondly, the toolmaker. Thirdly, Molly. Fourthly, Molly's parents. Fifthly, himself, and sixthly, Kate. The miner and the toolmaker insisted a portion of their fee be paid off shore and he liked to divide the rest of the money up into as many bank accounts as possible. This looked less suspicious than if a sizeable chunk of money suddenly landed in one account. He always did this, and had divided the money he'd syphoned out so far into his account, Kate's, and some even into his boys' bank accounts.

After leaving the gold buyer, he went to the shops and bought some groceries for Kate. She had given him a list of things they could no longer get in Zimbabwe. He purchased a few of the items on her list and decided he'd buy the rest over the next few days, as he would have little else to do. From the supermarket, he proceeded to the

Cloud's End Hotel, where he would stay until they had completed all the financial transactions. It always took time for all the bank accounts to receive and deposit the gold payment.

On arriving at the Cloud's End Hotel, he took a quick nap and then freshened up for dinner. He knew the owner of the hotel well by now, and they exchanged a few pleasantries as he sat in the bar enjoying a beer before dinner. He went into the dining room afterwards and was deciding on whether he should try the oxtail stew on the á la carte menu or the full table d'hôte menu, when the hotelier came scurrying across the dining room to his table.

'Excuse me, Martin. You have a telephone call,' he said.

Martin looked at his flustered face and his heart sank. 'From Zimbabwe?' he asked, as his head spun with thoughts of another catastrophe that may have occurred back home.

'No, it's a local call. You can take it in my office. No one will disturb you there.'

'Thank you.' No one ever telephoned him here, and his stomach lurched as he wondered why anyone would phone him. He placed his napkin on the table, took a sip of the drink the waiter had just brought him, and walked into the reception with a smile, acknowledging the hotelier who was now conversing with the receptionist behind the counter.

'Through there,' he said to Martin, pointing to a door next to the gents' toilet. Martin closed the office door behind him and strode across the room to the desk on which the hotelier had placed the telephone receiver.

'Hello,' he said.

'What's your game, Martin?'

'Sorry? Who's…?'

'It's me,' the gold buyer said. 'We've smelted the tools and discovered they were just fucking chrome plated metal.'

'What?' The room spun as these words sank in. Martin put his hand on the desk to steady himself.

'Metal. They're just metal.'

'They can't be.'

'I can assure you, they are. We chipped the chrome off all of them, and smelted each tool, one at a time, like we always do... and there is not one sniff of gold in any of them.'

'But... I weighed them once I collected them. They were exactly the same weight as the gold I handed over, considering the chrome plating, of course, and... well... you know, there's never been a problem before.'

'Well there is now,'

'I can't believe it.'

'Believe it, boet, believe it. Come here now and see for yourself.'

Returning to the Cloud's End hours later, Martin spent a sleepless night trying to figure out who had stolen the gold.

Was it the gold miner? No. If the miner had given him gold plated metal, the toolmaker would have told him. He would have noticed this as soon as he smelted the gold bars.

And no one could have stolen it when he was driving from the miner to the toolmaker. He'd gone straight from the one man to the other without stopping.

So was it the toolmaker then? Bloody hell. Stealing the gold would have been a simple task for him. It wouldn't have been difficult to make the tools the exact weight they needed to be. All he had to do was add a bit more metal or chrome plating here and there to get the weight right. The rat. No wonder it had taken him longer than usual to make the tools, if he was tinkering with the weights.

But they'd become good business associates. Would he do this to him?

Maybe it wasn't him? Maybe it was the gold buyer in Louis Trichardt? They'd weighed the tools together when he'd handed them over, and they'd weighed them again, tonight, when he'd gone to check out the molten mass of metal they'd become. Had that bastard exchanged the gold for steel before he phoned him? He could have added a bit here, or taken out a bit there, so the weights matched. It had sometimes worried him that he never let him watch the process. Maybe his outrage about the tools being made of metal had just been an act.

Martin felt sick to the stomach. He found it hard to believe that something like this had happened, especially as there'd never been a problem before.

He groaned as he thought of the mess he was in. It wasn't as if he could go to the police and report the theft. He'd be arrested if he did. He didn't like to think how many laws he was breaking on both sides of the border.

What was he going to do? He still had to pay the miner and the toolmaker their off shore fees, because he couldn't categorically point a finger at either of them. And what was he going to do about Molly? She would go ballistic if he said, "Sorry, someone has stolen the gold I bought with your money." But surely he didn't have to pay her out? This was a risky business, and she knew it. He'd been doing her a favour, so why should he suffer? She would understand when he told her he'd lost a lot of money too.

He travelled back to Bulawayo the following day, his head fuzzy from lack of sleep, his stomach churning with nerves. Kate burst into floods of tears when he told her his story.

He decided the best way to approach the miner and the toolmaker was to call a meeting as soon as possible with the two of them together. The miner was the first person he phoned, and he immediately said he could meet him the following day. He sounded surprised and concerned when Martin told him there was a problem, certainly not guilty. However, when he phoned the toolmaker, his telephone rang and rang. It was four o'clock in the afternoon by now, but he got into his car and drove to his workshop in the industrial sites to find him, only to discover that his workshop was empty, with the security guard at the gate telling him, 'the boss moved out yesterday.' Martin did a quick calculation. That would have been the day after he'd collected the tools. He knew where this man lived, near Amanda's, in the suburb of Ilanda, so now, in a panic, he left the workshop and rushed there, only to find no one answering the gate bell when he rang it. The gate was shut, but not locked, so he opened it and went into the property. He walked around the house, peering in all the windows, seeing nothing but scraps of discarded rubbish. The fucking thief must've done a runner as soon as the transaction was complete, Martin thought. He's been planning this for a long time. Martin wanted to shout out loud that this crook had taken him for such a ride. The bastard, the fucking thieving bastard.

He didn't know him socially, so did not know who his family or friends were. The miner had recommended him and introduced them, so Martin rushed home to telephone the miner again, to see if they could meet now. He was desperate to gather information about where the toolmaker might have gone, and the miner was his best bet right now. Martin knew he lived in Hillside, and he asked if he could meet him there. The miner appeared as shocked as Martin had been when he heard that someone had stolen the gold and the toolmaker had disappeared. He had no idea where this man might have gone. He would ask mutual acquaintances, but he doubted they'd find him. He suspected he'd left the country and got as far away as possible.

Martin's only consolation was that he would not need to pay that thief his off shore fee. But he'd blown his wonderful scheme to get money out of the country to smithereens, and he wondered how he'd move the rest of his money. After being taken for such a ride, he didn't think he'd be able to trust anyone else ever again.

By now he was exhausted, but he still had to tell Molly what had occurred and he decided the best place to do this was at Bea's house. This would avoid him facing Molly and her parents alone. He phoned Bea to check she was there and ask if they could all meet at her house now, as he needed to speak to Molly as soon as possible.

Serena, Bea, Molly, Molly's parents and Martin gathered in Bea's sitting room an hour later. Martin dreaded telling them what had taken place, but there was nothing for it. He had to do it, so he launched into his sorry tale straight away. Disbelief turned to shock and then to anger as they listened to what he was saying. Like Kate earlier, Molly burst into tears, and feeling exhausted, exasperated and wretched, Martin started crying too. Serena couldn't believe what she was seeing. He had not cried in front of her since he was a little boy, and, feeling desperate for him, tears rolled down her cheeks as well.

Eventually, they all regained their composure, but the reality of the disaster was sinking in.

'What am I supposed to do?' Molly wailed. She had given Martin half of her portion from the sale of the farm. 'How am I supposed to set myself up in Natal with only half the money I was expecting to have? And I have to pay Tom's university fees for the next three years on top of everything else.' Molly's mother stroked her arm, nodding in agreement. 'And how am I going to get the rest of the money out of the country, now that your "fool proof golden tools" scheme has backfired on us, Martin?'

'All this has been going through my head, Molly, I can assure you.' Martin took his glasses off and wiped his eyes. 'I'm just as upset as you. Remember, I have lost thousands too.'

'You told me there wouldn't be a problem, Martin,' Molly shouted.

Serena noticed both their tempers rising, and she quickly intervened. 'Okay, you two. I think we all need time to digest what has happened and meet again this time tomorrow to discuss how we go forward from here.'

Her intervention surprised them, but no one argued. Martin was so tired by now he could not think straight. He hoped that maybe, by some miracle, he would receive some information in the interim about where the toolmaker may have gone. There were a few more people he needed to talk to who had vouched for him, but because what he'd done was illegal, he could only talk to people he trusted, or at least, thought he trusted. He'd been reluctant to tell many people what he'd been doing, and he was just as reluctant now to let them know how he'd been ripped off.

It turned out it was wishful thinking that he'd be able to trace the whereabouts of the toolmaker. When the family reconvened the next day, he knew nothing more about where he might have gone.

Oliver and Will were at the meeting this time, much to his irritation. Serena had asked Oliver to join them, and Will had rushed down from the Victoria Falls when his mother told him what had happened.

Once they had been through the hopelessness of retrieving any of their money, Oliver spoke. 'I've thought long and hard about all this since Serena telephoned me last night and she and I have discussed it at length this afternoon. We both think that Martin needs to pay Molly some of the money she's lost through his hair-brained scheme.' Martin gasped when he heard this and was about to speak, when Oliver put up his hand. 'Hear me out, please, Martin. The main points I want to make here are these. The first one is that if it wasn't for your insistence and actions, we would not have sold the farms and been forced to leave our homes.'

'But Molly was happy to go along with it.'

'Please Martin, I haven't finished. Molly had only just lost her husband when you started pushing your agenda, which leads me to the next reason we think she needs to be compensated by you. She's a widow now, with no one providing for her. You can get a job, while Molly will have difficulty finding one that pays well. As you know, she married John when she was just a teenager, so has no qualifications or work experience, whereas you went to agricultural college and have spent many years working in agriculture.' Martin tried to butt in, but Oliver spoke over him. 'The last thing I want to point out is this; if it hadn't been for you telling her about your scheme and assuring her it was a fool proof way to get her money out of the country, she wouldn't have gone along with you.'

Martin's face was cerise with rage and he barely controlled his anger as he replied. 'Molly was more than happy to sell the farm when I suggested it to her. And secondly, only an idiot wouldn't realise there are risks to getting money out of the country by smuggling. But Molly didn't have to take the personal risks I had to take. If someone had caught me, I would have ended up in jail.'

'You didn't tell me I was being an idiot to go along with your scheme when you offered to help me, Martin,' Molly said.

Martin ignored her. 'And another thing, I've lost just as much money as Molly has and I will need every cent I have when I move to South Africa. I doubt it'll be as easy as you think for me to find a job there. I don't have the contacts like I have here.'

'Then why are you leaving?' Oliver said. 'Why don't you stay here and help keep the community together? As you say, you have the contacts, you have the expertise, you have the wherewithal, so why are you turning your back on us?'

'Because, like most people, I have no confidence in this country, Oliver. Can't you see what's happening? When I was in the industrial sites yesterday all I saw were industries closing, previously busy factories, empty. Everyone is leaving, and I don't want to be the only one left behind.' With this, he leapt up and strode from the room before anyone could say another word to him.

There was silence for half a minute once he'd slammed the front door behind him, and then Molly spoke. 'I've always thought he was a total bastard. John did too,' and with this she burst into tears again.

Serena heaved herself from the sofa she'd been sitting on. 'Come with me, Bea. I think we need to pour everyone a stiff gin and tonic.'

They returned five minutes later, with Bea carrying a tray filled with glasses clinking with ice. Molly rushed over to Serena and flung her arms around her. 'Sorry Serena, I know he's your son. I shouldn't be rude about him in front of you, but I had so hoped he'd at least agree to give me part of what I've lost.'

'It is difficult,' Serena said. 'I also hoped he'd feel he had enough money to give you some too. Unfortunately, he has never been as family orientated as the rest of us. He and Val have both been this way from when they were young children. I think this may partly be because I sent them off to boarding school when they were too young, only five. They both also felt the death of their father far more than John and Bea did, perhaps because they were that much older when he died.'

'Well, I think he's being selfish and miserly, only thinking of his wife and children now,' Will said. 'But we'll work something out together, Mum,' he said to Molly.

'I don't know why I bothered coming all this way to talk to him,' Oliver said.

'Well, thank you for trying.' Serena said, giving him a weak smile.

CHAPTER 21

DESPITE LILY'S best efforts, Oliver remained unwilling to lend a hand with their impending move into town. Their search for a house remained fruitless, as he continued to decline every house they inspected. Oliver always found a reason why none of them were suitable. Lily was at her wit's end. With only a few weeks left before they had to leave the farm, she asked Amanda if they could revert to their original plan and stay with her until they found a place Oliver approved of. Although she had disposed of most of their excess furniture and belongings, she knew they still had too much to fit in Amanda's garage. She had to approach Bea about using her garage for storage as well.

It was all very inconvenient and she would have liked to throttle Oliver if she hadn't been so worried about him. As their departure day drew closer, his despondency and unhappiness deepened.

Looking back, his family wondered if Oliver had had a subconscious inkling of what was to come. Surely not? Yet it was astonishing how right he had been to delay finding a home in town, because their lives took a dramatic turn one Friday afternoon in March when Siphas Ngwenya arrived at Brightside House in his old Peugeot truck.

Prince was the only one who noticed him parked in the driveway, and he went out to greet him. Siphas said he'd come to see Dominic, so Prince showed him to the veranda. Despite the mess of cardboard boxes and wooden crates, the armchairs and coffee table were still arranged in their usual place, and Prince asked him to sit there while he looked for Dominic. Siphas perched himself on the edge of one armchair, feeling uncomfortable sitting there alone.

'Ah, there you are. Sorry to have kept you waiting. Prince couldn't find me, at first, because I was in a barn,' Dominic said when he arrived ten minutes later. 'Can I get you something to drink?'

'No. No, thank you. I have come here to discuss an important matter with you.'

'Ah. And what is that?'

'I wanted to ask you if you'd be interested in buying my farm?'

'Whispering Plains?'

'Yes.'

There was a long silence while Dominic processed this information. 'I didn't know it was for sale,' he eventually said.

'It wasn't until a few months ago.'

'So why have you decided to sell it now?'

'Did you hear my brother was killed in a car crash at the end of last year? My brother who was involved in politics.'

'Yes. I did, and I was very sorry to hear that. My father told me when I returned from a trip to Botswana. I've been so busy since then, I didn't get around to visiting you to give you my condolences. My apologies.'

'Thank you. His death has persuaded me to leave this country. Politics is a dangerous game here.'

Dominic raised an eyebrow.

'My daughter is now living in the UK. She has married an Englishman,' Siphas said. 'She met him when he came to work here in 1980. They have invited me to live with them in England.'

'I am sorry to hear this. Do you want to live in England?'

'Oh yes. I will have a much better life there. Bad things have been happening to us Ndebeles here in Matabeleland since Independence. I now believe I come from the wrong tribe and I cannot enjoy a good life here. I am lucky I can go to my daughter in England.'

'It's sad you feel this way. I thought the whole reason for the war was to elevate the lives of all Zimbabweans.'

'Correct, but only some will prosper. The Ndebele people will struggle. Therefore, I am going.' He cleared his throat, changing the subject. 'I asked the government if they wanted to buy my farm and they said no. They have issued a "Certificate of No Interest" in it.'

'That's good.'

'Yes. No one has ever developed Whispering Plains like your family have developed this place, but I am sure you can make it more productive.'

Dominic's mind was racing. He knew Whispering Plains well. His parents had been friendly with the Beamishes, from whom Siphas had bought it, and he'd visited the place countless times. He liked the idea that it was rougher than here. Over the last few months, while he'd helped Will renovate the lodge in the Matetsi hunting concession, he had dreamed of working with wildlife. He still didn't know how, though. Unlike Will, he wasn't a professional hunter, and he did not want to become one, despite believing that controlled hunting had a place in Zimbabwe, because it gave wild animals a tangible value and encouraged people to conserve them rather than just kill them for meat. Now Siphas was offering him his rugged farm. He wondered if it was possible to make it into a wildlife conservancy and instigate projects that would give the wildlife in this area some value.

'How much land do you have, Siphas? I know Whispering Plains is big, but I've never known the actual acreage?'

'Thirty thousand acres.'

That would be big enough for a wildlife conservancy, Dominic thought, his heart racing with excitement. 'And how much are you wanting to sell it for?'

'Five dollars per acre.'

'You've certainly got me interested. Can I take my father there so we can look around?'

'Tomorrow? I want to sell as soon as possible.'

*

When Dominic told Oliver that Whispering Plains was for sale, Oliver said he was too old to start again. However, Dominic's suggestion of turning it into a wildlife conservancy, as opposed to keeping it going as a cattle ranch, intrigued him.

Oliver leant back in his veranda chair and placed his hands behind his head, staring out at the garden, mulling this over for a long time.

'You're right,' he eventually said. 'It would make a fine wildlife area. I'm not sure how you could make a living out of it, but we can look at the place tomorrow with this in mind.'

Whispering Plains was an extensive property with a seasonal river running through it, but it had no irrigation, other than some wells and boreholes. Because of this, the Beamishes had always limited their farming activities to cattle ranching and Siphas did the same, but he soon discovered this was not easy. Leopards and hyena ate the calves, cows died from an array of tick borne diseases, fences collapsed, cattle disappeared and diesel engines kept breaking down, leaving the animals with no water. He had encountered one problem after another, and, on top of all this, he found that cattle ranching did not give him a steady income. It took too long to breed a calf up to slaughter and he didn't have the money to tide him over, as he'd used everything he had on buying the property. He soon discovered he had no money for day-to-day living, let alone for repairs and maintenance, and the farm fell into disrepair. So he tried bringing in a regular revenue by renting out sections of the farm to other aspiring farmers, but this created new problems. The natural vegetation in this part of Matabeleland should only carry one livestock unit per ten acres with cattle, if the grass is to be safeguarded, but Siphas charged his lessees per head, so he encouraged them to bring as many animals as possible. These, on top of his own cattle, soon overgrazed the farm, and the succulent, nutritious grasses disappeared, leaving barren areas and bitter grasses, until thick *uGaju* bush grew up and suffocated all remaining vegetation, reducing the grazing further.

When Siphas told the Craigs his tales of woe, they understood why, politics aside, he was so keen to pack up and move to England. He would certainly have an easier life there.

Siphas suggested the Craigs look around the farm on their own.

Viewing it as a wildlife area, they could see past the problems he had encountered. Without cattle, they wouldn't have to worry about dips, dipping, handling facilities and internal fences, and there would be less pressure on the grass and water.

The homestead would need to be renovated, but they knew, of old, the potential it had, and Dominic had had enough renovating experience.

'You and Mum can live there, and I'd use it as a base until I build something for myself,' Dominic said. 'I've always thought it was an interesting old house.'

'It is, and big too' Oliver said. 'We enjoyed coming to the Beamishs' for dinners and lunches over the years. I never thought I'd end up living in their house, but now it's being presented to me, I can see myself happily settling here. Mum would especially enjoy reviving the garden.'

'Yes. She'd soon put some life back onto the bones of Mrs Beamish's old garden,' Dominic laughed.

Seeing his father so absorbed filled Dominic with relief. Oliver had shown so little interest in anything for months.

An array of outhouses lay behind the main homestead – a garage, barns, a workshop, sheds and storerooms – and as they walked around these, Dominic's mind buzzed with ideas.

Oliver was making his own plans. 'There's enough space around here for me to keep a few of my prize cattle, after all, which means I can continue breeding my bulls.'

Dominic gave him a sceptical look. 'I thought we were turning it into a wildlife area?

'I'd only use a few paddocks around the house, dear boy. You know how much I enjoy my pedigree breeding, and I wouldn't need much land. It would give Mum and me a small income as I'm sure my loyal customers will still support me.'

Domnic relented, knowing his father would need an interest of his own. 'Yes, Dad, they would.'

They continued their drive around the property, observing how the vegetation changed from region to region. Stunted mopane trees grew in dark cotton soils in some spots, the *uGaju* scrub, caused from overgrazing, in the sandier areas, but, wherever they went, they saw a variety of mature, impressive-looking trees, in groups here, individually there.

'You'll need to hire gangs of people to remove all the *uGaju* if you want to regenerate the grassland plains,' Oliver said.

'I agree, Dad, but there's still so much potential. Yes, it's run down, yes, it's overgrazed, but we can sort all that out. What's great about the place is that it has hills and valleys, lots of beautiful old trees, and the river offers added interest. It would make an ideal wildlife area.'

They approached the river and drove through a forest of huge acacia galpinis, similar to the galpini forest on one section of Brightside. They stopped in a glade in the middle of this forest. It was more elevated than the surrounding area and the cliffs along the river bank were visible a short distance away.

Dominic switched off the Land Rover engine and both men sat for a long time, saying nothing, observing their surroundings, listening to the screeches of the Meyer's parrots high in the trees above them. Every now and then they'd see a flash of green and yellow as the parrots flew from one tree to the next. They'd brought Luna and Jimbo with them, and both dogs began to agitate to get out. Dominic told them they could and, without hesitation, they leapt off the back and rushed around, their noses down, their tails wagging, sniffing and scurrying around until they took off after a flock of guinea fowl.

'Eh! Come back here,' Dominic called to them. He turned to his father. 'I've been thinking about what we could do with this property, and I've come to the conclusion that, if we want to run it as a wildlife area, the only way we can make real money, is to have hunting. We wouldn't have to do too many, but we'd need some.'

'Yup. I agree.'

'Obviously we could arrange other types of safaris in the off season – photographic and birding, for instance – but the hunting would be the primary source of income. We could get professional hunters, like Will, to come here with their clients. There'll be leopard living in the hills, and we could offer plains game hunts as well. Will was telling me there are people in the Lowveld needing to relocate game from there to other parts of the country. We could take some of these animals, to top up the numbers here, and also reintroduce species that haven't been in this area for decades. Giraffe, wildebeest, and zebra, for example. It would be great to have them here again.'

'It would indeed.'

'The animals that are already in the vicinity will soon come back, without cattle,' Dominic continued. 'If we're going to have hunts and safaris, we'll need a camp, and this clearing would be an excellent place to build it, don't you think?'

Oliver's face lit up. 'We could offer the people at Brightside jobs. Building the camp, fixing the roads and fences. There'll be a host of things for them to do. What a relief that would be for me. Especially the old timers who've been with us for so long.'

'A number of them have told me they'd prefer to carry on working for us, so, yes, we'd now have jobs to offer them. But, we digress Dad. I was talking about building the camp here.'

'Yes dear boy. I can see how appealing this area is. A natural clearing in the middle of all these impressive trees.'

'And it's close to the river too. Of course it will be dry for a lot of the year, but look over there, Dad.' Dominic pointed to a spot a hundred or so metres away. 'Can you see, there's a borehole? We could knock down the cattle trough and pump water to that sunken area over there,' he pointed to another place. 'It's a natural pan in the rainy season, but if we pumped water in the dry season we'd create a permanent waterhole below the camp for the animals to drink from all year round.'

'I like your vision, dear boy. We need to sit down and work out how much all this is going to cost us.'

'There's lots of materials on this place that we can use. When we were walking around all those outhouses, I thought we wouldn't need so many. We'd probably just need the workshop, some storerooms and the small barn, so we could dismantle the other buildings and salvage the materials for other projects, like a camp. We could even use the bricks if we chiselled the buildings down carefully. And then there's all the other stuff; the window frames, door frames, doors, corrugated iron sheets, roof timbers. Did you notice those wooden floors on the mezzanine level of the big barn?'

'Yes.'

'It's really good quality wood. Much better than anything we can buy in the shops these days. We could use that wood in our camp. We would need to buy very little besides cement and plumbing materials.'

'You're right. I even noticed electrical fittings in those outhouses. We could use the cable and wiring at the camp too.'

Dominic called the dogs back to the Land Rover and started the engine. He and his father continued making plans all the way back to Brightside, and they were like an excited pair of schoolboys by the time they got there. Lily came out of the house to greet them and saw, from the looks on their faces, that it was a done deal. They were going to buy Whispering Plains. She heaved a sigh of relief, even though she knew there would be a lot of hard work ahead of them.

'There's one more thing I need to do,' Dominic said.

*

After speaking to Dominic on the phone, Will drove to Freedom High School. He went there to check if Cassia was interested in going out to Brightside with him the next day. He told her that Dominic had invited them.

'Wow. Yes, please,' she said. 'But let's go in Graham's car. I'll come and fetch you early tomorrow morning. Has your mother moved into her new house yet, or is she still with her parents?'

Molly's plans had changed after the fiasco with moving money out of the country. Bea and Amanda had convinced her she had enough money to buy a lovely house in Bulawayo, much better than anything she could get in South Africa for the same price. Bea had also heard, from one of the ladies in her tennis group, that Whitestone School needed a new receptionist, and she suggested Molly apply. Initially hesitant, Molly changed her mind when she and Bea discovered a beautiful thatched house near Whitestone School at an incredibly low price. Within weeks, she had successfully applied for the job at Whitestone School, and she had purchased the house. Better still, the previous owners had already left the country, so the house was unoccupied, allowing her to move in as soon as she had signed the Agreement of Sale with the lawyers.

'Yes, she's living in her new house,' Will said. 'She'll be starting her job at Whitestone School next term, so she's finally feeling settled again.'

'No regrets she won't be near Tom in Natal?'

'I told her Tom's a student. He doesn't want his mother cramping his style. Did you hear, by the way, that Uncle Martin deposited ten thousand dollars into Mum's South African bank account? I think Granny convinced him that he needed to do something?'

'Granny told me. It's better than nothing, I suppose. So is she talking to Martin and Kate again?'

'Nah. Only Granny and Bea are in comms with them, but they'll be gone soon, once Martin's found another way to syphon more money out.'

'Exactly. So do you stay with your mum when you're in Bulawayo?'

'Yes. I'm there now.' Will gave her the address and suggested she arrive early the next morning so Molly could show her the house before they left for Brightside.

*

Dominic was waiting for them when they arrived at Brightside House. He'd packed canvas deck chairs and a picnic basket in the back of his Land Rover. He'd also put in a cooler box. Will and Cassia wondered what Dominic had planned, but he refused to say where he was taking them. Cassia was relieved she was wearing her old khaki shorts, a button-up shirt with a collar, and her now well-worn *veldskoens* as she envisaged a long day out in the bush. Surely not to spray cattle? She'd been told they'd sold most of their beef herd.

After a quick hello to Oliver and Lily, they set off, the dogs in the back, the three of them on the front seat, with Cassia wedged between the men. Will and Cassia's curiosity increased as they left the farm and continued down the main dirt road, before turning off at the signpost to Whispering Plains.

'Where the heck are you taking us?' Will said. 'This place belongs to the Ngwenyas'.'

Dominic drove past the old homestead and on towards the river.

'I hope Ngwenya won't give us any gyp for trespassing,' Will said. 'Although he'll struggle to find us. These roads sure are fucked.'

Dominic didn't mind as he bumped along a narrow track. They arrived at the galpini forest. He changed gear and drove down a path near the river, twisting and turning to avoid dongas and bushes. When they got to the glade, he stopped the vehicle and turned off the engine. Cassia and Will stared in bewilderment through the windscreen.

'And?' Will said.

'I'm going to build a camp here.'

'On Mr Ngwenya's place?'

'He's selling it. My dad and I are buying it, and I'm going to turn it into a wildlife conservancy. We'll do some hunts and other safaris to make money.'

'Boy. I wasn't expecting you to tell us something like this,' Will said.

'Neither was I,' Cassia agreed. 'But how exciting for you.'

'Perhaps for you, too, because I'm inviting both of you to be a part of the project. Will to do hunts and safaris here, when he's not hunting in Matetsi. Cassia to handle the marketing and camp operations.'

Will and Cassia were silent. They were too surprised by what Dominic had said. Their minds raced with what this would mean.

They slid from the cab and the dogs jumped off the back. Dominic removed the chairs and placed them in a half moon facing the river.

'How about we have a cup of coffee here and I can fill you in on more of the details. Then we'll go for a long drive around the whole place and come back here for lunch afterwards. What do you think?'

*

They returned to the glade hours later. While driving around the property, Dominic had discussed his ideas with Cassia and Will, and they were now equally enthusiastic about his plans. Besides this, Cassia felt a combination of amazement and relief. At last, her dreams were being fulfilled. It was almost too good to be true – Dominic asking her to help him create a life she had only ever imagined in her wildest dreams. She kept glancing at him in admiration. Despite acknowledging that none of it would be easy, he appeared unfazed by the challenge. Her bare leg brushed against his as they jostled along the bumpy roads, and each time this happened, it sent tingles through her body.

Dominic found a shady spot on the edge of the glade and switched off the engine. He put his hand on Cassia's knee and gave it a sudden squeeze, making her jump.

'You guys hungry?'

'For sure,' Cassia said.

'Good, because I've brought boerwors, onions and some fresh rolls Prince made this morning.'

'Brilliant, I'm starving,' Will said.

'There's a frying pan in the basket to cook the boerwors and onions in, but we'll need to make a fire. Let's find some kindling and dry wood, Will, while Cassia sets up the table and chairs. It'll be good practise for when you're running our proper camp here, huh?' He winked at her.

She laughed. 'Oh yes. I have to start somewhere, don't I?'

THE END

Acknowledgements

This a work of fiction. The characters and events are made up. When places and historical figures are mentioned, it is in a fictional way.

Firstly, I would like to thank the following who helped with this novel:

Maureen Van Der Horn, Lyn Rawlins, Lisa Kaufman, Michael Bullivant and Tina Booth. They spent days reading the manuscript, followed by many hours with me, discussing every aspect of the book imaginable. From the plot, to individual words, to spellings, to the grammar and punctuation, everything was analyzed, dissected, corrected and deleted if we decided it didn't work. The input these people made was invaluable and I could not have completed the work without them.

I would also like to thank Nonhlanhla Mkhwananzi and Last Mlala for helping me with the Ndebele words and sentences.

Also, thank you to Duncan Watson for producing another stunning cover, and to Frankie Kay for allowing me to use her beautiful photograph on the front cover.

Last, but not least, I would like to thank you, the readers who have been following this Sunrising Series, rating it and writing reviews. I am absolutely delighted there are so many people enjoying this family saga set in Africa.

Glossary

arb	abbreviation for arbitrary
bakkie	pick-up truck
boet	(Afrikaans) brother
boerwors	a type of spicy sausage
braai	barbeque
cossies	abbreviation for swimming costumes
dunno	abbreviation for I don't know
gook	(slang) guerrilla
howzit	(slang) hello
kopje	(Afrikaans) small hill or mound
jawl	(slang) good time
lekker	(Afrikaans) good or pleasant
mealie	maize
okes	(slang) guys
skrik	(slang) fright
stoep	(Afrikaans) small veranda
veldskoens	(Afrikaans) a type of lace up shoe made of leather
vlei	(Afrikaans) a grassy plain
dwala	(Shona) hill or rock
hayi	(Ndebele) no
khaya	(Ndebele) house
khiwa	abbreviation for white people/person
litshonenjani	(Ndebele) good afternoon
madala	(Ndebele) old man
makhiwa	(Ndebele) white people/person
ngixolisa	(Ndebele) sorry
sadza	(Shona) a thick porridge made from maize meal
salibonani	(Ndebele) hello
siyabonga	(Ndebele) thank you
uGaju	Ndebele abbreviation for a type of bush
Yebo	(Ndebele) yes

Akula muntu phandle, ngaphandle komfazi wakhe – there is no one outside except his wife

Vula. Sijahile	Open. We are in a hurry
Ungaphi uZachariah?	Where is Zachariah?

Reviews

I found this book difficult to write, mainly because of the period in which it is set. However, I would be interested to read what you have to say. Your reviews are important so please, if you are able, write a review or give the book a rating. This will be most appreciated.

In the meantime I will be working on the final book in the series, a story about the next generations of the Craig and Brooke families in the 2000s.

About the author

Susan Hubert was born and has lived in Zimbabwe all her life.
She has an English and Psychology degree from the University of Kwazulu Natal in South Africa, with Mathematics as a minor.

She taught Mathematics for 16 years at high schools in Bulawayo, Zimbabwe, before retiring so she could spend more time with her husband, who was working as a professor of Equine Surgery at Louisiana State University and then Colorado State University. It was during this time she started writing.

When she was back home in Zimbabwe she tutored Mathematics and looked after her husband's herd of cattle.

She now lives full time with her husband on a farm just outside Bulawayo, where they are establishing a pecan plantation. She has one son, Jack Allard.

Learn more on Facebook: Susan Hubert – Author

Made in the USA
Las Vegas, NV
09 April 2025

20732152R00163